MARVEL

SPIDER-MAN
Storybook Collection

MARVEL

Los Angeles · New York

Spider-Man
Just a kid from Queens.

Groot
I am Groot.

Rocket
Groot's best friend.

Hulk
Hulk . . . SMASH!!!

Rhino
Ready to squash bug boy.

Nova
Fighting for #1 Super Hero spot.

Lizard
Ready for Sssssspider-Man.

Doctor Octopus
Leader of Sinister Six.

Ms. Marvel
A hero in high school.

Ant-Man
Small hero. Big problem.

Falcon
Ready to fly.

Electro
The bug zapper.

Contents

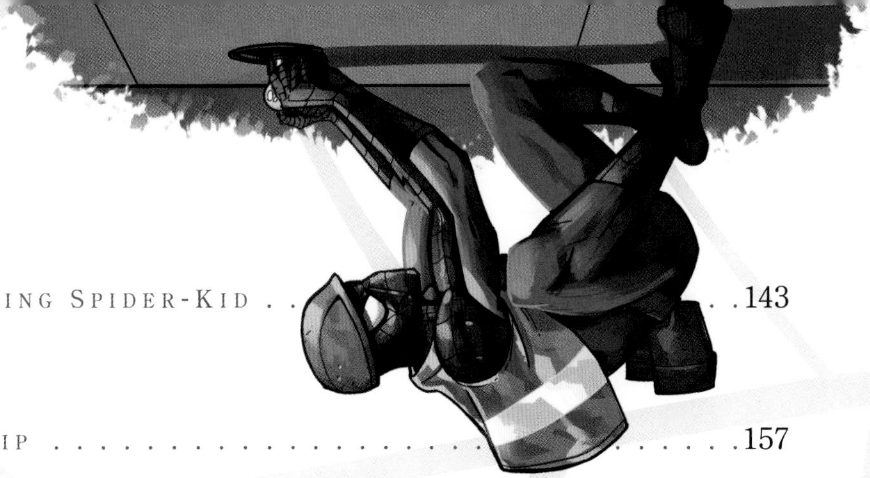

"Cause for Celebration" written by Andy Schmidt. Illustrated by Ron Lim and Matt Milla. Based on the Marvel comic book series *Spider-Man*.

"Science vs. Science" written by Andy Schmidt. Illustrated by Christian Colbert and Christopher Sotomayor. Based on the Marvel comic book series *Spider-Man*.

"Hulk Disposal" written by Colin Hosten. Illustrated by Khoi Pham and Matt Milla. Based on the Marvel comic book series *Spider-Man*.

"Last Days of Summer" written by Clarissa Wong. Illustrated by Ron Lim and Matt Milla. Based on the Marvel comic book series *Spider-Man*.

"Alone Against the Sinister Six!" written by Steve Behling. Illustrated by Khoi Pham and Paul Mounts. Based on the Marvel comic book series *Spider-Man*.

"Halloween Stampede" written by Colin Hosten. Illustrated by Ron Lim and Christopher Sotomayor. Based on the Marvel comic book series *Spider-Man*.

"Attack Off-Broadway! Guest Starring Rocket and Groot" written by Tomas Palacios. Illustrated by Ron Lim and Matt Milla. Based on the Marvel comic book series *Spider-Man*.

"Crazy Eights" written by Nancy Lambert. Illustrated by Khoi Pham and Christopher Sotomayor. Based on the Marvel comic book series *Spider-Man*.

"Love Bug" adapted by Clarissa Wong. Illustrated by Christian Colbert and Matt Milla. Based on the Marvel comic book series *Spider-Man*.

"No Room for Debate" written by Nancy Lambert. Illustrated by Ron Lim and Matt Milla. Based on the Marvel comic book series *Spider-Man*.

"The Amazing Spider-Kid" written by Cristina Garces. Illustrated by Khoi Pham and Christopher Sotomayor. Based on the Marvel comic book series *Spider-Man*.

"Power Trip" written by Nancy Lambert. Illustrated by Christian Colbert and Paul Mounts. Based on the Marvel comic book series *Spider-Man*.

"Black Ice" written by Nancy Lambert. Illustrated by Christian Colbert and Christopher Sotomayor. Based on the Marvel comic book series *Spider-Man*.

"A Hot Dog, a Real Dog, and an Octopus" written by Adam Davis. Illustrated by Ron Lim and Andy Troy. Based on the Marvel comic book series *Spider-Man*.

"Super BUGZ!" written by Colin Hosten. Illustrated by Khoi Pham and Christopher Sotomayor. Based on the Marvel comic book series *Spider-Man*.

"Sand Trap" written by Colin Hosten. Illustrated by Ron Lim and Matt Milla. Based on the Marvel comic book series *Spider-Man*.

"The Fastest Web in the West" written by Arie Kaplan. Illustrated by Ron Lim and Andy Troy. Based on the Marvel comic book series *Spider-Man*.

"Museum Madness!" written by Andy Schmidt. Illustrated by Khoi Pham and Matt Milla. Based on the Marvel comic book series *Spider-Man*.

"Climate Calamity!" written by Andy Schmidt. Illustrated by Khoi Pham and Andy Troy. Based on the Marvel comic book series *Spider-Man*.

"The Sensational Six!" written by Steve Behling. Illustrated by Khoi Pham and Paul Mounts. Based on the Marvel comic book series *Spider-Man*.

Cover designed by Marvel Press.

marvelkids.com
© 2016 MARVEL

For information address Marvel Press, 125 West End Avenue, New York, New York 10023.

Printed in the United States of America

First Hardcover Edition, May 2016
10 9 8 7 6 5 4 3 2 1

FAC-038091-16253

Library of Congress
Control Number:
2015901547

ISBN 978-1-4847-3215-1

SPIDER-MAN
Cause for Celebration

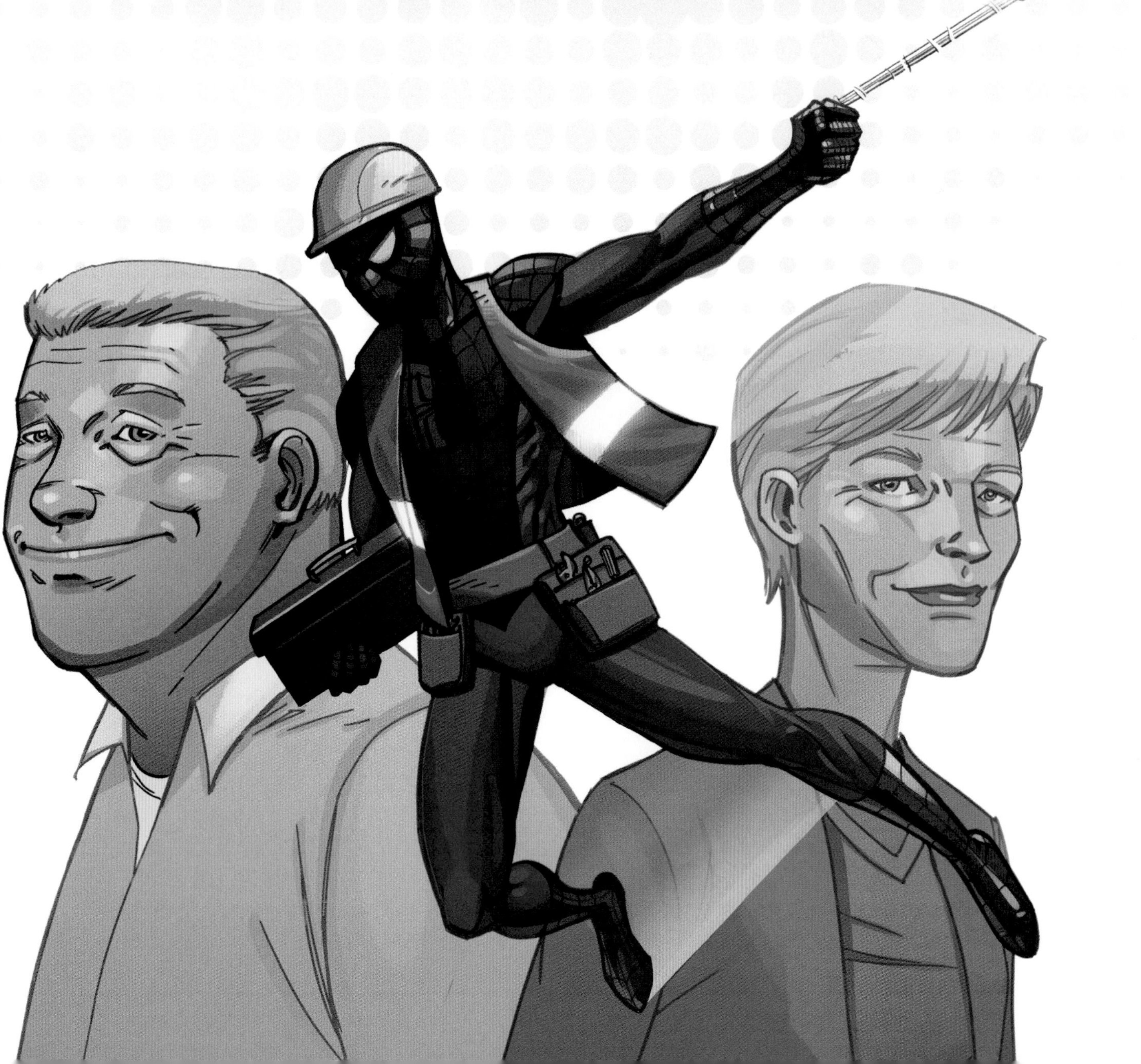

*I*t was Ben Parker's birthday. Every year, Peter Parker noticed that his aunt May got a little sad on her husband's birthday. Uncle Ben and Aunt May had raised Peter from a young age.

Aunt May put down the stack of old photos of Uncle Ben she was studying and said, "Peter, I've got to go to the store, but when I get back, maybe we can patch up this house a little. Your Uncle Ben would never let things stay in such disrepair."

Peter leaned down and said, "Aunt May, Uncle Ben isn't really gone. He is always with us. You'll see."

Peter looked around the house and saw a leaky faucet, a hole in the wall left after some plumbing work, broken light bulbs up high on the ceiling, and even a big spot where the carpet was coming up. *Yeesh!* Peter thought. *Aunt May is right. Uncle Ben would have fixed these things right away.*

Peter was determined to cheer up his aunt!

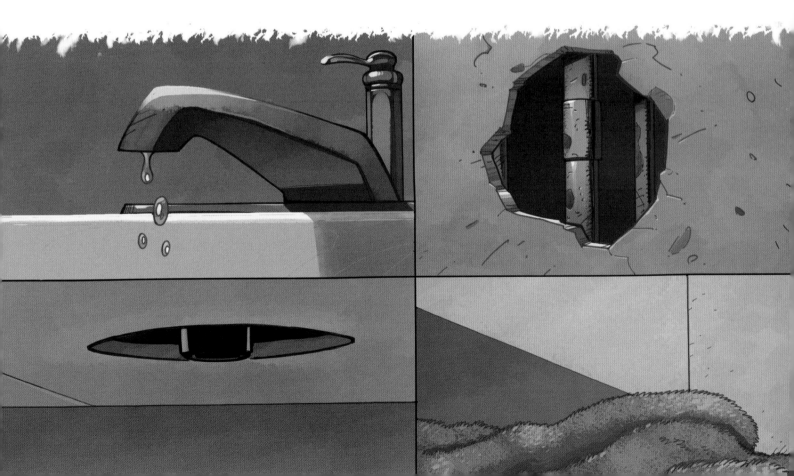

As Aunt May left the house to run her errands, Peter realized he had his job cut out for him. These were no small chores! He wanted to prove Uncle Ben lived on, and he'd have to get to work. Peter Parker couldn't complete all the tasks alone, but Spider-Man could—as long as Spidey was done before Aunt May returned home!

Spider-Man swung into action, heading to the hardware store to gather a few supplies. Swinging from building to building, Spider-Man would get back to Queens in no time!

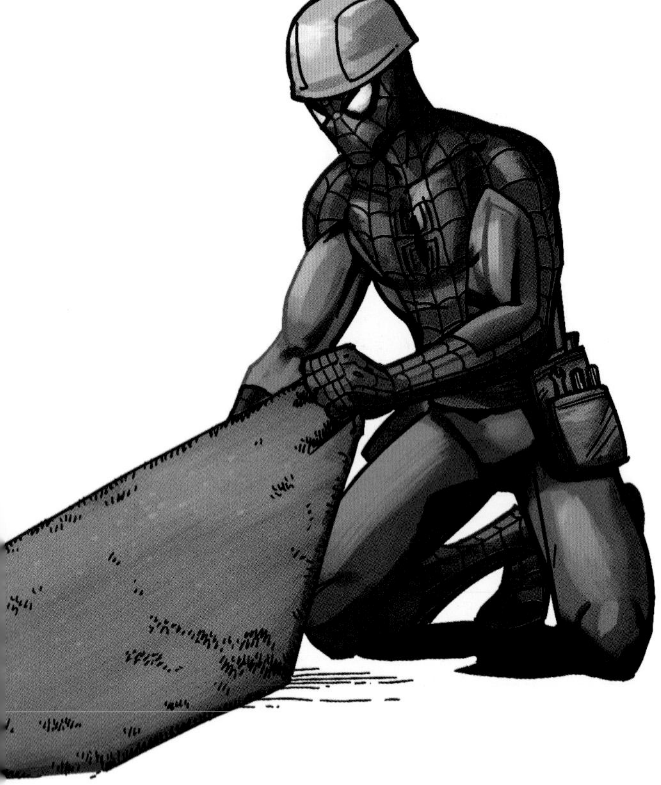

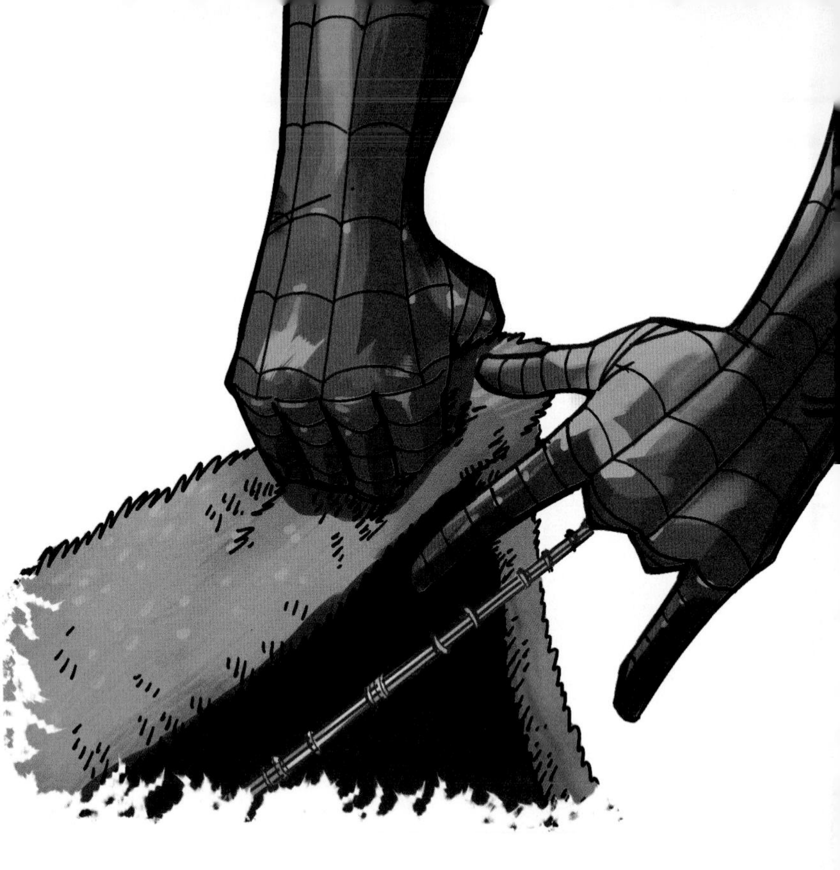

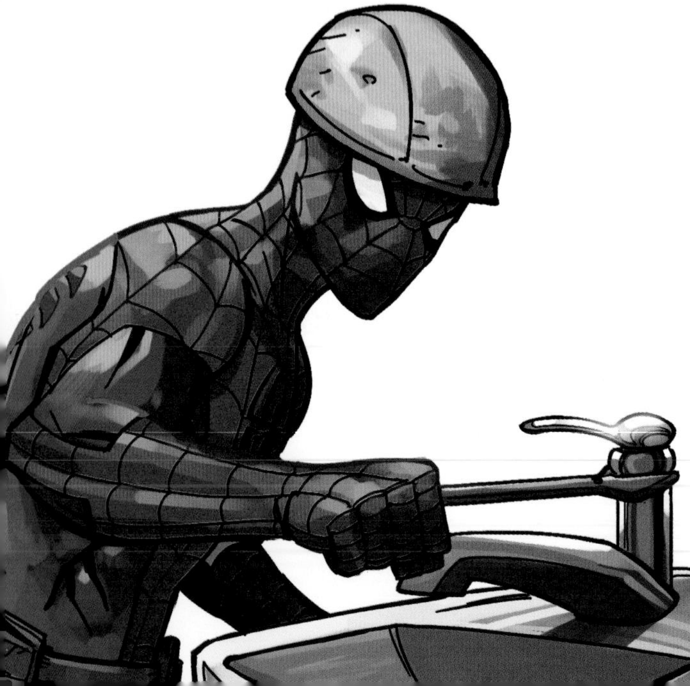

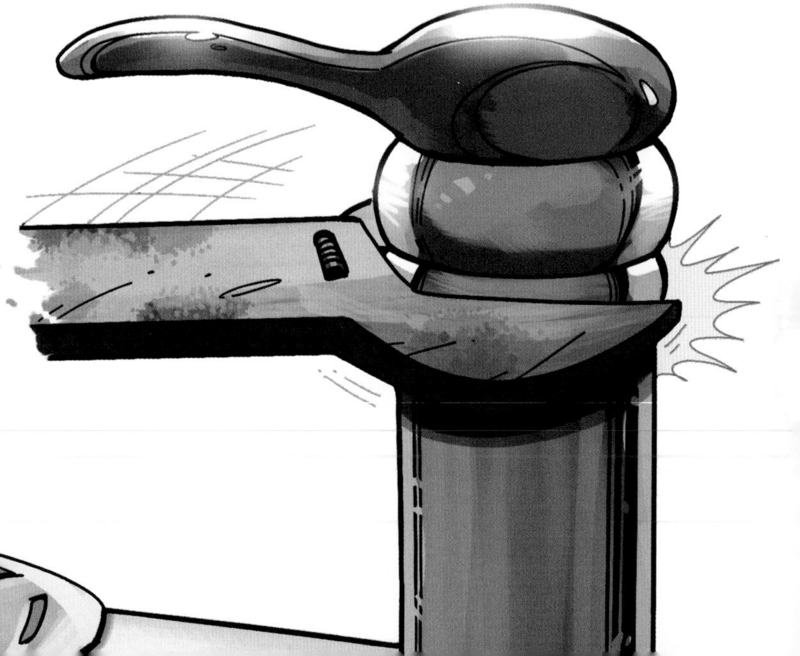

Once Spider-Man got back home, he went to work on the carpet. Using his webbing, Spider-Man stuck that loose corner down. *Thwip-thwip. Thwip-thwip.* Now it would stay down for good!

It took his spider-sized strength to tighten the pipes and fix that leaky faucet—well, his strength and a giant wrench! Spider-Man smiled under his mask. "Just call me DIY Spidey!" he said to himself.

It would have taken Peter Parker half an hour to get the ladder and fix all the light bulbs himself—but Spider-Man could walk on the ceiling! Presto change-o! But Spidey had to be careful not to leave any marks where he crawled. He thought it might be tough explaining to Aunt May why there were footprints on the ceiling.

Spidey webbed the wall patch in place from the inside, and Peter Parker smoothed it from the outside. It looked like there had never been a hole at all! And just in time, too. Peter's spider-sense began to tingle. Aunt May was about to come walking through the door! "Oh, no! I hope my last surprise is ready for her!" he said.

When Aunt May opened the door, she was met by Peter holding a roast—Uncle Ben's favorite meal—to help celebrate Ben's life and how important he was to both of them.

"Peter, you did all this for me?" asked Aunt May.

"I did this for us," Peter said. "This was Uncle Ben's house, too, and you were right. He wouldn't have liked seeing it fall apart. So we fixed the place up—just like Uncle Ben taught me!"

Just then, Peter noticed that his Spider-Man gloves were still on his hands!

"Oh, Peter, you always have your head in the clouds," Aunt May said. "And just who helped you do all this work? I didn't know you knew how to turn on the oven!"

Peter quickly hid his red Spidey gloves from his aunt. "Oh, just a friendly neighborhood handyman," Peter said. "Happy birthday, Uncle Ben."

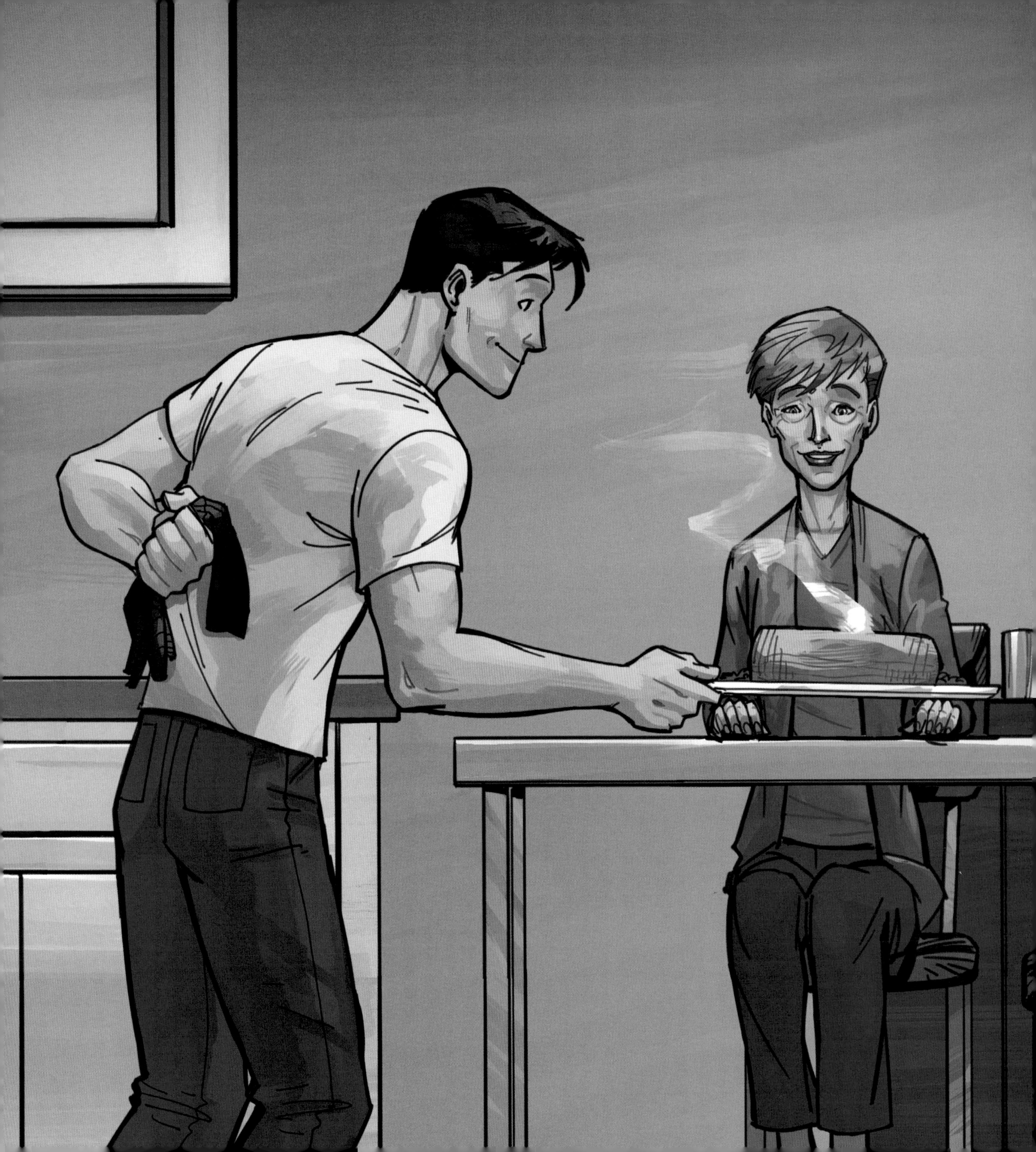

"Happy birthday, my dear Ben," Aunt May said with a smile.
The two of them laughed and told stories about Ben Parker for the
rest of the night.

SPIDER-MAN
Science vs. Science

Peter had stayed up all night prepping his science project—a steam-powered super potato launcher—for the school science fair. He was sure he'd finally get the recognition he craved!

Peter was exhausted, hardly able to keep his eyes open, but Aunt May spurred him on and took him to school.

While setting up his project, Peter looked at the other students' work. He was really impressed with Cameron's electrosphere, Ben's erupting volcano, and Nate's combustible chemistry set. It wasn't going to be an easy win for any of them!

Peter was introduced to the judges, one of whom was Dr. Curt Connors, a famous professor who had paved the way for major breakthroughs in science.

But Dr. Connors was best known not for his great scientific works but because one of his experiments went wrong and turned him into the reptilian creature called . . . the Lizard!

Fortunately, Dr. Connors was cured. He wouldn't change into the Lizard again. . . . Right?

As the judges examined each project, one student's experiment went haywire, releasing a strange green gas! Peter tried to help, but he was already too late! Dr. Connors was transforming!

Without a moment to lose, Peter ducked behind some solar panels. After a quick change, he leapt out as Spider-Man!

"Ladies and gentlemen—may I have your attention?" Spider-Man called to the crowd. "Please exit in an orderly fashion. We're about to have a showdown! Thank you!"

As Dr. Connors fought the transformation, the crowd fled the building. He thought he had cured himself of the monster inside, but something in that green gas had unleashed—the Lizard!

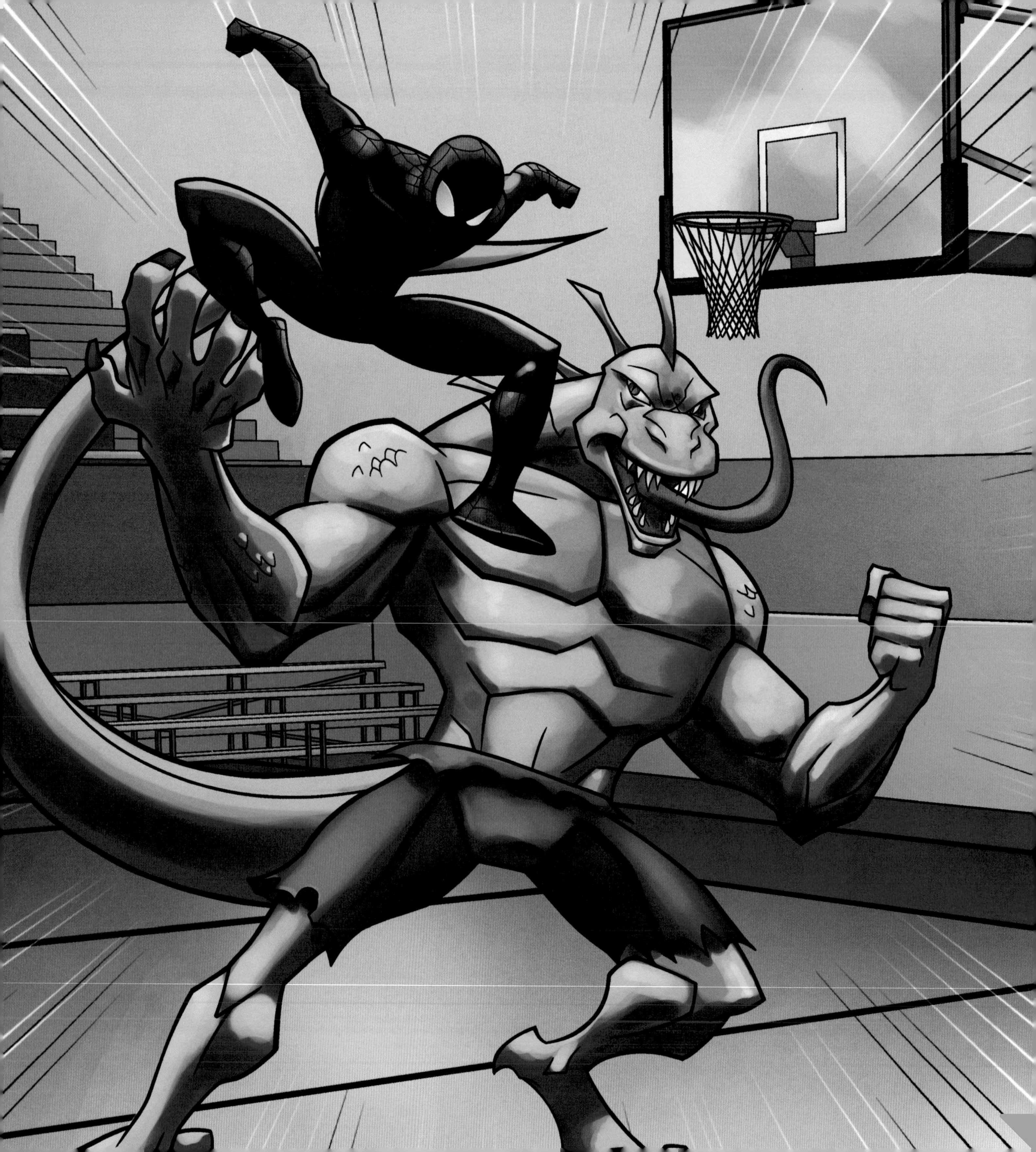

"Paging Doc Connors, paging Doc Connors. Can you stop yourself from changing? Just calm down now . . ." Spidey said, easing down his voice. "Think of all the great things you've done—the discoveries in science and genetics—all the hurt people you've helped! Remember you're a good person!" Spidey watched the scientist he admired struggle against the monster inside him—the monster trying to get out. . . .

"No one ever sseesss the good I've done, Ssspider-Man," Dr. Connors grunted back. "They only sssssee the horror I can unleashhh!"

Spidey wanted to help, but the transformation, once triggered, couldn't be stopped! And where Dr. Connors once stood, there now stood—the Lizard!

Spider-Man clenched his fists and prepared for the fight that was sure to come.

With the giant reptile barreling toward him, Spidey leapt into the air, spinning his webs as fast as he could. He wasn't going to let the Lizard trash all the science projects!

His webs slung from his wrists, each shot finding its target and preventing the projects from shattering on the ground. The Lizard roared! While the green reptile's mouth was wide open, Spidey spun a web right around those powerful jaws and pulled them shut! "Put a sock in it, Lizzy!"

Struggling to rip the web off his face, the Lizard staggered back a step and shredded his jaws free. "You barely sssssslowed me down," he hissed. "Why must you alwayssss get in my way?"

"Gee, let me think about that," Spidey said. "Oh, I know! It's because you're always trying to ruin everybody's day!" Spider-Man dropped back down to the gym floor. "Why don't we just skip the whole fighting part and get to you turning yourself in?"

The Lizard lunged at the webbed hero!

"I'll take that as a no," Spider-Man said as he slid between the Lizard's legs.

As Spidey popped up behind the Lizard, an idea came to him. The Lizard's thick skin made him too tough to defeat by pushing him around. He wouldn't feel a thing! "It's science that turned you into the Lizard, so let's fight science with science!" Spidey said.

Spider-Man used the projects around him: he swung Cameron's electrosphere at the Lizard! "This should give you a good jolt!" Spidey cried. Lightning lashed out from the electrosphere and struck his opponent!

ZRRAAKT!

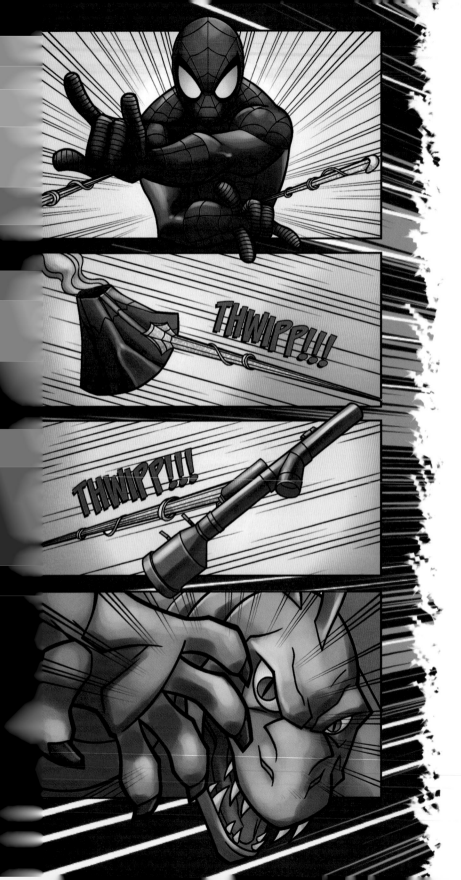

The Lizard growled at the wall-crawler as his massive, scaly green tail swatted Ben's volcano.

"All right," Spider-Man said. He slung a couple more webs, catching Ben's project and at the same time grabbing Peter's potato launcher and hurling Nate's combustible chemistry set through the air—raining flames down on the Lizard! "Let's see how you like playing with fire!"

Spider-Man realized he needed to outsmart his adversary, not just throw things at him. The Lizard put out the flames on his tough skin, hardly even noticing the heat. "Issssss that the best you can do, Sssssspider-Man?"

"Not by a long shot, Liz!" The web-slinger triggered Ben's volcano to erupt and aimed it directly at the Lizard's eyes. While his ornery opponent was temporarily blinded, Spidey grabbed the science project that would put Lizard down for the count—Peter Parker's potato launcher!

Boof! Boof! Spidey launched a couple of sweet potatoes, but they weren't strong enough! Spidey had a tough decision to make. "I'll miss you, my dear potato launcher," he said. He took his invention by the barrel and smashed the Lizard over the head with it!

The Lizard fell to the ground. But Peter was more concerned about his broken project. Now there was no way he'd win the science fair!

Spider-Man put everyone's science projects back in place while he waited for the Lizard to revert to human form. When he did, Dr. Connors was so sorry for what had happened. "Will I never be free of this terrible curse?" he asked Spider-Man.

Spidey considered the question. "I don't think you're responsible for what the Lizard does, Dr. Connors," he said. "You'll figure out how to get rid of the Lizard someday, and then you'll be remembered for all of your scientific work."

"That would be nice, Spider-Man." Dr. Connors smiled a little. "Thank goodness no one was hurt—not even the science projects."

"Well, one project broke," Spider-Man mumbled.

"It was that invention that stopped the Lizard! And I'm grateful for that." Dr. Connors replied.

The police and a group of doctors rushed into the auditorium to take Dr. Connors away and help him.

Peter sighed. "Well, I guess I'm off to make potato salad!"

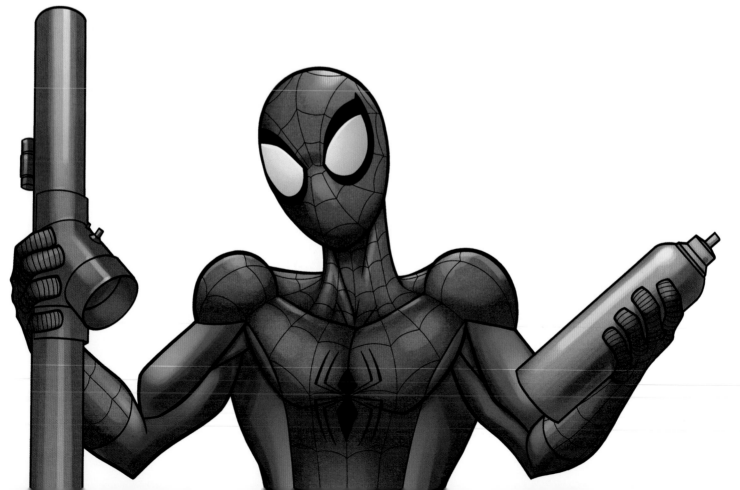

SPIDER-MAN
Hulk Disposal

Peter Parker was pretty excited when his boss, J. Jonah Jameson, called him in.

"I'm trusting you, Parker," JJ barked. "This job is major!"

Peter hopped on his bike and followed JJ's directions . . . right to the city dump!

Jameson's "major" assignment was to take pictures for a profile on Mack Scalese, the city's new head of Waste Management.

"Well, this stinks," Peter mumbled. "Literally."

A large bald man with a MACK SCALESE name tag called out to Peter from a trailer office. "You the kid they sent from the paper?"

"Yes, sir. My name is Peter Parker."

"Well, come on and take your pictures. I don't have all day."

Peter started clicking away on his camera, but he couldn't shake the feeling that something wasn't right. His spider-sense was tingling! But why? He looked around and saw a few men unloading some gray barrels from a nearby truck.

"Maybe we can get an action shot over there by those barrels?" Peter suggested.

"Never mind those barrels!" Mack yelled back. "I think we're through here. You got enough pictures."

Peter took one last picture—of the faded symbol on one of the barrels. He had an idea what it meant, but Spider-Man knew someone who could say for sure.

"No doubt about it—that's nuclear waste," Dr. Bruce Banner said as he examined the photograph Spider-Man had given him. "This could be very dangerous if not disposed of properly. What are they doing with it at the city dump?"

"Good question," said Spidey. "I think I'll go find out."

"I'll come with you," Bruce said. "We may need to get a sample for testing."

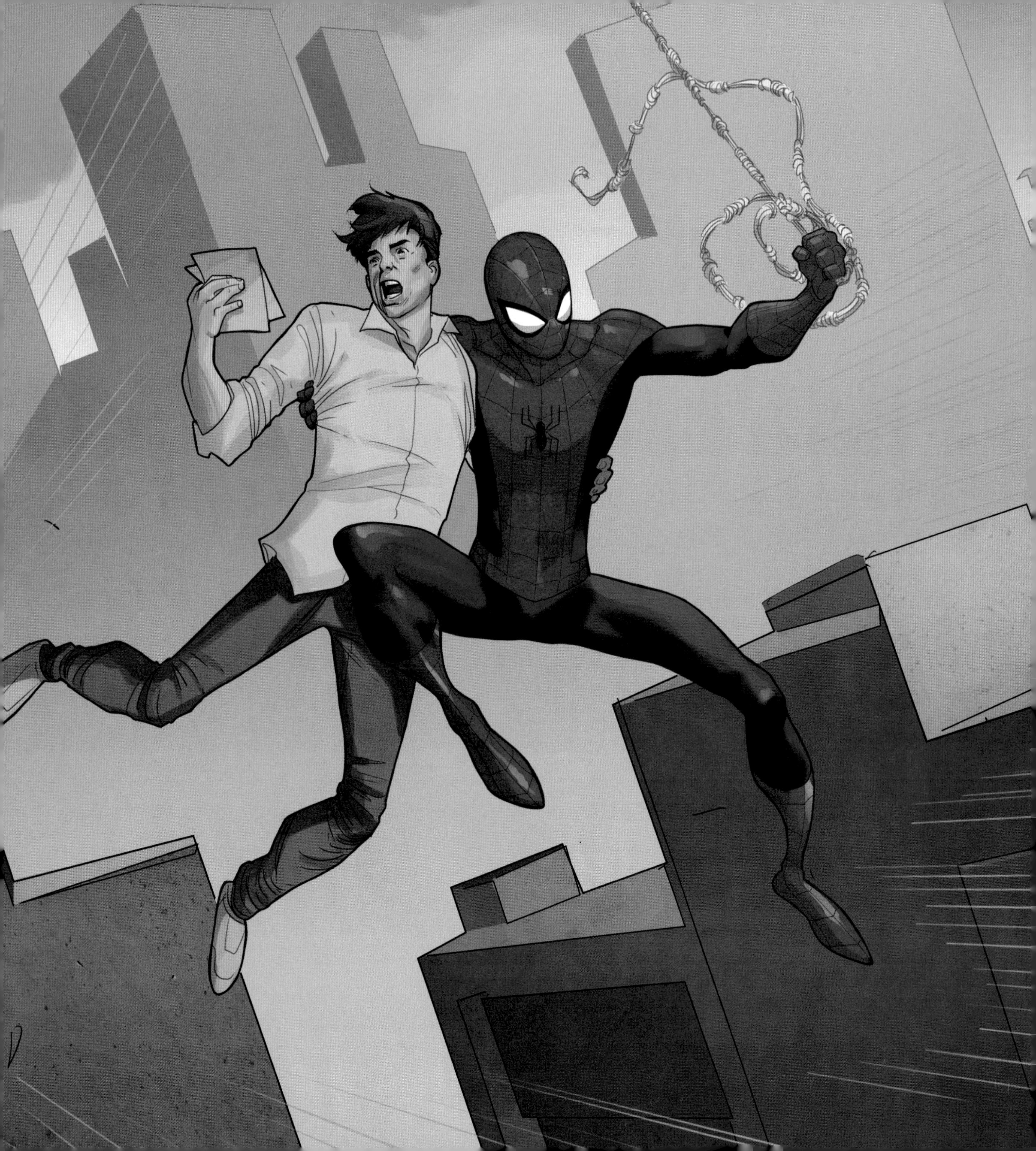

Back at the dump, Spider-Man tried to open a barrel for Bruce.

Just then, a spotlight blazed on, temporarily blinding them both. Spidey heard a voice that sounded familiar.

"Spider-Man! What are you doing here? I knew nothing good would come of that reporter. Get rid of them!"

It was Mack Scalese! Seconds later, Spidey and Bruce fell through a trapdoor. Before Spidey could web his way out of the pit, the steel door slammed shut again. There was no escape!

"It'll take more than that, Mack," Spider-Man said, starting to climb up one of the walls to get to the top. Maybe it was his imagination, but the wall seemed to be moving!

Spidey sighed. It wasn't his imagination. Both walls were moving closer, with the two of them stuck in the middle. They were in a giant trash compactor! They would be squished into a Spidey and Bruce sandwich in no time!

Spider-Man pushed against one of the walls. It slowed down a little, but it kept closing in. "I hope you're not claustrophobic," he said, turning to Bruce. "Getting out of this won't be easy."

"I am," said Bruce. "And trust me, it will be."

Mack smirked, happy to be rid of Spidey. Suddenly, he heard a loud explosion. He turned around just in time to see the trapdoor flying into the sky, and Spider-Man and a huge green giant emerged from the pit.

"Naughty, naughty, Mack," Spider-Man said, dusting bits of garbage from his shoulder. "Hulk, do you want to let him know what we do to people who don't recycle?"

"Hulk *SMASH*!"

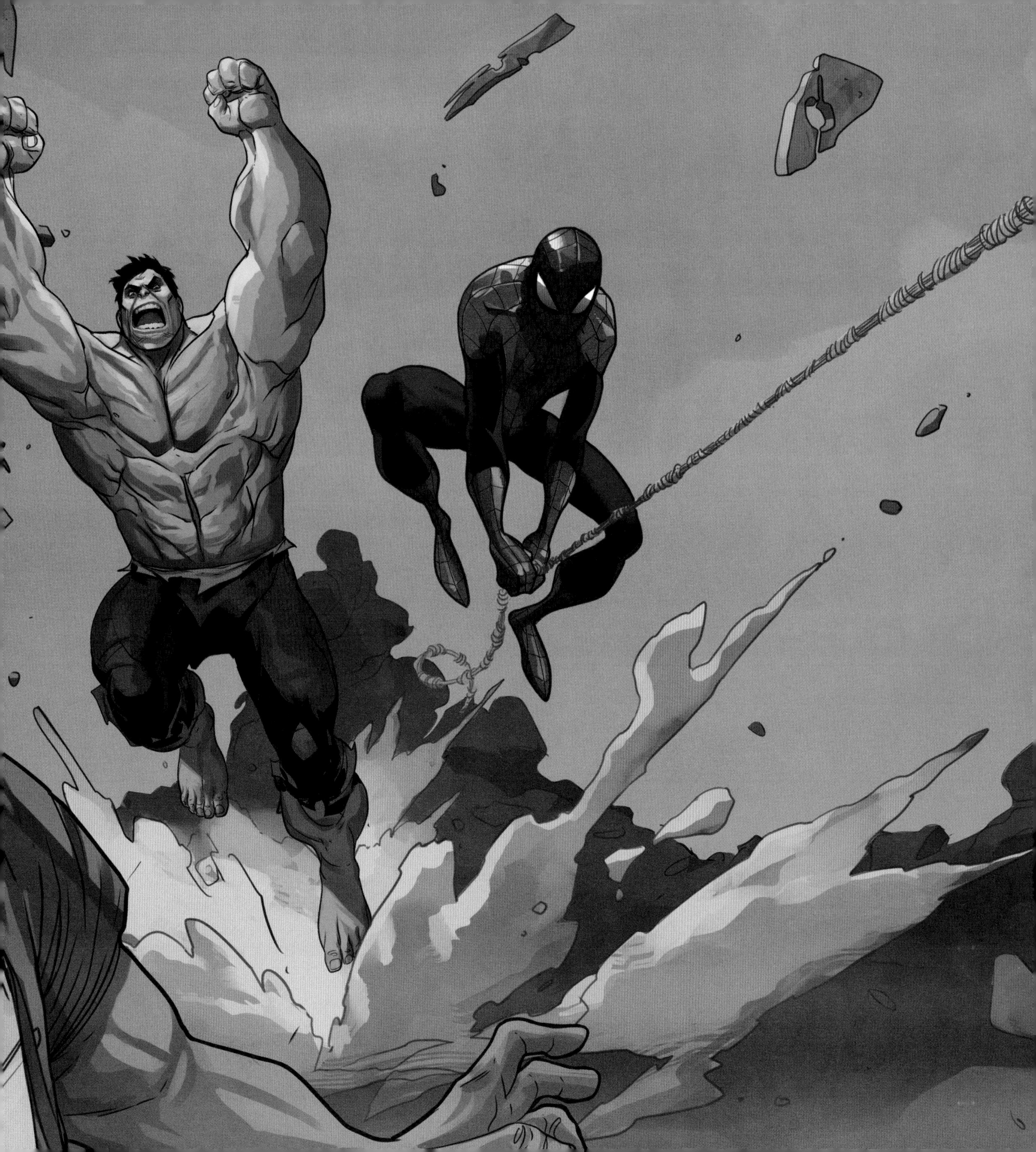

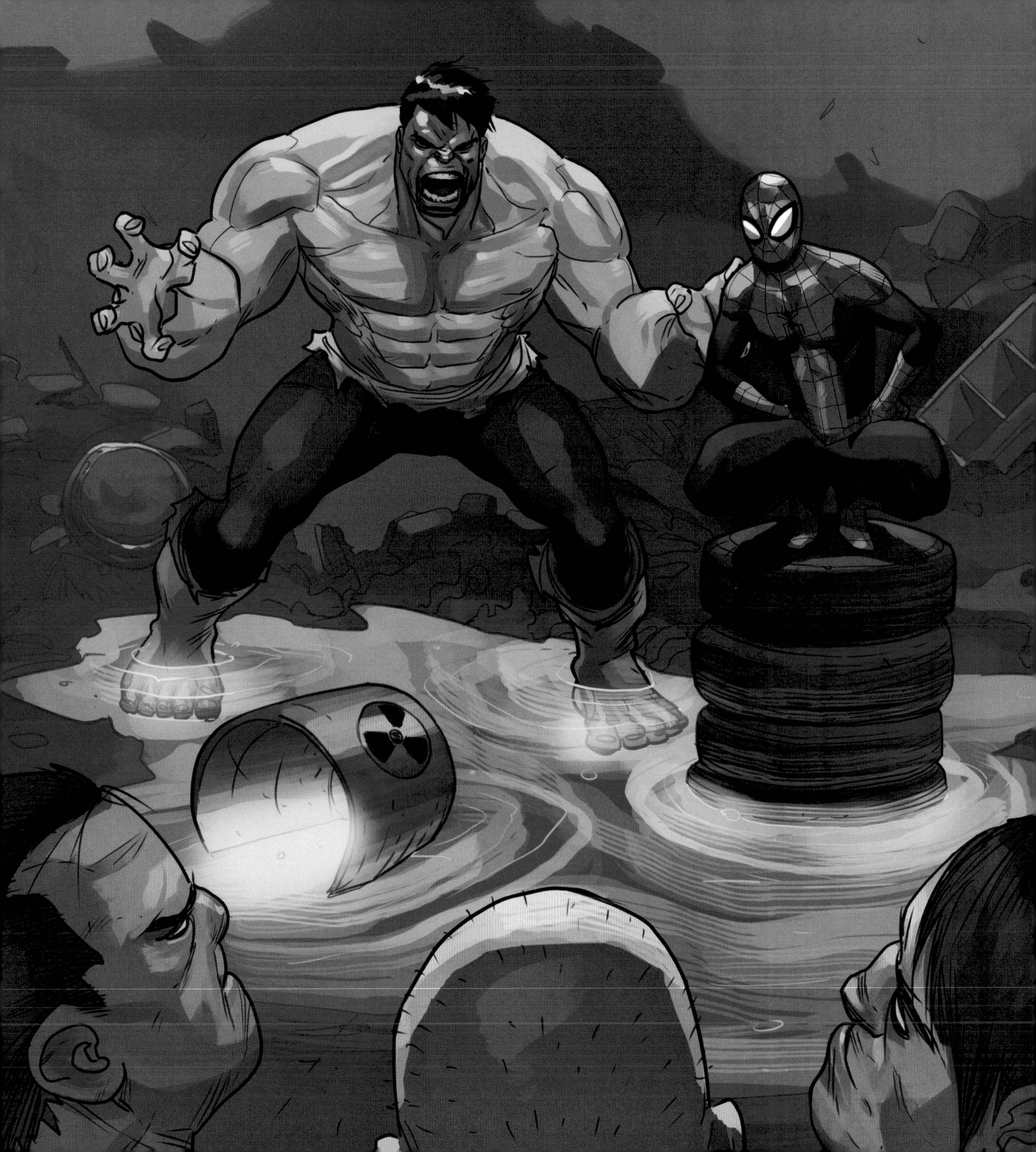

"Get them!" Mack yelled, waving his hands wildly at his henchmen.

About a dozen men in gray overalls surrounded Hulk and Spider-Man. One of them kicked over a barrel of nuclear waste in the direction of the Super Heroes.

Spider-Man swung himself up onto a nearby pile of tires to get out of the way, but Hulk just stood there as the toxic goo flowed over his feet. The nuclear waste had no effect on him. His tough, regenerative skin made him immune to it. The men gasped and drew back in fear.

"Now you've gone and done it," Spidey said. "He hates getting his feet dirty."

The men tried to turn and run away, but Hulk had other plans for them. With an incredible roar, Hulk charged toward the goons. It was not going to be a good day for them.

Hulk grabbed
each henchman
and threw him into
the open trash-
compactor pit. Once
the last one was
in, Hulk grabbed a
giant piece of scrap
metal and slammed
it over the opening,
trapping them inside.

"Sorry, guys.
We can't recycle
garbage," Spidey
joked.

Meanwhile, Mack was making a break for a garbage truck. Thinking quickly, Spider-Man grabbed an empty barrel and swung with all his might. It landed directly on top of the large man, and he fell over with a crashing *thud*.

"I think it's time to take out the garbage. What do you say, Hulk?"

"Hulk *TRASH*!"

The next morning, Peter Parker stood in J. Jonah Jameson's office as his boss held up a copy of the *Daily Bugle*.

"The Hulk?" Jameson yelled. "You couldn't even get me one lousy picture of Spider-Man?"

"I'm sorry, JJ. He took off too soon. But I'm sure you're happy that we exposed Mack Scalese's illegal dumping operation."

Jameson didn't seem to be listening to him. Peter could still hear him mumbling as he backed out of the office. "Garbage . . . just garbage."

SPIDER-MAN
Last Days of Summer

Peter stretched out his arms and leaned back. He was at Brighton
Beach with his friend Mary Jane on one of the last days of summer.
And he was going to make sure it was a blast!

"Ugh, I *can* wait for school to start," MJ grumbled.

"Not now, MJ. Let's enjoy our last few days of *freedom*," Peter joked.

But MJ continued to whine. "We are going to have to wake up super early to catch that stinky bus, suffer through gym class, and then come home to a pile of homework!"

That got Peter thinking. Going back to school would mean less time as Spider-Man, which was the most amazing part of his life.

Who would want to be Peter Parker when he could be Spider-Man instead? The famous wall-crawler could take on the biggest, baddest villains; help others in need, swinging from skyscraper to skyscraper through New York City; or just chill out and reflect on life.

What a bummer! Peter thought.

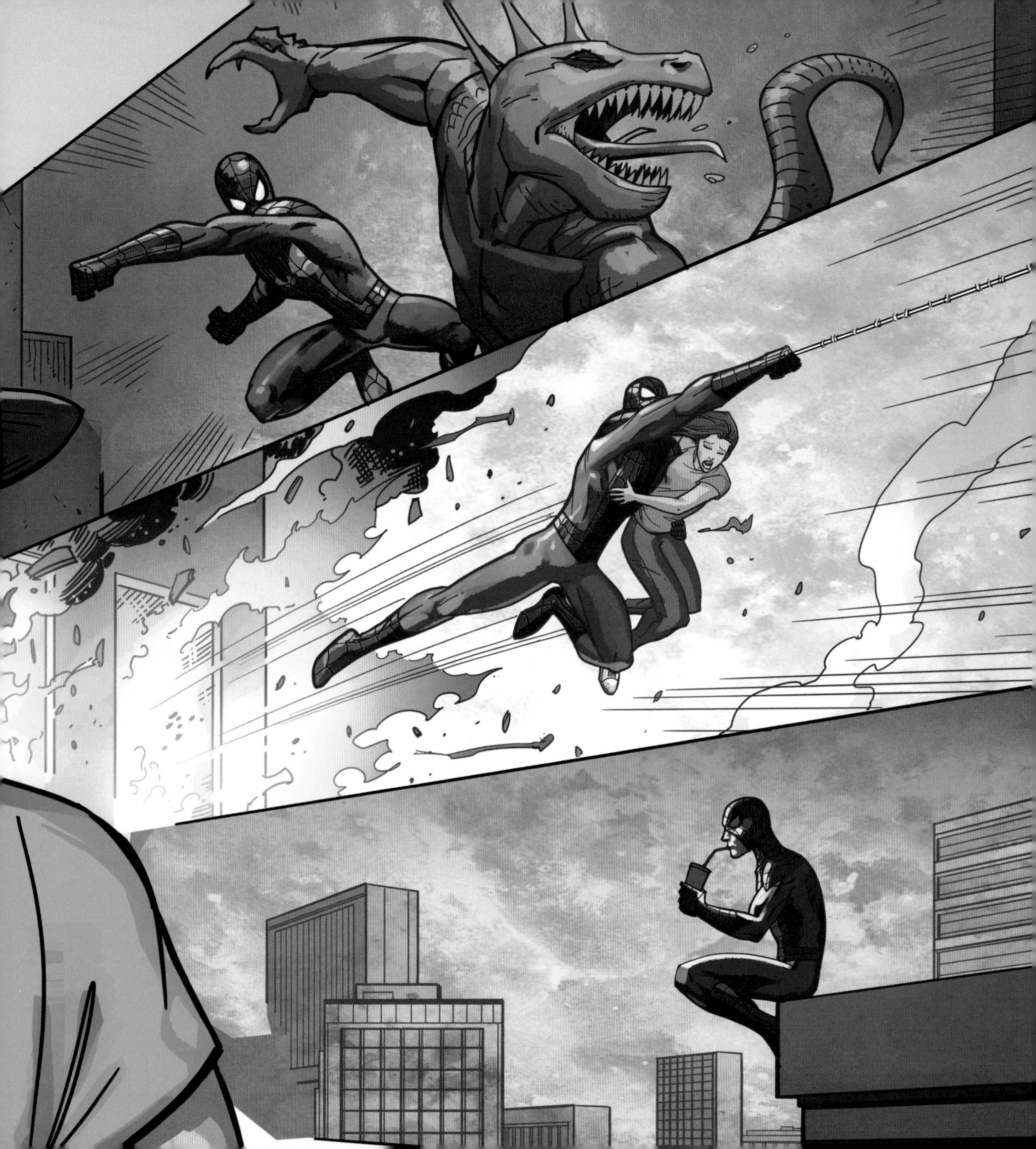

"No more hanging out at the beach or staying up late watching TV . . ." MJ went on.

"Well, we're still going to stay up late, but working on homework instead," Peter said with a smirk. MJ playfully kicked sand at him.

"Hey, look at that clown!" Flash yelled, pointing at Peter.

"And dealing with Flash five days a week!" MJ said. "Are you nervous?"

Of course Peter was nervous! Super Villains such as Rhino and Doc Ock were meaner than ever before. Spidey barely survived battling them in the summer heat. How was he going to add Flash Thompson to that list now? Flash didn't have super powers, but he did have a way of getting under Peter's skin. Peter had to admit, dealing with a bully—whether jock or Super Villain—was tough.

But Peter also had to remember the bigger picture: if they were so set on bringing him down, he must be doing something right . . . *right*?

Suddenly, his spider-sense went off.

"Hey, twinkle toes! I bet you can't catch this!" Flash yelled as he threw his ball right at Peter's head. Peter knew that with his spiderlike reflexes he could easily dodge the football. But then he realized someone else would get hit. So he let the ball hit him squarely in the head. *THUMP.* Peter's hat flew off and landed in the sand.

Peter took a deep breath as the surrounding kids laughed and pointed. He suddenly remembered why bullies stunk. He clenched his fists tightly and his face became red with anger. MJ looked frustrated, too. *I have to do something,* Peter thought.

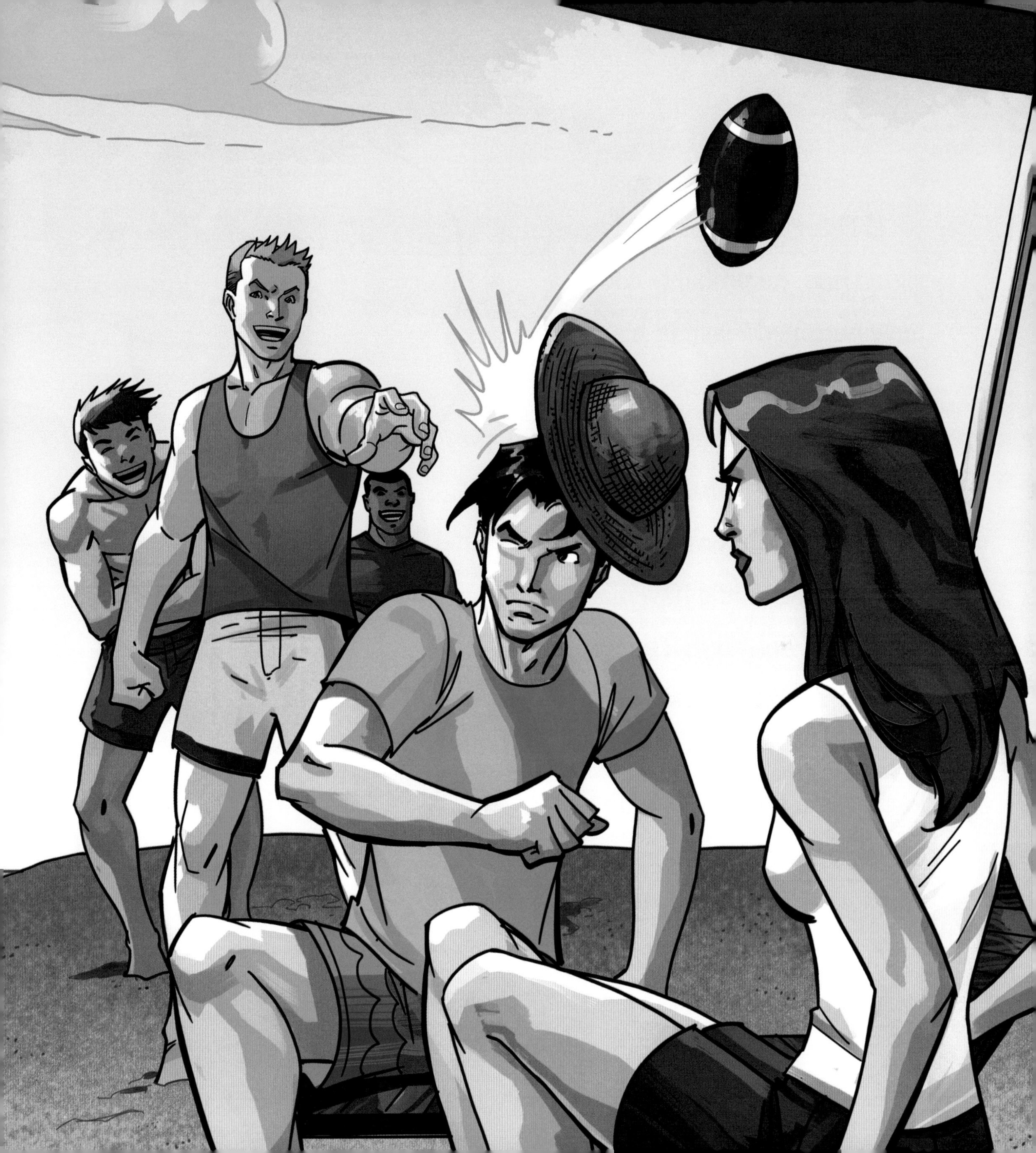

If Peter were Spider-Man right then, he probably could have wrapped Flash in his famous web burrito—maybe even dangled Flash over some hungry sharks. *I heard sharks love burritos*, Peter thought. And then he would have had the last laugh, not Flash Thompson.

He closed his eyes and slowly reminded himself that Peter Parker had powers, too: he could control who annoyed him and who didn't.

Peter let out a sigh and relaxed his fists.

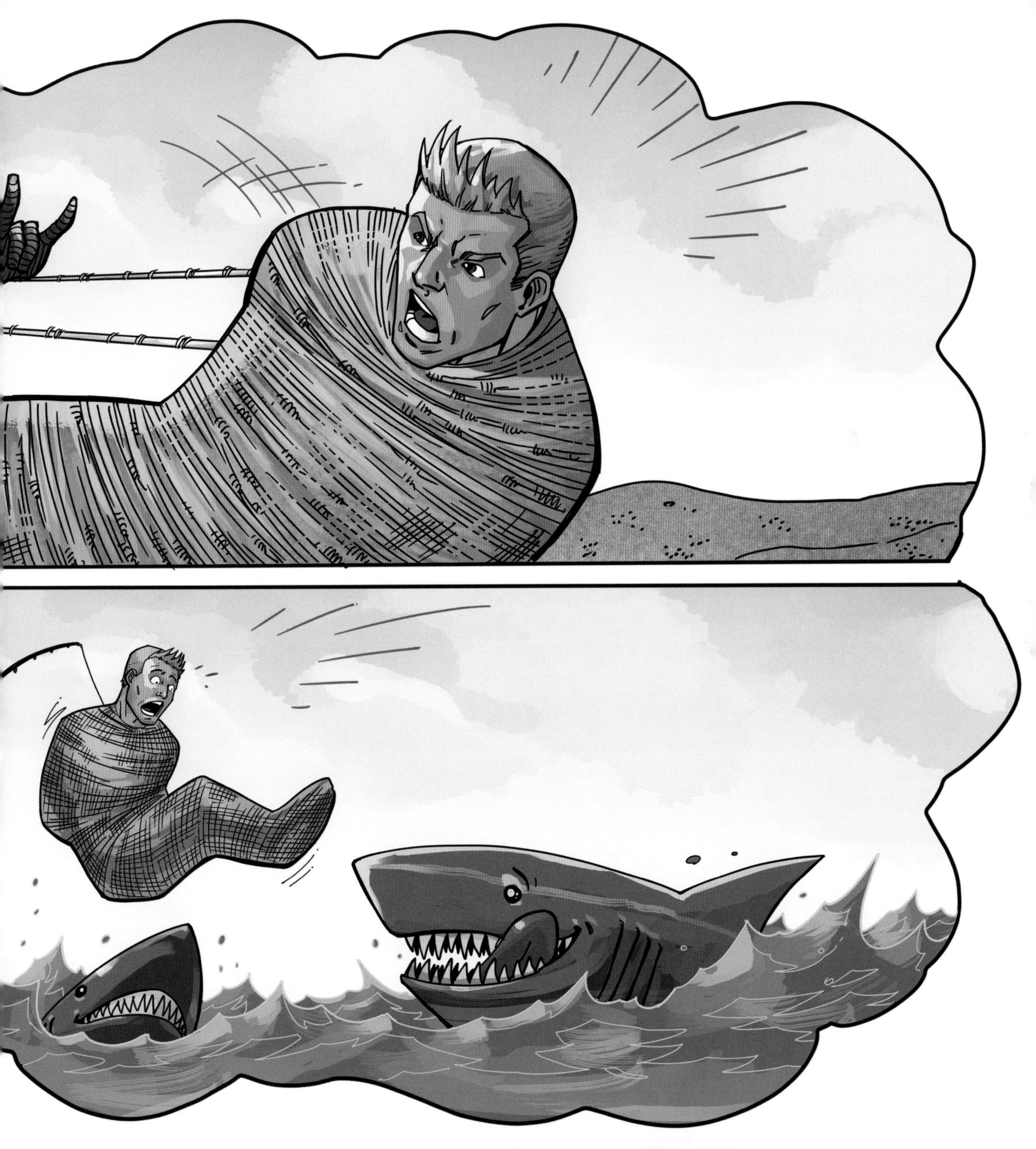

"Guess you're still a jerk on your days off, huh, Flash?" MJ shouted.

Peter looked up at MJ. He was surprised to hear his friend stand up to the biggest bully in school. She picked up Flash's ball and threw it into the ocean.

"With a friend like you, I'm good," Peter said as he high-fived his hero. In the end, it wasn't so bad to be Peter Parker.

SPIDER-MAN
Alone Against the Sinister Six!

*I*t was an average day for the amazing Spider-Man—you know, the kind of day when a Super Villain like the Looter breaks into a museum and tries to steal a rare meteor. As Spidey snared the Looter in his web, the criminal sprayed the wall-crawler with a strange mist.

"Wait. Did you just spray me with *perfume*?" Spidey asked. "I am officially done."

"Now wait here for the police like a good little Looter. I'm going home to take a bath—*yuck!*" said Spidey. The masked hero swung away just as the police arrived.

Unknown to the web-slinger, a curious group had gathered across town. Beneath an abandoned dock on the East River, Doctor Octopus spoke to a collection of Spidey's most fearsome foes.

"The Beetle, Electro, Kraven the Hunter, the Lizard, and the Rhino—Spider-Man has defeated each of you," said Doctor Octopus.

A bored Electro zapped a nearby computer screen, causing it to shatter. "Tell us something we *don't* know!" said Electro.

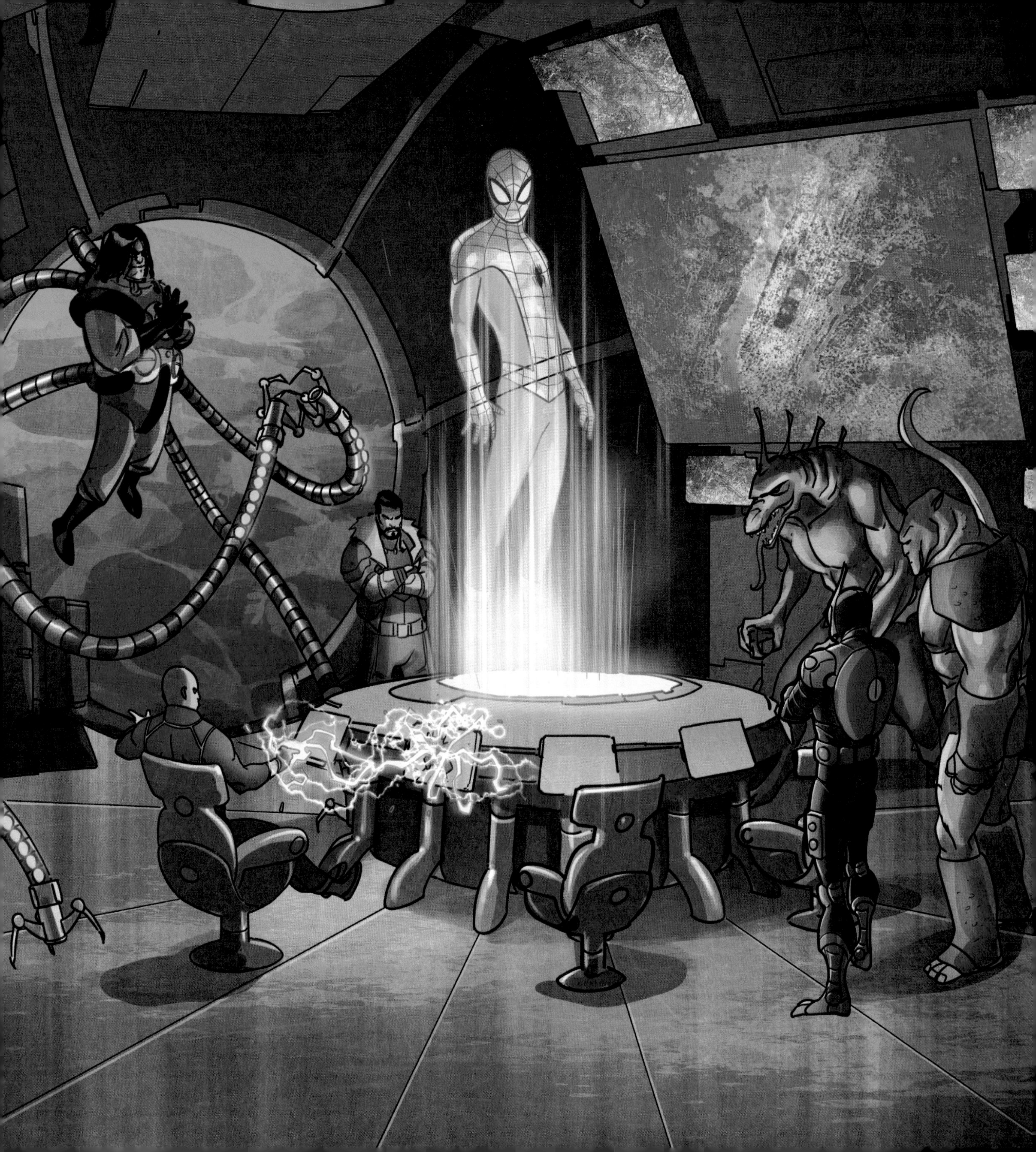

"What if I told you I have the perfect plan to stomp Spider-Man?" Doctor Octopus asked with a terrible smile. The other villains looked at the doctor and smiled their own terrible smiles.

"What do you have in mind, Doc?" said the Beetle.

"Spider-Man has beaten each of us. But what if we act as a team? How can one tiny bug hope to stop . . . the Sinister Six?"

"You make it sound easy," said Kraven. "But what is your plan?"

Doctor Octopus pointed to a huge screen.

"The Looter owed me a favor. He sprayed Spider-Man with a mist that carries tiny, almost invisible robots— Octobots!"

"What are itty-bitty robots gonna do?" asked the Rhino.

"The Octobots will track Spider-Man wherever he goes," said Doc Ock. "We can attack at any time!"

Spider-Man couldn't wait to get home and take a bath! But suddenly, his spider-sense began to tingle.

"Uh-oh!" said Spidey. "That means danger is near. But I don't see any—"

Before he could finish his sentence, a spear sliced through his web line. Standing on a nearby rooftop was Kraven the Hunter! Spider-Man spun another web to break his fall and landed on the same rooftop.

"Hey, if it isn't my old friend Kraven!" said Spidey. "You're up past your bedtime!"

"I do not find your so-called jokes amusing," said Kraven.

"Oh, come on! My jokes are at least as amusing as your vest!" said Spidey.

The Hunter threw a net at Spider-Man, but the hero dodged it with ease. Then he trapped Kraven in his web.

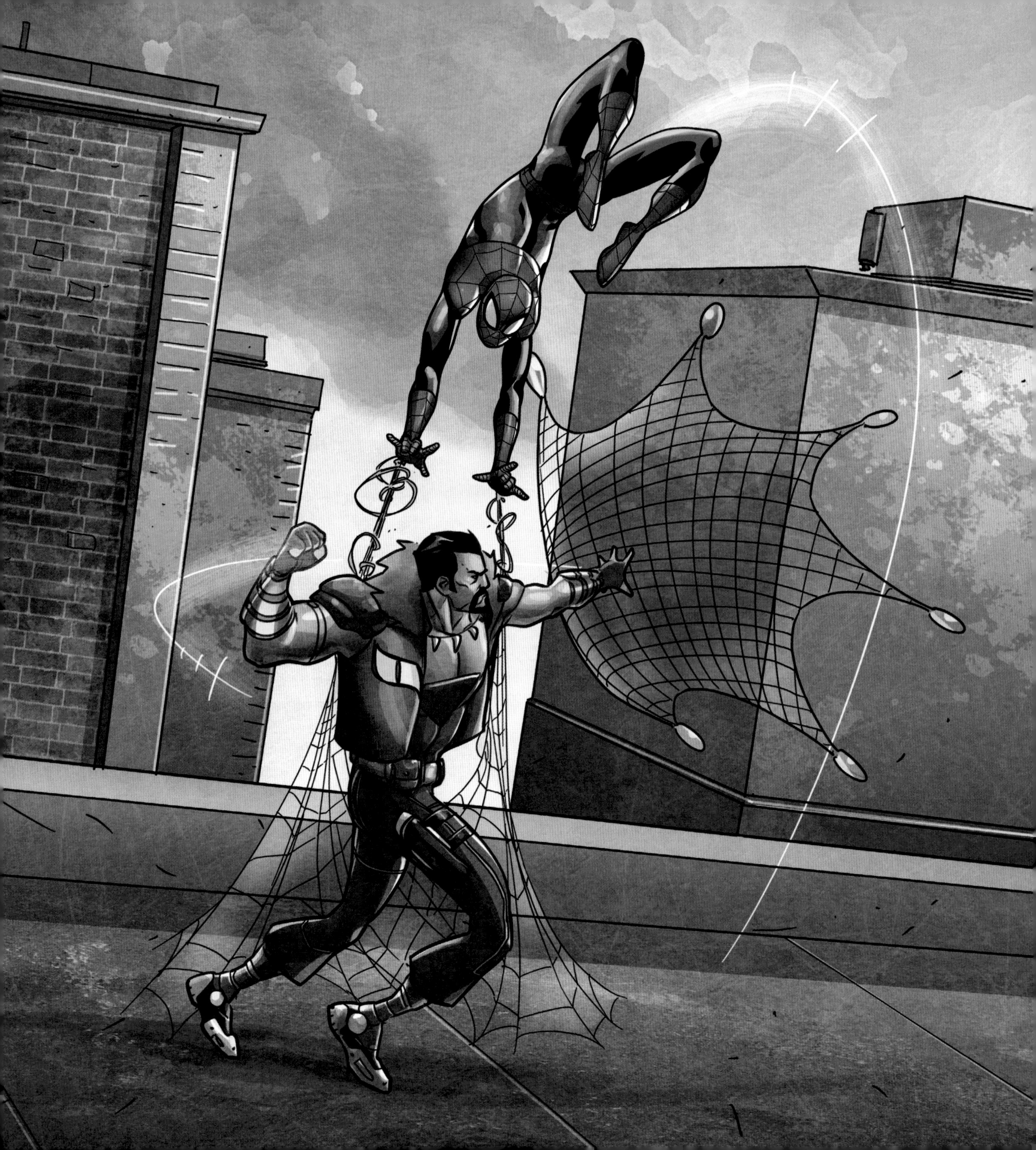

But as soon as Spider-Man swung away, he ran right into the Beetle! The armored villain blasted Spidey with rockets. Dodging and ducking, the web-slinger escaped—only to be cornered by the Lizard!

"What is this, Pick on Web-Head Week?" Spider-Man said as he struggled against the Lizard's claws.

"More like Desssssstroy Sssssspider-Man Day!" the Lizard hissed.

Using all his strength, Spider-Man broke free from the Lizard.

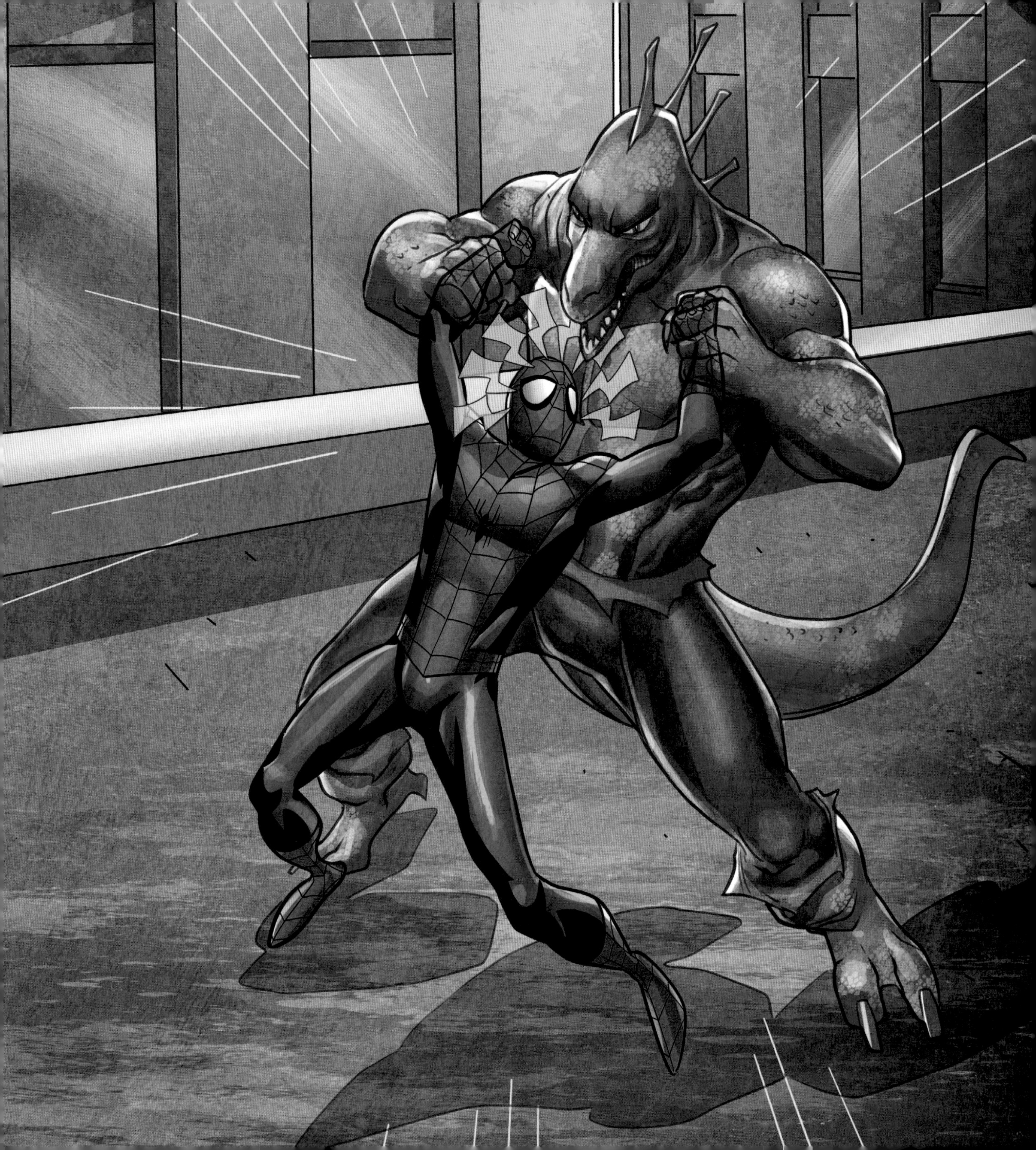

"I need to catch my breath and think this through," said Spider-Man. Swinging to a nearby alley, he quickly changed into Peter Parker. "That ought to throw them off my trail," said Peter.

But it didn't! The Rhino rumbled right by him.

"Hey, kid! Did you see Spider-Man?" said the Rhino as he stopped and looked around for the hero. Peter shook his head.

At home, Peter sat in his bedroom and stared at his Spider-Man costume.

"That stuff the Looter sprayed . . . that must be how my worst friends forever keep finding me! Let's have a closer look."

Peter studied his costume under a microscope. He made a shocking discovery.

"Well, what do you know? Mini tracking robots!" said Peter. "This gives me an idea!"

"It's time for another member of our crew to say hello to that webbed weasel!" said Doctor Octopus.

He turned on the monitor and saw Spidey running across a rooftop. Then Spider-Man stopped. To the Super Villains' surprise, they could suddenly hear Spidey!

"Hey, Doc!" said the hero. "Say good-bye to your little friends!"

Spider-Man took out a bottle and sprayed something all over his costume. Doctor Octopus's monitor turned to static.

"Hey!" said the Rhino. "What happened to the big TV?"

"The bug figured out the Doc's plan, horn-head," said Electro.

The Sinister Six were in shock—but not Doc Ock. He just smiled.

"No matter. My Octobots have done their work. Soon Spider-Man will be ours!" Doctor Octopus said.

"Dear Diary," said Spidey. "Worst. Day. Ever."

Though he had stopped the villains from spying on him, he knew Doc Ock and his gang were still out there.

Spidey spun a web and swung off into the night. Somehow, he would need to stop the Sinister Six. But Spider-Man knew he couldn't do it alone. *Perhaps I'll find a few friends,* he thought. But who?

To be continued . . .

SPIDER-MAN
Halloween Stampede

*P*eter Parker loved watching the Halloween parade every year—especially since, as Spider-Man, he always had the best seat in the house. He really got a kick out of seeing how many people tried to imitate their friendly neighborhood Super Hero.

One year, the grand marshal of the parade was Arthur Van Buren, the billionaire tech wiz whose latest invention was a phone that worked underwater. Spider-Man saw him at the front of the parade, wearing his costume: a fish holding a phone in its fin.

"I wonder if it's called an iFin," Spidey said, chuckling as he continued to scan the crowd.

Behind the grand marshal were several varieties of princesses, monsters, and even what looked like an entire army of costumed zoo animals. He counted a dozen gorillas, a few grizzly bears, and even one very realistic rhinoceros.

Almost *too* realistic, Spidey thought. He didn't have a good feeling about it. And that's when his spider-sense started tingling.

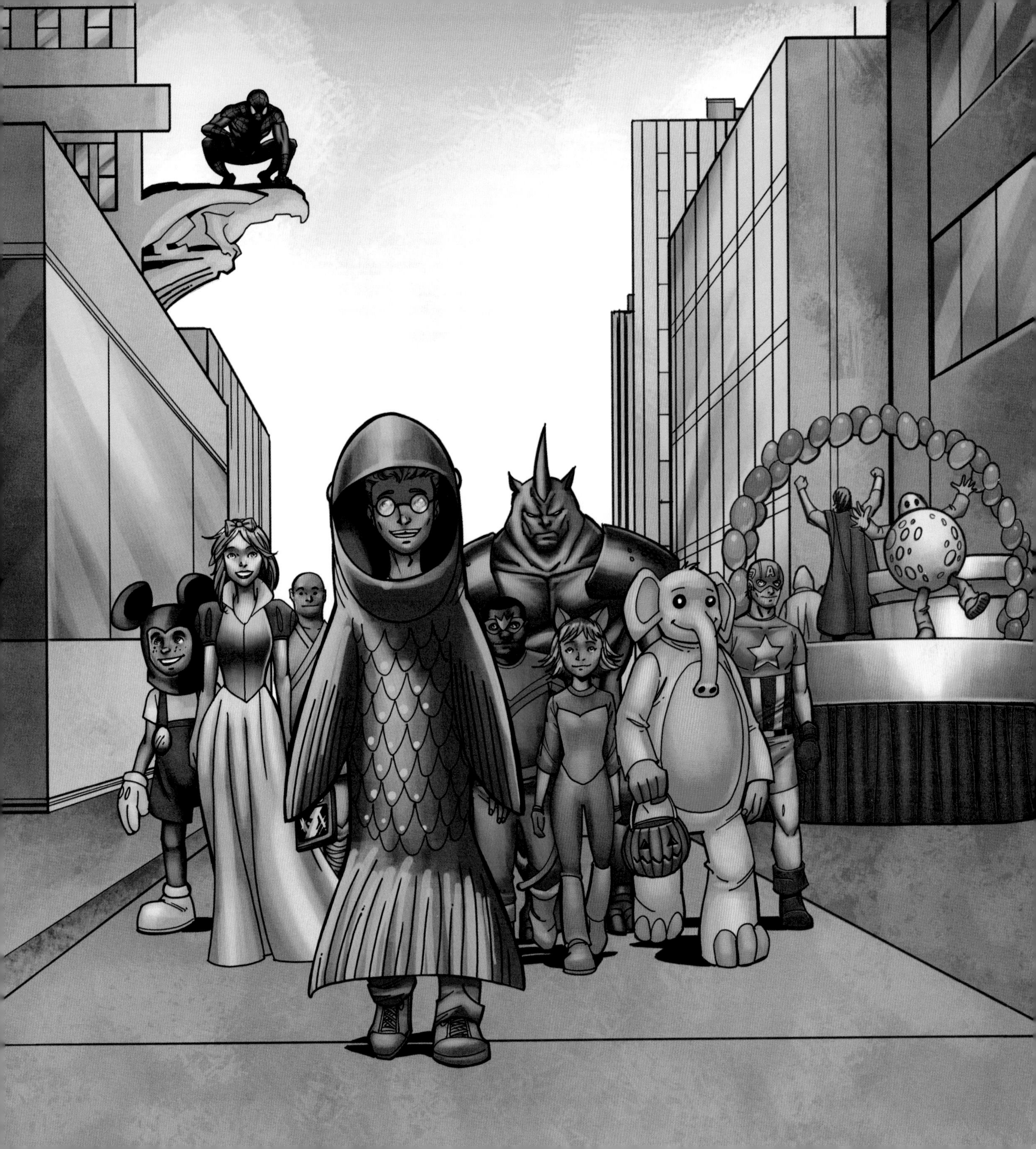

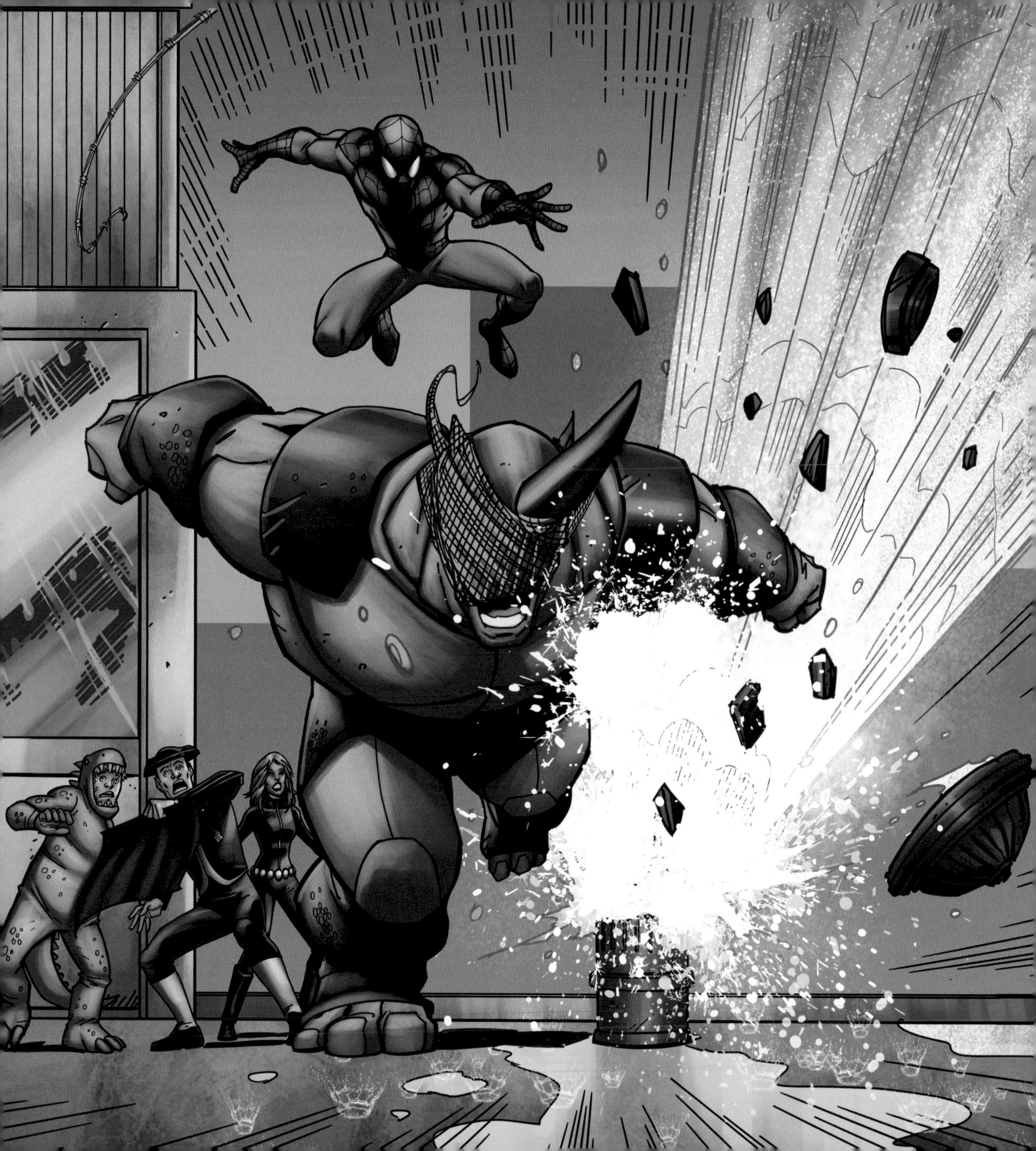

Just then, the person in the rhinoceros costume broke away from the other animals and charged toward the front of the parade. Spider-Man was surprised that anyone could run so quickly in such a heavy costume. Whoever it was looked like he or she was heading straight for Arthur Van Buren! Finally, Spidey put it all together.

"That's not a rhinoceros costume! It's *Rhino*!" Spidey yelled before swinging down into the parade and blasting some webbing into the Super Villain's eyes. "What a surprise! I didn't know you were a big fan of Halloween, horn-head."

Rhino was blinded, but he kept charging—straight into a fire hydrant!

"Oh, great, it's spider-bug," he grumbled, rubbing the top of his hard head.

Spidey landed on top of a streetlight above Rhino. "Now, what could you possibly be up to? Is it treats? Or tricks?"

"I'm busy, web-head!" Rhino snarled, grabbing the spout of the fire hydrant. "But since you asked, how's this for a nice trick?"

Rhino ripped the fire hydrant open! Powerful jets of water shot into the parade, and the crowd started to panic! Even Spidey got caught in the watery geyser!

"Hope you brought your swimsuit," Rhino said with a sneer. "Now, where's that rich kid? I have a ransom to collect." He turned and ran into the chaos at the front of the parade, leaving Spider-Man to take care of the watery mess.

"Why does he always have to be such a party pooper?" Spidey groaned, looking around for a way to plug the fire hydrant. His eyes landed on one of the parade banners. "That's it!"

All Spider-Man had to do was find a way to secure the banner over the top of the hydrant. He flicked a strand of web at one corner of the tarp, then swung himself through the air. "Geronimo!"

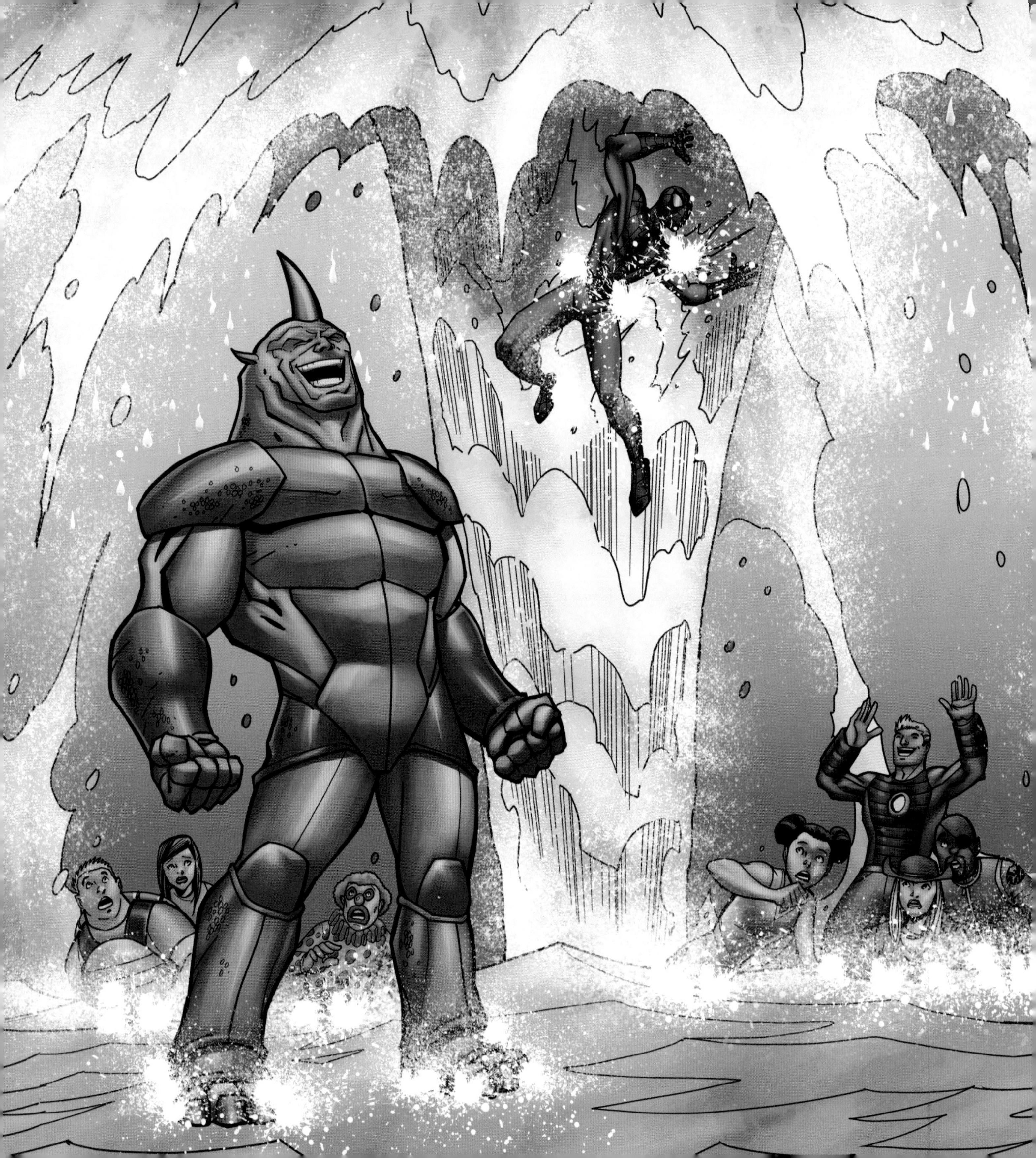

Spider-Man flicked three more strands of webbing onto each of the remaining corners. Then, using the tarp as a parachute, he floated down over the geyser. When he landed, he tightened the tarp over the hydrant, tying a knot at the base.

"That should hold it until they can turn off the water," he said, looking around to make sure no one was hurt. "Now, did I hear something about a ransom?"

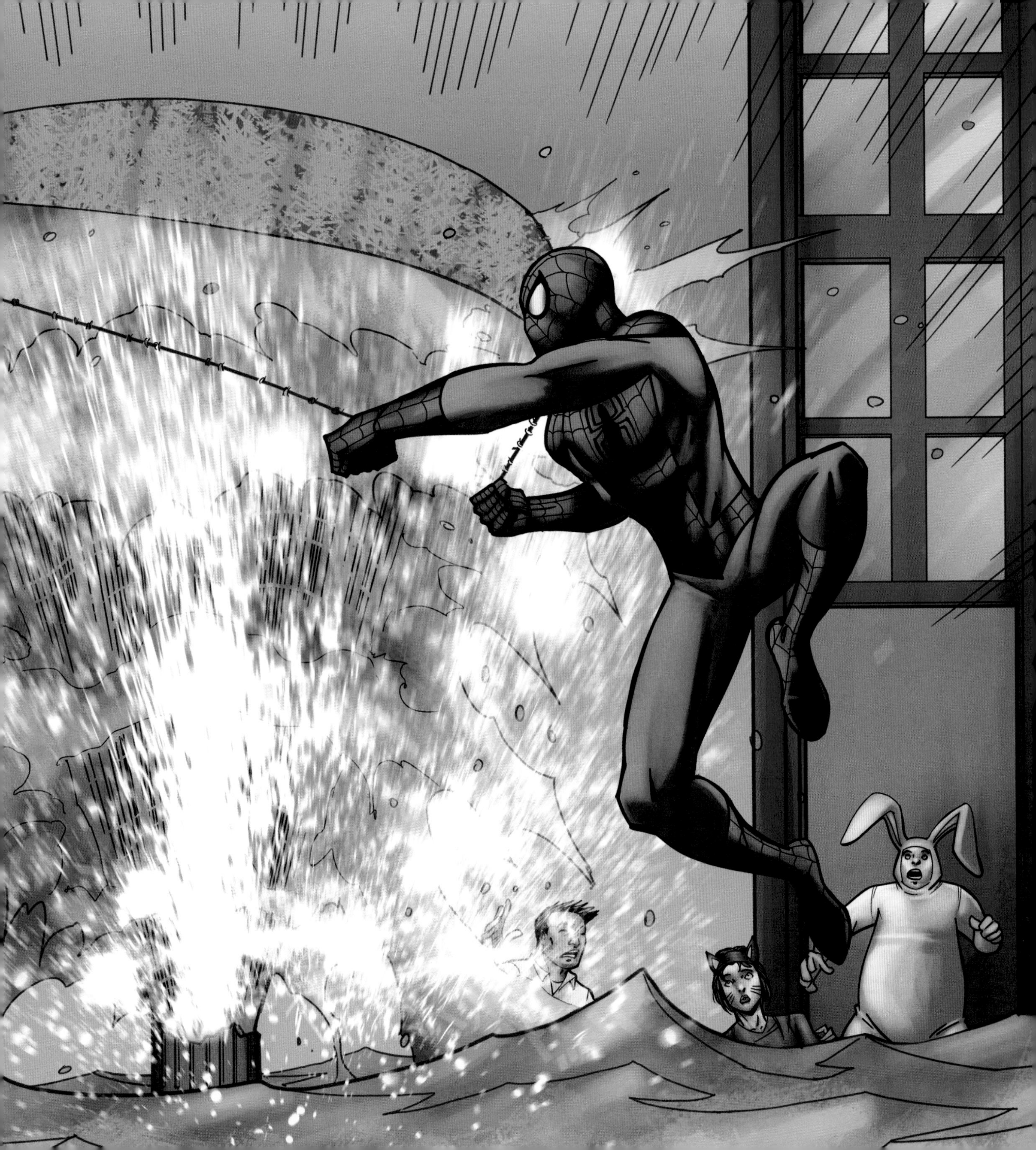

Spider-Man saw Rhino at the front of the parade, carrying a large fish over his shoulder.

"You're too late!" Rhino growled. He turned and charged through the crowd, with Arthur Van Buren trapped in his grasp.

Spidey needed to act fast, and he had the perfect idea. Flicking a web at the street sign on the corner, Spider-Man swung ahead of Rhino. Then he quickly created a thin stretch of webbing between two light poles. "I hope that fish costume has a lot of padding!"

Rhino saw Spidey's trip wire, but it was too late.

"*WHAAAHH!*" Rhino cried. The gray Goliath ran right into Spidey's trap and went sprawling in the street, sending Arthur Van Buren flying through the air. The tech mogul landed in the middle of a small fountain in the park.

"Are you okay?" Spidey called out.

"Don't worry, Spider-Man," Van Buren replied, waving his fin. "My phone is waterproof!"

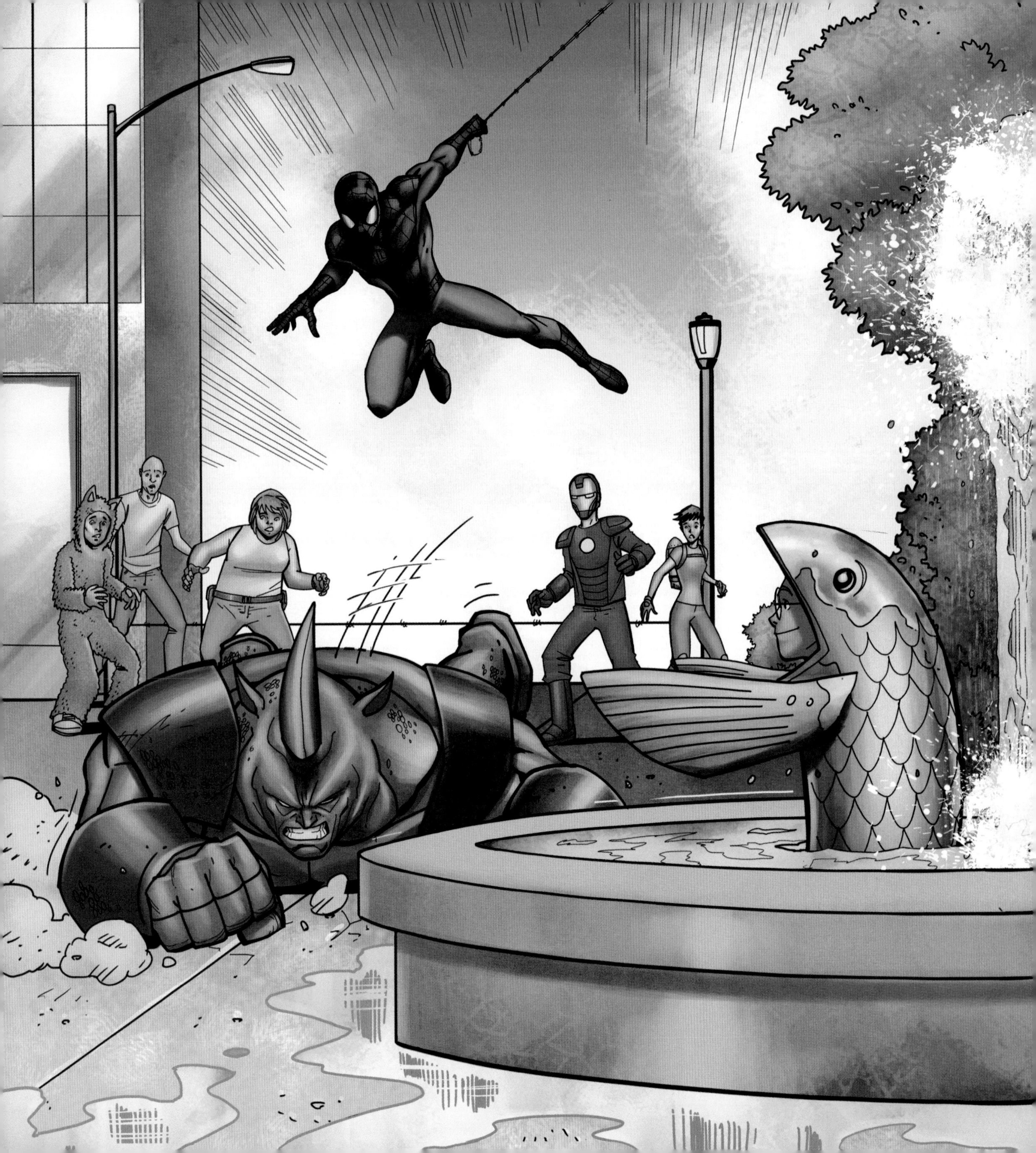

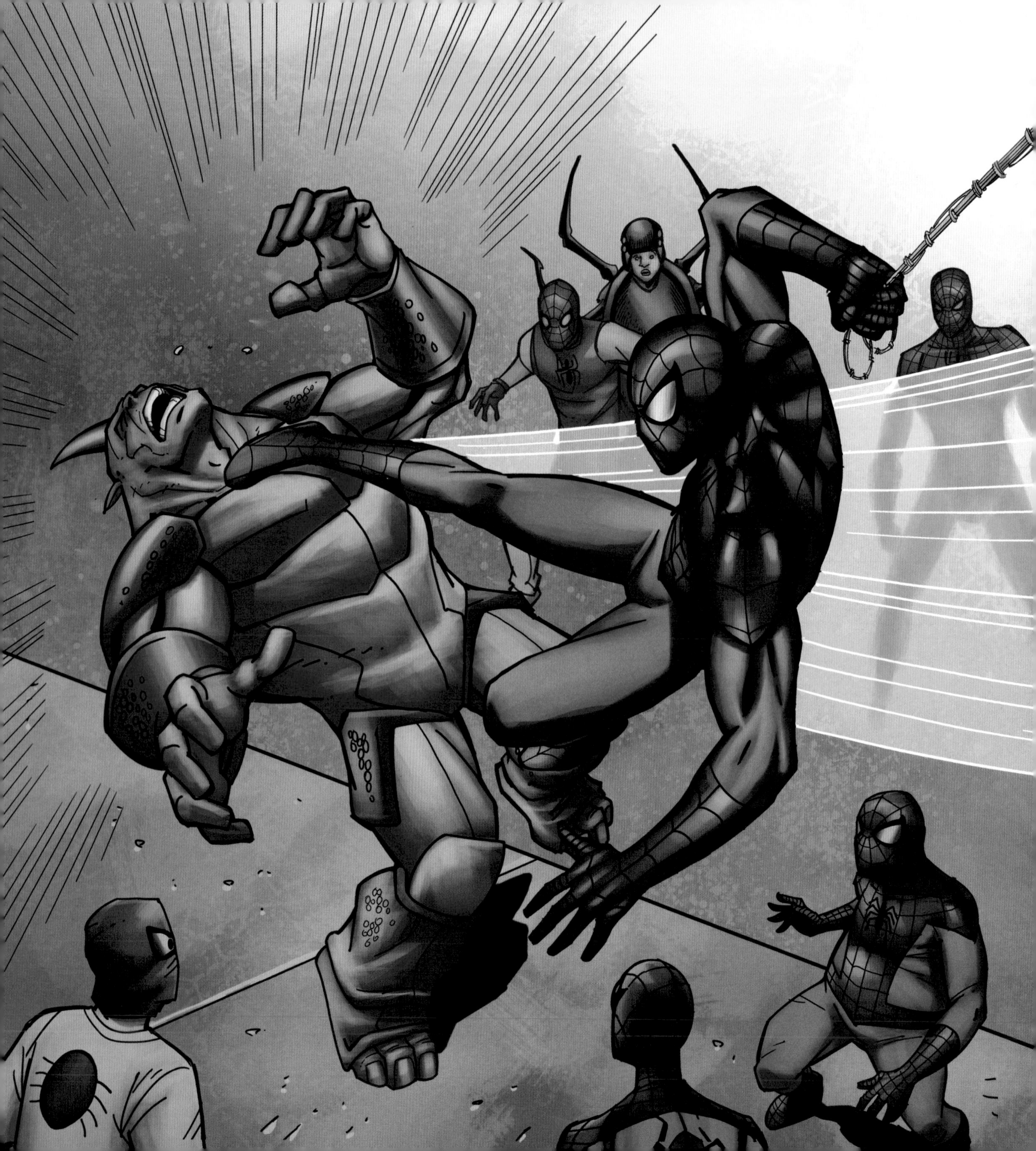

"You'll be sorry you did that, bug-brain!" Rhino growled.

"'Bug-brain'?" Spidey asked. "Is that the best you can do?"

By that time, the people in the parade had started to gather around them, so Spidey decided to have some fun.

Rhino rushed toward the Super Hero, but this time the wall-crawler was ready.

"Wrong way, buddy. I'm over here!"

Rhino looked up to see Spider-Man to his right.

"Now I'm over here!"

Rhino spotted another Spider-Man, but to his left.

"Over here!"

Every time Rhino started to charge, he saw another Spider-Man!

"Stop! You're getting me dizzy!" the large villain cried.

Just then, the real Spider-Man swooped in from above, knocking Rhino directly in the chin. He teetered for a moment before falling squarely on his face again.

A few minutes later, Arthur Van Buren was leading the parade again. Right behind him, a group of people in different Super Hero costumes escorted a large float. On the float, a handcuffed Rhino, surrounded by police, scowled and grumbled.

High above, back on his perch on a tall building, Spider-Man couldn't help smiling. "Best Halloween parade *ever*!"

SPIDER-MAN
Attack Off-Broadway!
Guest Starring Rocket and Groot

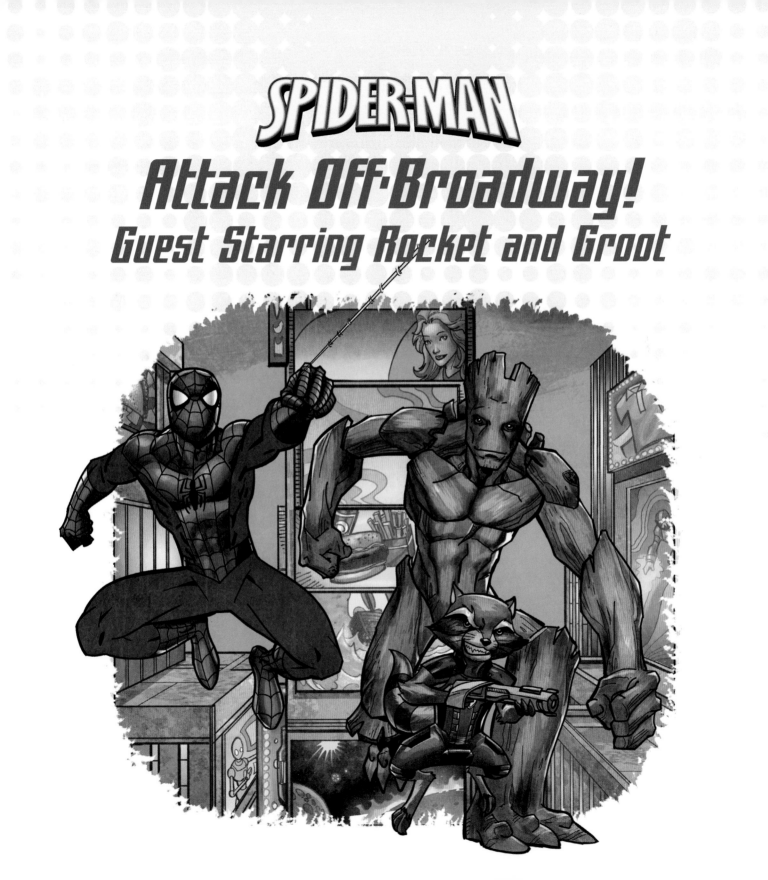

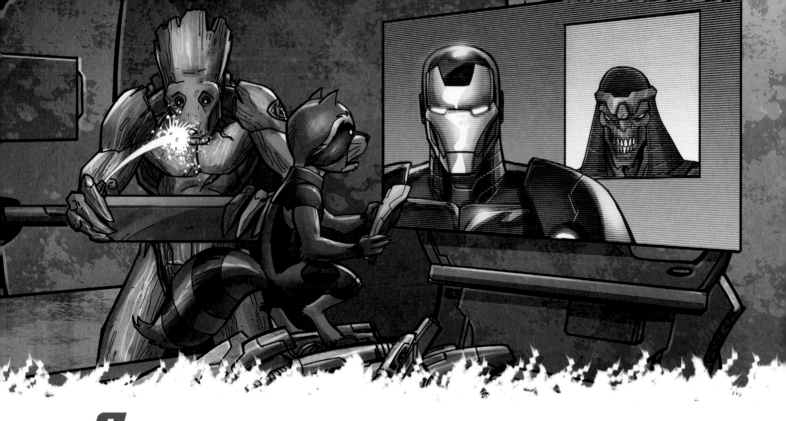

After fighting giant space piranhas all weekend, Rocket and Groot needed a vacation. But before they could think about tanning on Saturn, a familiar face came on their telemonitor.

"Fur ball. Iron Man here. Need help. A Chitauri space pirate is causing mischief in New York. The Avengers and I aren't around, but . . . you two are!"

Groot smiled. "I am Groot!"

"He means we'd love to help!" Rocket said. "I haven't had a New York hot dog in ages!"

Rocket set the coordinates for Earth and they blasted off.

"I wonder if the Hulk would mind if I crashed in his room for a few days," Rocket said as they flew past Avengers Tower.

Groot shook his head. "I *am* Groot."

"Yeah. I guess you're right," Rocket replied.

They landed in Times Square and parked their ship.

Rocket grinned. "It's like Disney World! Only really dirty! . . ."

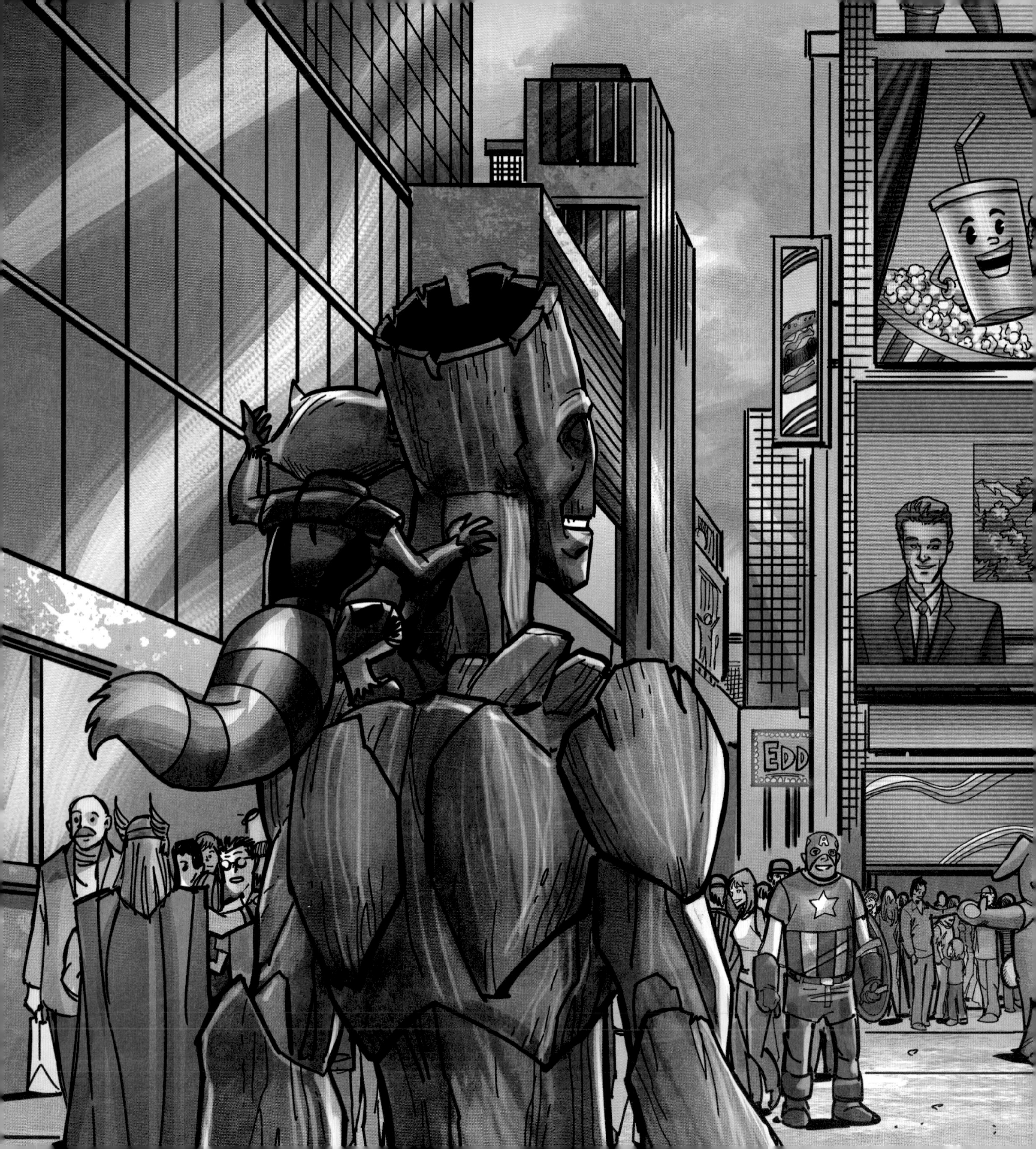
EDD

Rocket climbed Groot's branches and leaned out in excitement. "Times Square! The center of the universe! The city that never sleeps! The Big Apple!"

Groot frowned. "I am Groot!"

"Don't worry. I won't eat it," replied Rocket. "Now, if I was a Chitauri space pirate, where would I be?"

"*Wow!* Look at those costumes!" came a voice from above them.

They turned and saw a friendly neighborhood Super Hero suddenly swinging down to meet them.

"I am Groot!" Groot said, recognizing their old friend.

"And I'm Spider-Man!"

Rocket sighed, "That's what Groot *just said*. . . ."

"It sounded like he said, 'I am Groot,'" Spidey replied.

"He did, but . . . never mind. Listen, we need help finding a Chitauri space pirate. We think he wants to sneak into Avengers Tower and steal top-secret information."

Spidey nodded. "Okay, time-out. *Where* did you kids get these costumes?" He tugged at Rocket's whiskers. "They seem so real! Like, the *real* Rocket Raccoon real!"

"I am *not* a raccoon, and I *am* real."

"Whoa!" Spidey cried. "Rocket! Groot! Long time no see!"

But before the friends could catch up, screams rang out from Forty-Sixth Street. The Chitauri villain was about to destroy a street-performing Iron Man!

"He thinks that's the *real* Iron Man!" Spider-Man said. "Let's take care of this before the eighty-seven-year-old Thor over there is next, shall we?"

The three heroes jumped into action! Spidey swung toward the Chitauri and blasted him with webbing. Groot charged forward with battle-ready fists! And Rocket . . . well, Rocket ate a New York City hot dog. His mission was complete . . . or so he thought!

"He's heading down Broadway!" Rocket cried.

"Let's cut him off," Spider-Man replied. "Follow me!"

The three raced down an alley and through a door. Suddenly,
they were onstage in a Broadway play! The Chitauri fired his
plasma cannon at Groot and Spidey, then ran offstage. Rocket
paused to bow to the crowd as he received a standing ovation!

The Super Heroes chased the Chitauri into the subway.

They jumped in the train as dozens of people scattered and ducked for cover. Groot politely nudged the passengers to one side to protect them as Rocket aimed his laser cannon at the Chitauri.

"No drinking, no eating, and *no* radioactive weapons on the train, dude!" Spidey said.

"Oh, *fine*!" Rocket replied as the train stopped and the Chitauri jumped out. "But he's getting away!"

The Chitauri raced up the steps to the surface, and everyone scrambled in panic as he blasted his plasma cannon.

By the time Spidey and the Guardians got to street level, it was a sea of running people. They had lost the Chitauri! But then something caught Groot's eye.

"I . . . am . . . Groot?" he said, pointing to a giant storefront window. On display was a beach scene with all the trimmings: a mannequin lifeguard, beach balls, towels, mannequin kids playing, mannequin parents watching—and a Chitauri in sunglasses.

Spidey shrugged. "I'd say that's weird, but we're in NYC."

"Enough!" Spidey yelled. "We've been through Times Square, a Broadway play, the subway, a window display . . ."

"And a hot dog stand," Rocket said. "Don't forget that."

"Let's end this now!" Spidey said. "I wrap him up, Groot knocks him out, Rocket takes him down. Ready?"

"I *am* Groot!"

"I totally agree!" Spidey replied.

Spidey helped load the Chitauri onto their ship as Rocket tipped the valet.

"Guys! We need some pics!"

"I am Groot?"

"Yes, we can get pics of the Statue of Liberty, Central Park, and the Bronx Zoo."

"That's not what he said," Rocket replied.

"I know," Spidey said. "But I'm getting close."

"Nowhere near," Rocket said.

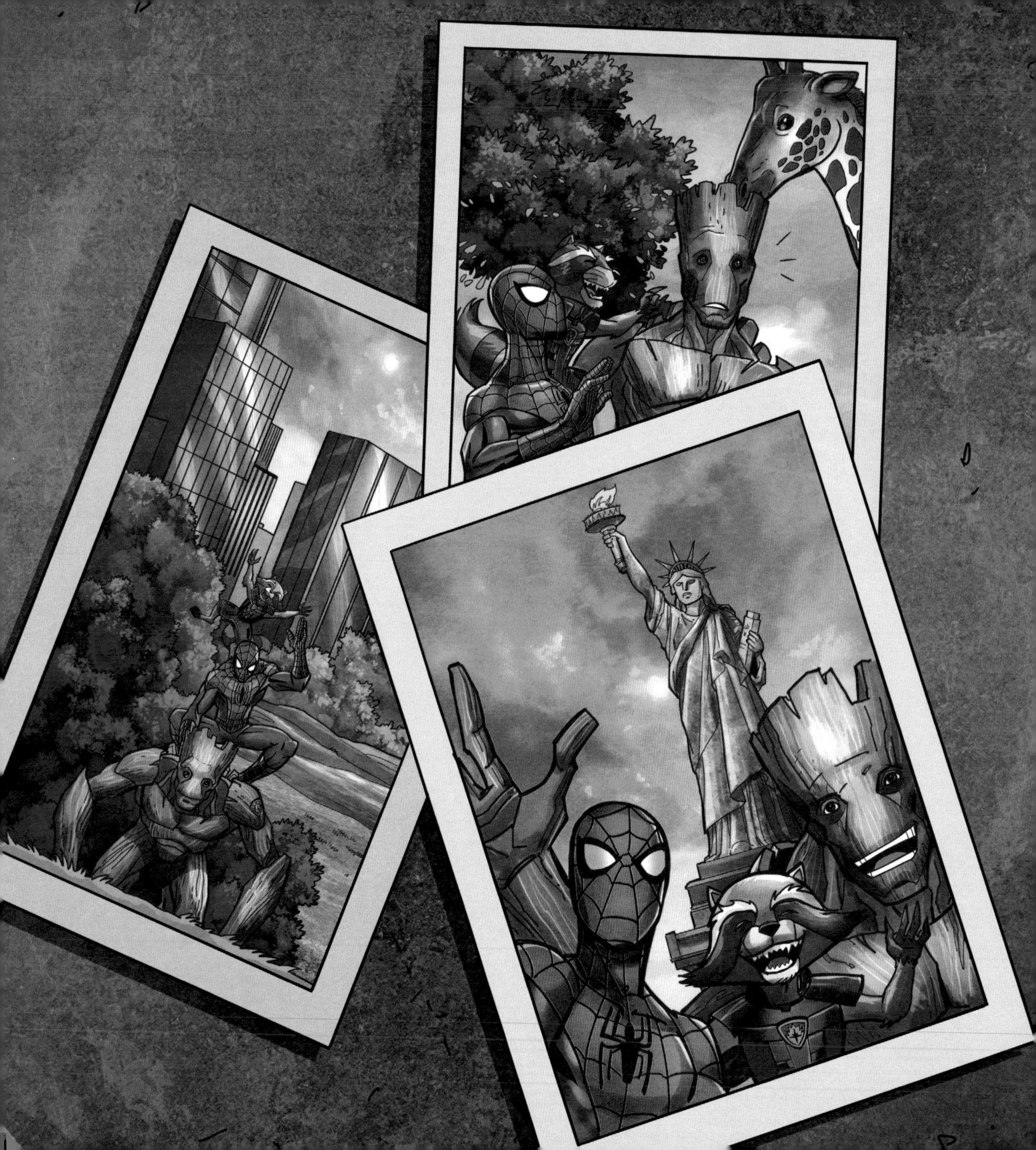

SPIDER-MAN
Crazy Eights

"**W**hoa." Peter Parker stopped in front of the Spider-Man Appreciation Day Festival. He smiled when he saw all the Spider-Fan gear. There were signs and banners everywhere! Some read THANK YOU, SPIDER-MAN! and others WE LOVE YOU, SPIDEY! By the looks of it, everyone in New York City was there to celebrate!

But Peter knew at least one person who would not be attending: J. Jonah Jameson, Peter's boss at the *Daily Bugle*. "It won't be long before JJ has half the city convinced again that Spider-Man is a menace," Peter said with a sigh. JJ had assigned Peter to take a few photos of the festival—but only so he could ridicule the hero in the next day's paper.

After snapping some shots, Peter looked for a place to change into the hero of the hour. He saw some men handing out rubber Spidey masks.

"Here," said one of the men, offering Peter a mask.

"No, thanks. I, uh, brought my own," Peter replied with a smirk.

"Just *take* it," the man hissed through gritted teeth, shoving it into Peter's hand. "Put it on before Spider-Man gets here."

But Peter tossed it in a trash can as the man walked away.

At first Peter wasn't sure whether the sudden edginess he felt was his spider-sense tingling or just nerves about his upcoming speech. But when he got onstage as Spider-Man, he realized it was definitely his spidey-sense. The festival was in chaos!

The fans who had been celebrating moments earlier were rampaging! They knocked down food stands and vendor kiosks, and they trashed banners and displays.

I was expecting Spider-Fans, not Spider-Foes! the web-slinger thought as he glanced around. Then he noticed something even odder about the suddenly angry crowd: every single one of them was wearing—a Spider-Man mask! Before he could figure out what was happening, he heard a familiar voice behind him.

"How quickly they turn, eh?" Doctor Octopus said as he stepped out from behind the curtains on the stage.

"I thought something was fishy," Spidey said, waving his hand in front of his face. "I didn't know it was an octopus I smelled."

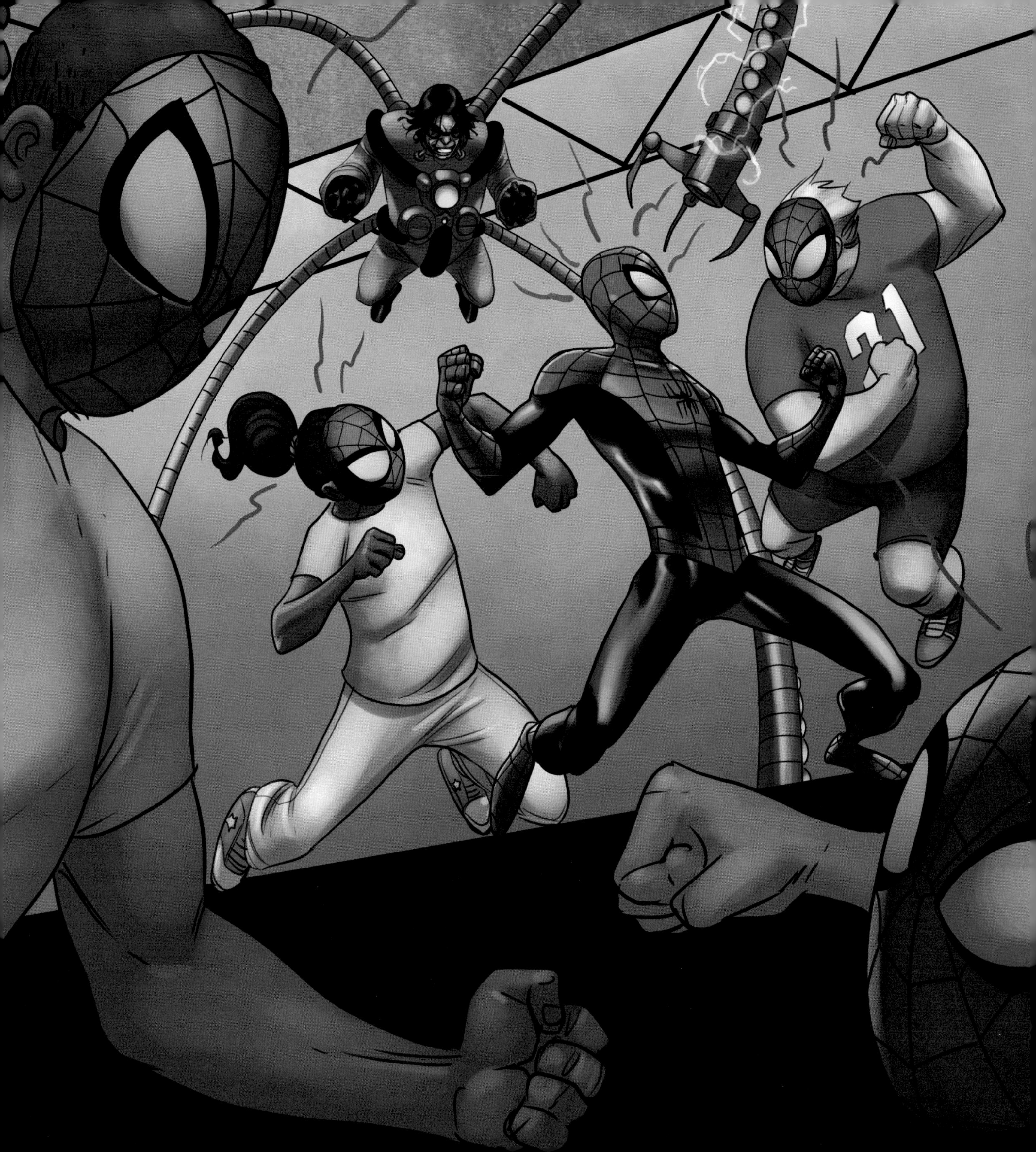

"Sorry to crash your party." Doc Ock laughed. "Actually, no, I'm not. This is the only way I could be sure you wouldn't interfere."

The super villain punched a few buttons on a controller wrapped around one of his tentacles. The device flashed, and everyone in the crowd roared at once. They all charged the stage. "Sorry, Spidey—looks like your fifteen minutes are up."

As Doc Ock lumbered toward the Nanotech Research Center, the crowd of masked Spider-Foes swarmed the real Spidey.

Trying not to hurt anyone, Spidey shot a web toward the rafters above the stage and pulled himself free. But the moment he landed, another group of Spider-Foes began to chase him.

Spidey quickly ducked around a corner. There seemed to be nowhere to hide. *Except in plain sight,* he thought. Spidey pressed up against a life-size poster of himself, striking the same wall-crawling pose. The Spider-Foes ran right past him!

With a quick *thwip*, Spidey pulled a mask from a nearby kid and examined it. The kid looked bewildered.

"Ha! Mind-control sensors—knew it." Spider-Man said, pulling a small round electrical node from the mask.

"Spider-Man?" The kid rubbed his unbelieving eyes. "Whoa. Spider . . . everyone?"

"Somehow, Doc is controlling the people with these masks," Spidey said. "I have to stop him. But first I need to do something about these Spider-Shams."

Spidey tried to remove the masks from as many people as he could. He shot webs left and right, all while dodging capture. But there were just too many of them! He crouched behind a snack stand. "I'll be here all day if I try to do it this way," Spidey said, watching an abandoned cotton candy machine spin a pink ball of fluffy sugar. Suddenly, he had an idea!

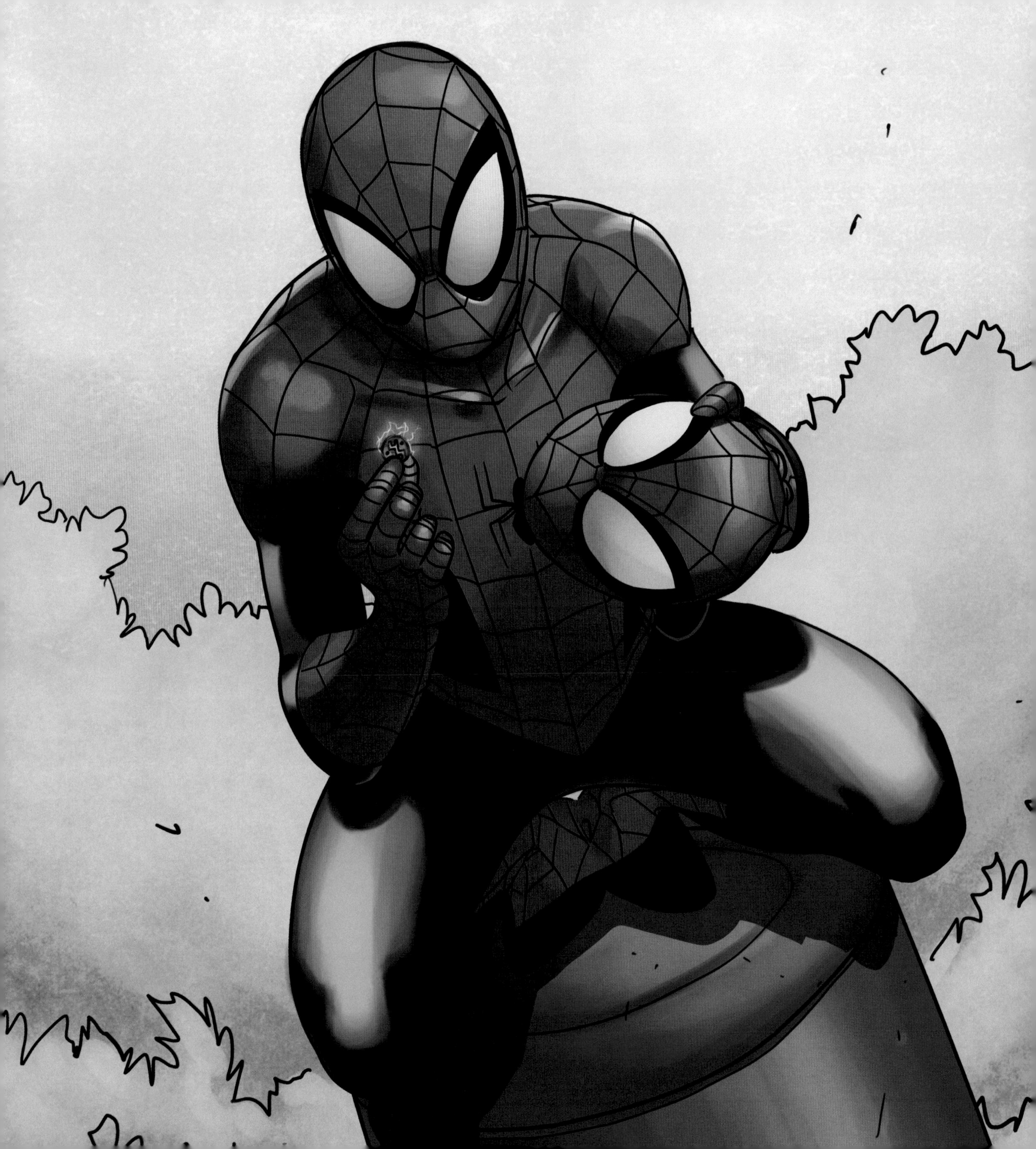

Spider-Man jumped onto the cotton candy machine. He balanced carefully on its rotating center and began to spin rapidly with it. Spidey pointed his web-shooters at the crowd.

"This round is on me!" he shouted. While the machine spun him round and round, Spider-Man was able to quickly cover the crowd with a thick net of webbing, trapping them. *THWIP! THWIP! THWIP-THWIP!* "That oughta keep them busy for a while," he said, jumping off the spinner. "Now, let's see what Doc's up to."

When Spidey entered the nanotech labs, he found Ock tapping furiously on a computer keyboard. His masked minions flanked him.

"Once I've hacked into this system, I'll have the technology I need to bring my mind-control powers to the entire city!"

"No way, Doc," Spider-Man said as he shot his webbing at the villain—but the minions blocked the webs!

"You're right!" Doc laughed. "Why stop at the city? With my mind-control nodes, I can play everyone in *the whole world* like a deck of wild cards."

"You wouldn't want to hurt your fans," Doc Ock said, pressing a button. The minions protecting him regained control of their minds.

"Spider-Man! Help!" they shouted. Doc Ock pressed the button again, and they fell silent.

"Time for a meet and greet!" he cackled.

"Let me roll out the *web carpet* for them," Spidey said. He shot a thick layer of webbing at the minions' feet.

Doc Ock growled and reached for Spider-Man with his tentacles.

With a *thwip*, Spidey ripped a cluster of electrical wires from one of the computers and smacked it into Doc Ock's metallic arm! The mind controller fell from his tentacle and slid across the floor, stopping at Spider-Man's foot.

With a mighty stomp, Spidey crushed the controller. The minions returned to normal and began taking off their masks.

Spidey had saved the day!

The next morning, Peter wasn't surprised to see the headline on the front page of the *Daily Bugle*: SPIDER-SCAM!!!

"I guess Spider-Man Appreciation Day won't be an annual event," Peter said, sighing.

SPIDER-MAN
Love Bug

Peter Parker was running late to school. Good thing web-slinging took half the time to get to class! While the teacher's back was turned, Peter swung into the room and slipped into his seat.

"Oh, Peter! I didn't realize you were here," said Mary Jane, his crush.

"Hey, tiger!" Mary Jane said to Peter after class, using her special nickname for him. It always made him smile when she called him that.

"Listen, there's a free play in Central Park this afternoon. I know you wouldn't usually be interested, but this one's about a scientist who is scared of his own shadow!" Mary Jane said.

"I'm not scared. Do I look scared?" Peter said quickly.

"Um, no," MJ said, giggling. "But you do love science."

Peter couldn't believe it. Was Mary Jane really asking him out on a sort-of-maybe date?

"Of course I'll come!" Peter said. Then he curbed his excitement just a little and added, "I mean—*ahem*—that sounds great."

"Good! Let's head over there together so we can grab a slice of pizza before the show," Mary Jane said.

Just then Peter felt a tingling in his head. It could mean only one thing. . . .

"You go ahead, MJ," Peter said. "I just remembered that I have a Science Club meeting. I'll catch you at the park."

"Okay, but don't be late, tiger!" she said with a wink.

Peter emerged as Spidey after a quick change on a nearby rooftop. From above he spotted Electro breaking into a power plant!

"You can't stop me, web-head!" Electro snarled.

"Wanna bet?" Spider-Man webbed Electro into a cocoon.

Moments later, Electro was dangling over the reservoir in Central Park. "I have a date, but don't worry—the cops will be here any minute!" Spidey said with a wave.

"Sorry I'm late, MJ! I got tied up with something!" Peter said.

"Don't worry about it! Hurry, the play is about to start." MJ grinned. Peter smiled back. He didn't want to blow his one chance!

They took their seats. Everyone was ready for a good show.

"I'm pretty excited! I've wanted to see this play for forever!" MJ told Peter.

Peter smiled. But he started to feel that familiar tingling during the first act of the play. *Something's wrong,* Peter thought, *and I'm not sure it can wait until intermission.*

"I'll be right back," he whispered to MJ before disappearing. He hoped she wasn't annoyed.

A moment later Peter came out as Spider-Man!

"I think I've done as many costume changes as the lead actor!" Spidey grumbled. He searched the park to see what had set off his spider-sense. Soon he found it!

"Look who escaped from the zoo!" Spidey joked.

Rhino did not look happy to see Spider-Man! He roared and charged at the hero.

"C'mere, Spider-Boy!"

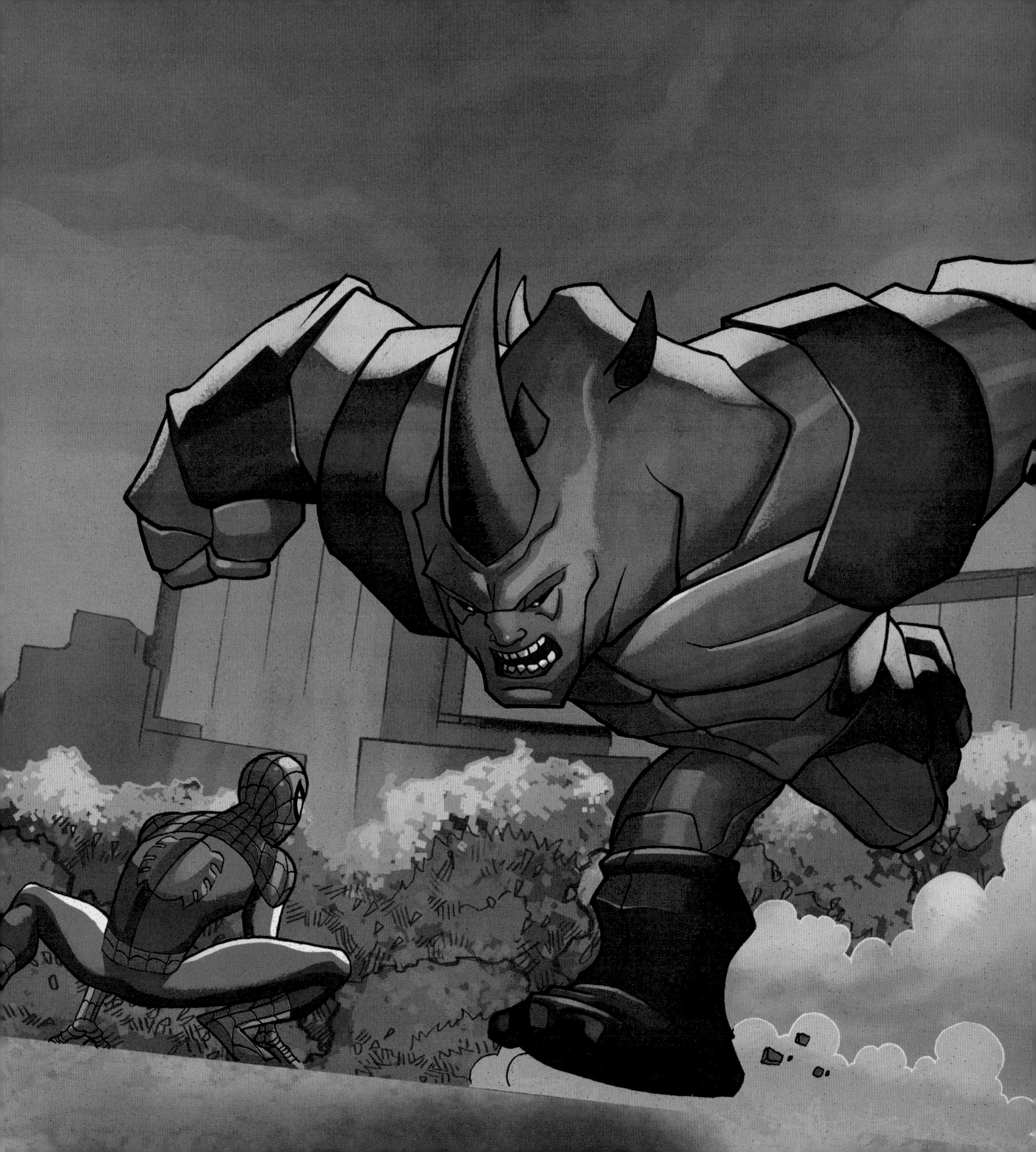

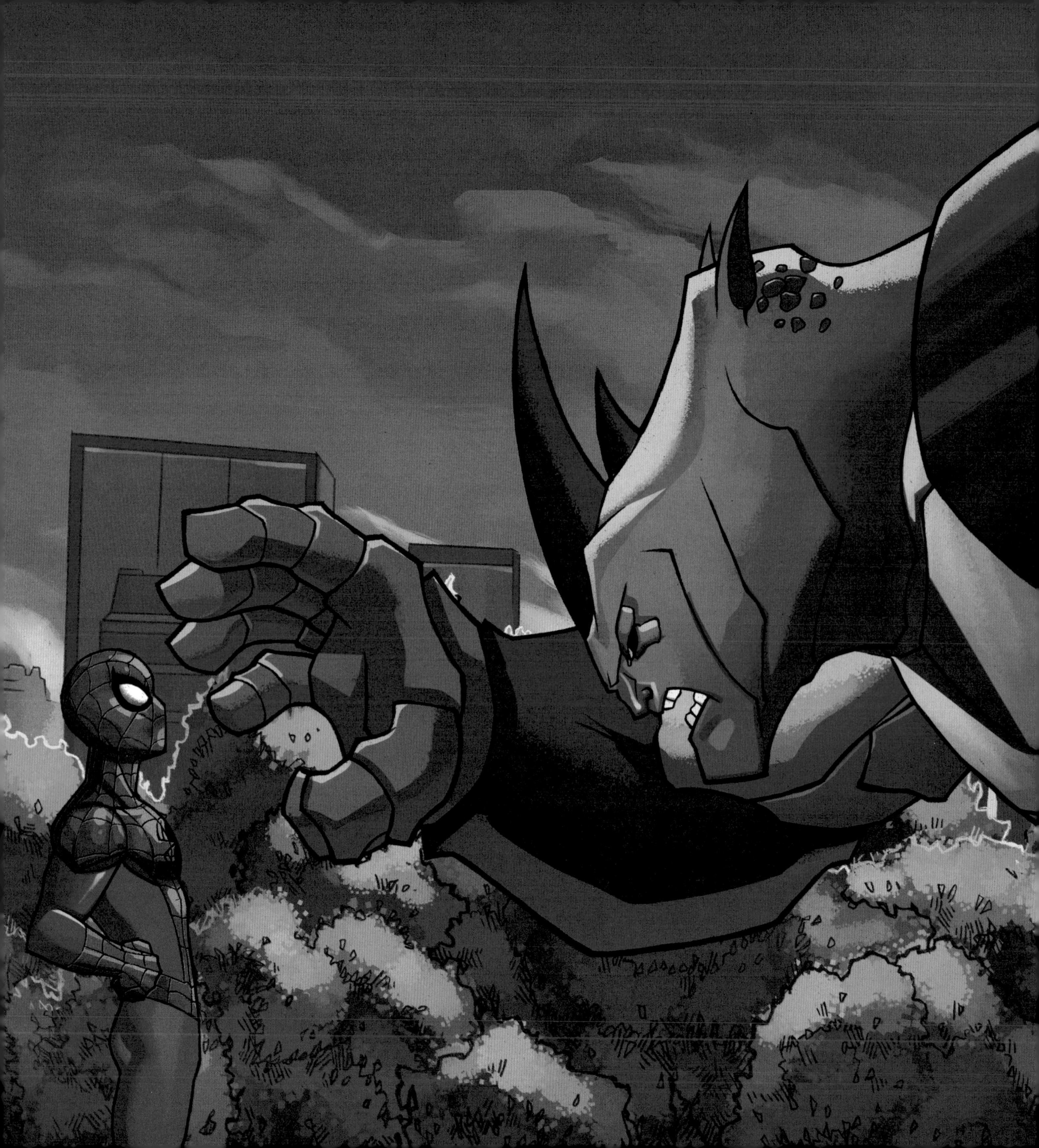

Yikes! There are too many people to get out of the way in time! Spidey realized. Swiftly, he made his webbing into a slingshot for Rhino to run into.

"Ha! You don't think I can break your little webs? Look at my size!" Rhino charged headfirst at full speed.

"I bet your head is as thick as your skin!" Spidey said, taunting the beast. Then, under his breath, he added, "Hope this works."

Rhino stampeded right into Spider-Man's webbing.

A second later he was shot into the air, and soon he was a tiny speck in the distance.

"Now back to the play!" Spidey said as he dashed off.

"What happened, Peter? You're sweating! Are you okay?" MJ asked, concerned.

Peter pulled at his collar. "Yeah, it got really hot. I had to step out for a minute."

"Well, you missed a show!"

"I know . . . I'm so sorry, MJ." Peter felt really bad. That was not how he had wanted his date to go.

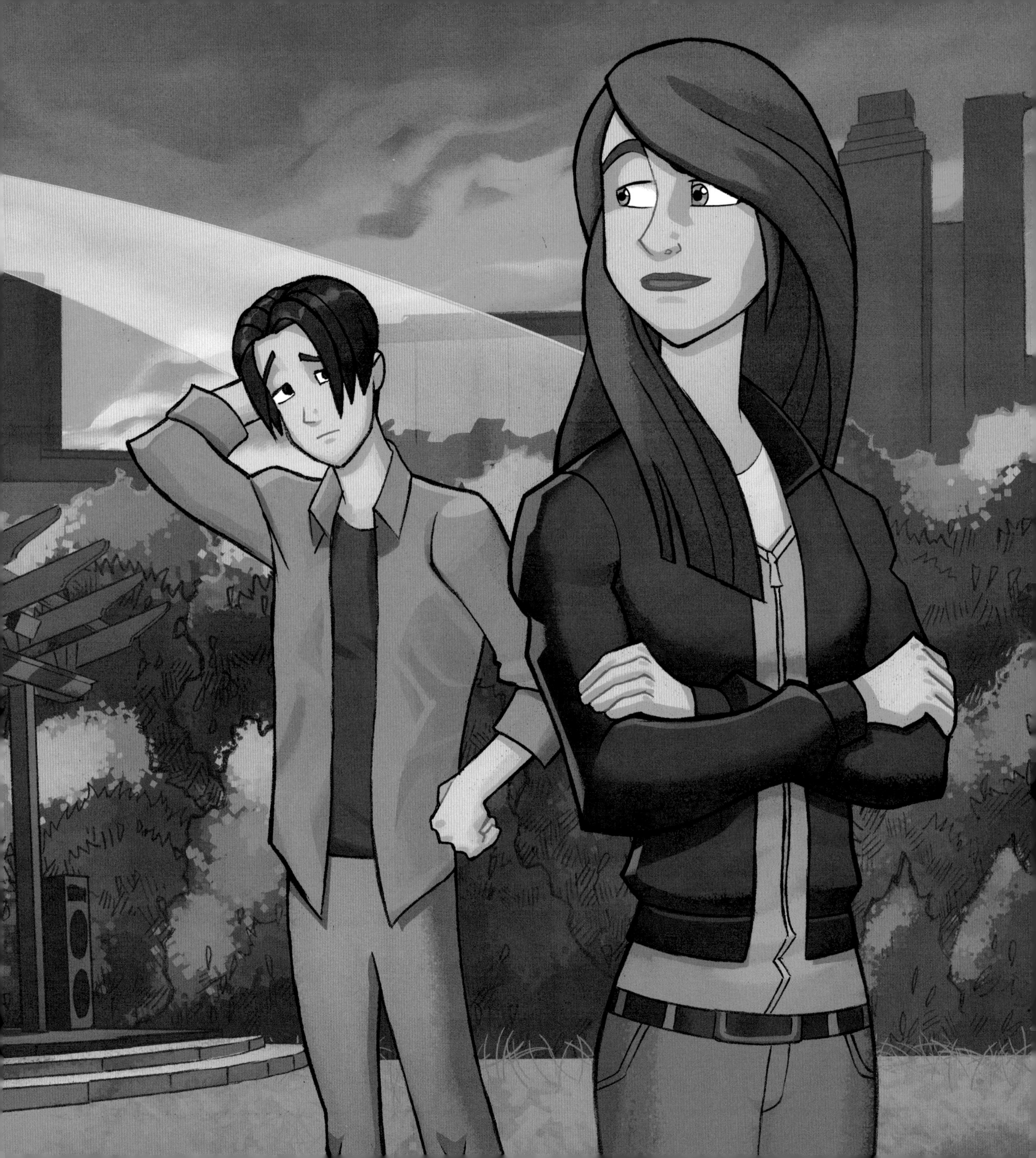

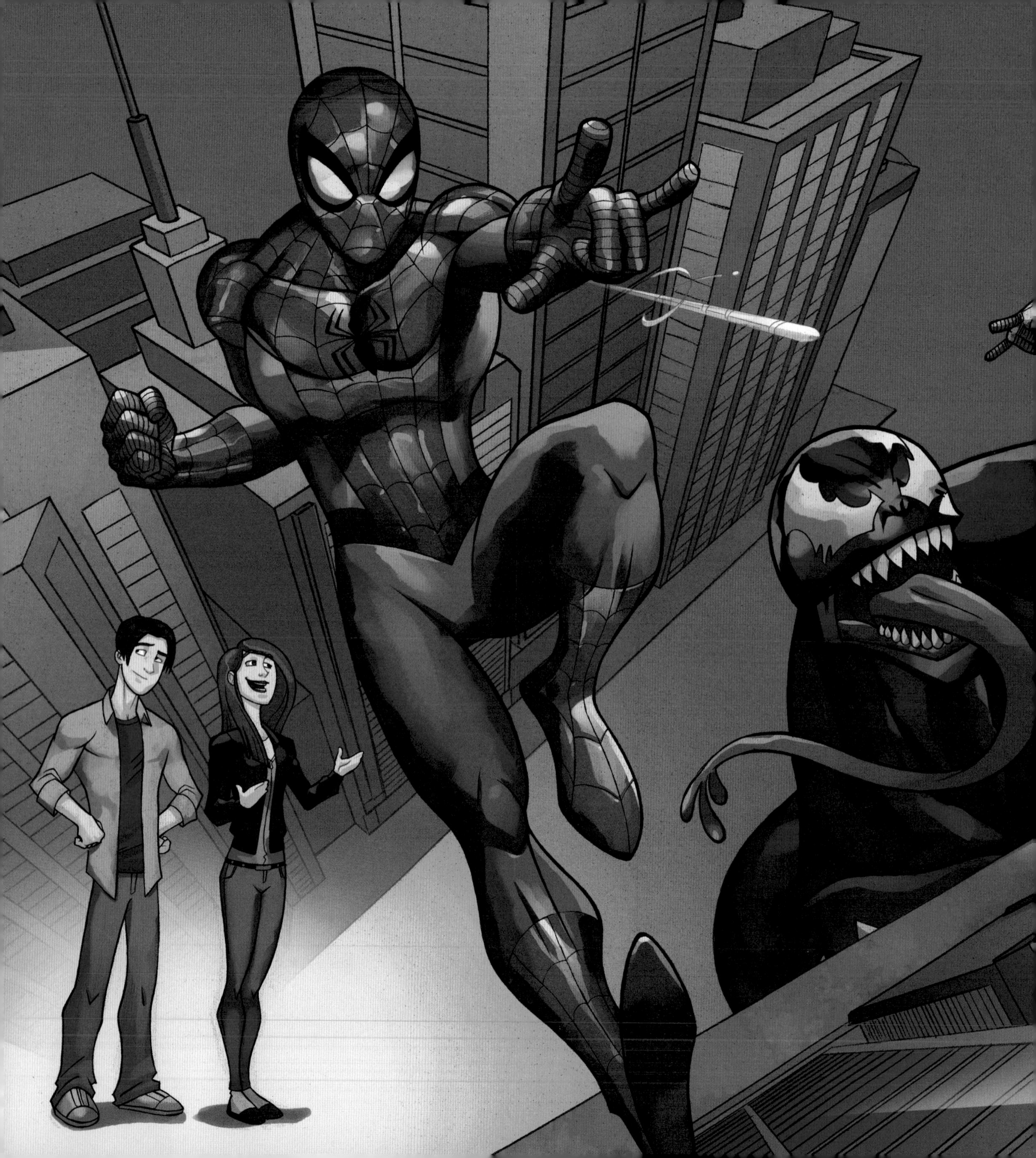

"No, I mean Spider-Man was here," MJ said excitedly. "There was all this commotion outside, so the play stopped. Turns out it was Spider-Man battling Rhino!"

"Oh, he's not bad." Peter tried to play it cool.

"'Not bad'?" MJ replied. "Spider-Man swings through the air, battles Super Villains, and has a Spidey bike!"

That made Peter smile . . . but then he remembered no one knew he was Spider-Man.

"Don't worry. You're not so bad yourself . . . but you have real bad luck with timing," MJ said with a laugh.

"Tell me about it," Peter replied, shaking his head.

SPIDER-MAN
No Room for Debate

Peter Parker tried to calm his nerves as he entered Oscorp's fancy new media center. Oscorp was hosting the big debate match between Midtown High and Coles Academic, and Peter was in the first group to compete. As the Coles Academic kids got settled at their table, a cute brunette smiled at Peter. He blushed deeply.

Just when I thought I couldn't be more nervous, he thought.

"For our first match," the announcer said, "Peter Parker, representing Midtown High, and Kamala Khan, representing Coles Academic."

Peter groaned. His opponent was the cute girl he'd just noticed!

Right as the announcer opened her mouth to share the topic of the debate, the lights went dark. The audience murmured and there were shouts of confusion before a raspy voice boomed over the intercom: "I'd like to announce a surprise guest . . . me!"

It was the Green Goblin!

Peter knew it was time for Spidey to make an appearance. He fumbled in the shadows, looking for a safe spot to change.

"I need Spider-Man for a few tests," the Goblin growled. "So here's something to debate: do you think capturing an entire audience will lure Spider-Man into my trap?"

The audience screamed. Spider-Man prepared to swing out and surprise the Goblin, but someone grabbed his arm in the dark.

"Stay down, sir—let me handle him," a girl whispered.

"I can handle him," Peter replied. "I'm Spider—"

Just then there was a loud cracking sound. An eerie green force field began to encase the horrified audience.

"Now, keep your arms and legs inside the vehicle at all times!" Goblin said with a cackle.

There was a deep humming as the force field charged brighter and brighter, and then with a *SNAP* the audience was gone—and so was the Green Goblin!

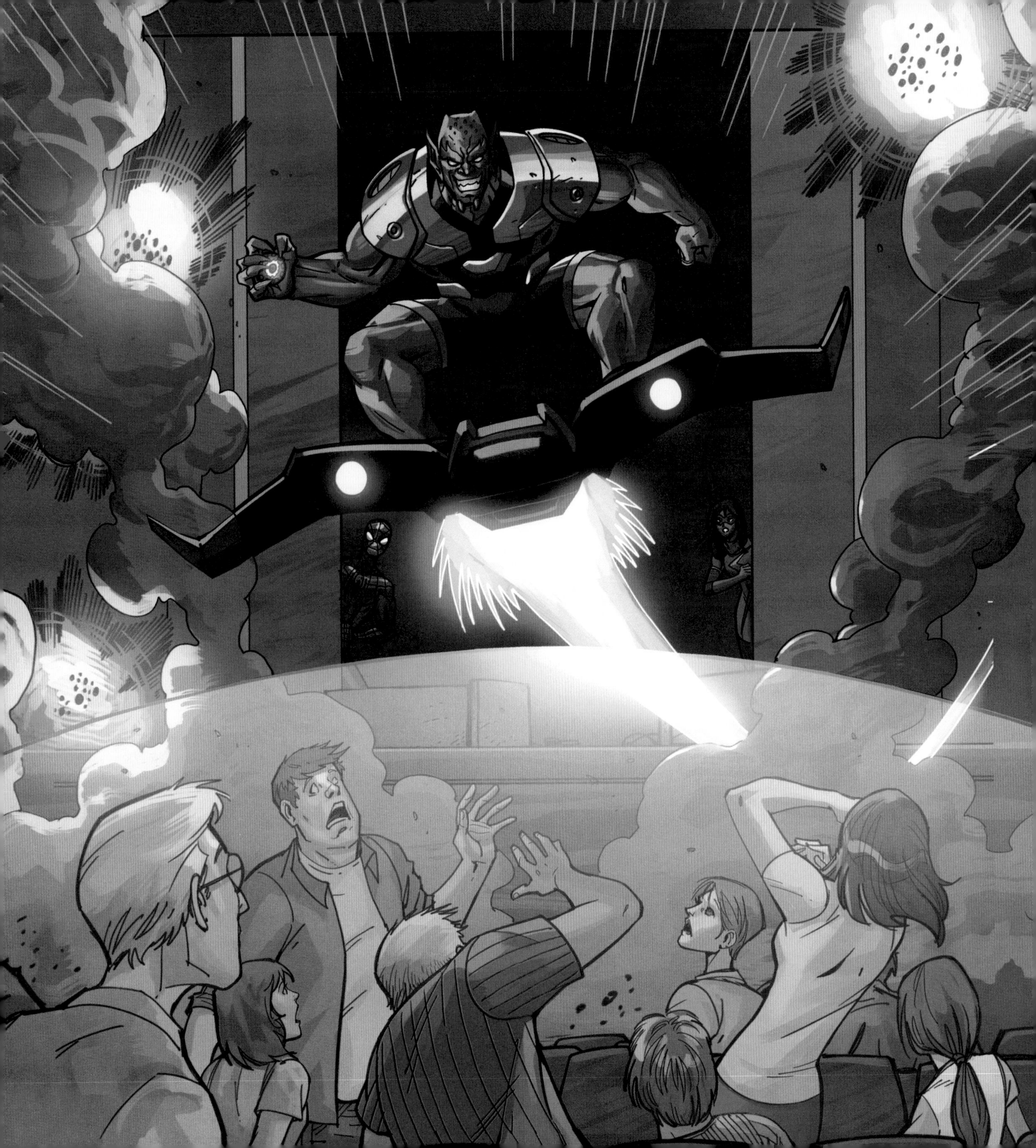

The lights flickered back on.

"Spider-Man!" the girl said.

Spidey looked at her and gasped. "Ms. Marvel?"

She adjusted her mask. "I could have stopped him if I hadn't been trying to stop *you*." She sighed. "I'd love to chat, but I've got a Goblin to catch."

"Hold up," Spidey said. "Goblin set the trap for me, so obviously I should be the one to handle it."

"Maybe we should work together," Ms. Marvel suggested.

Spider-Man grinned under his mask. "Okay, we have three advantages. One, there are two of us and only one Goblin. Two, we know this is a trap. And three, Goblin's not expecting either of us to be in the building already."

"And I bet he doesn't know I can morph into any shape or size!"

The lights flickered again. But when Spider-Man and Ms. Marvel looked more closely, they realized that the whole room was flickering a little.

There was a bright flash; suddenly, they saw the debate room as it really was—a windowless steel cell! There was one door, but it had no handle and was shut tight.

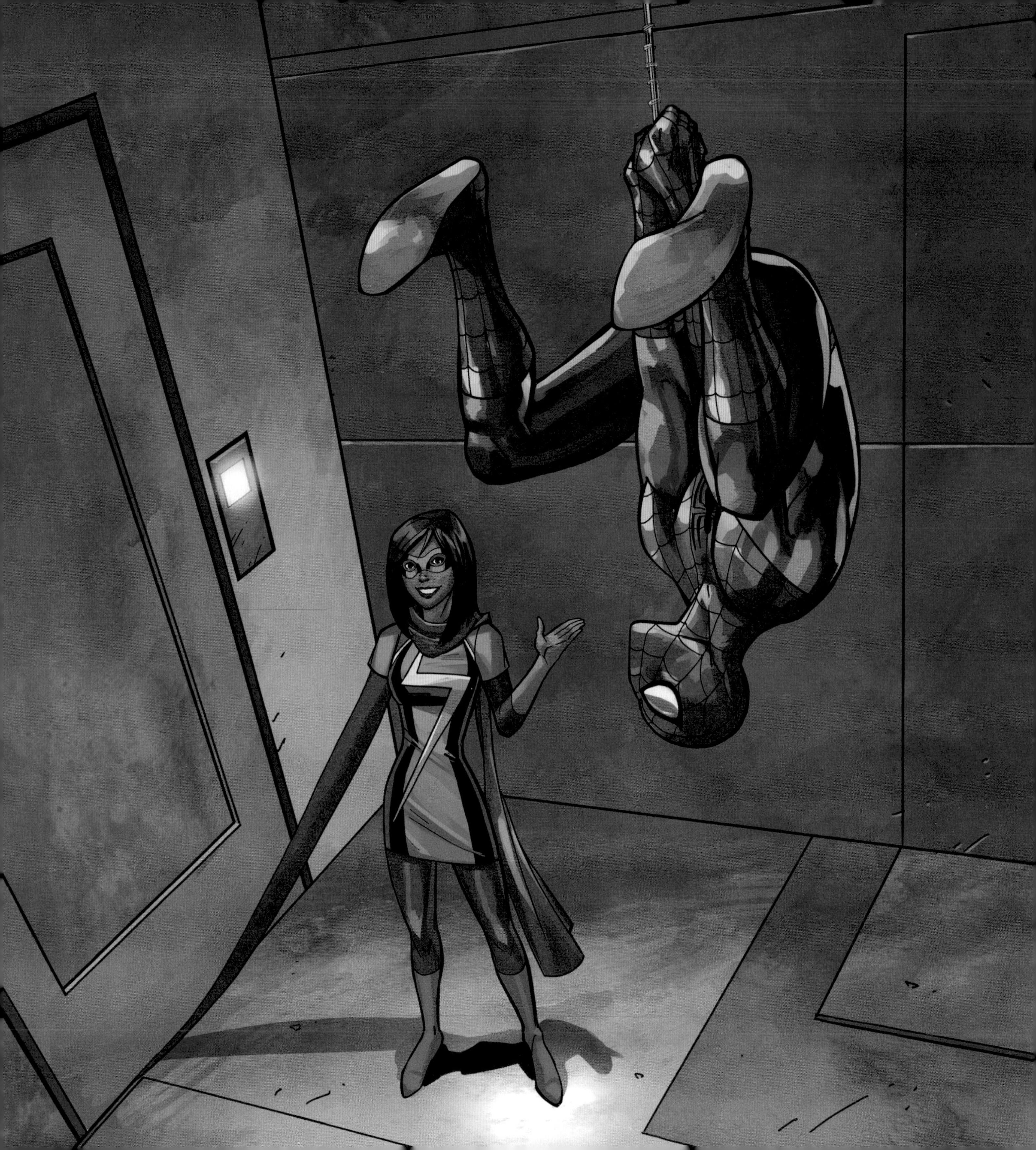

"The Goblin must have built this trap under Oscorp's new media center and used holograms to disguise it as the debate room," Ms. Marvel said as she felt around the seams of the closed door, looking for some way to open it.

Spider-Man dropped down beside her. "But if we're already trapped, Goblin wins—right?"

"We may not be trapped," Ms. Marvel said, eyeing a thin sliver of light that shone through a crack under the door. "Goblin's expecting you to come in from the outside, so I bet the trap hasn't been triggered yet. Hang on. I'll be right back."

Ms. Marvel shrank down super small and carefully crept through the crack under the door.

"Spider-sized! I like how you think," Spidey said.

In a few moments, the door slid open with a hiss. Ms. Marvel was waiting on the other side; she was back to her normal size.

"Ready to grab a Goblin?" she asked.

As soon as Spidey passed through the door to join Ms. Marvel, bright green lasers crisscrossed behind him.

"That was close!" Spidey said, waving his hand over a small motion detector mounted above the doorframe. "That room was more than a trap. This door has a motion detector set to trigger those stun lasers."

Ms. Marvel held a finger to her lips. "Listen. . . ."

They heard shouts for help.

"I have an idea," Spidey said. "How much do you know about holograms and lasers?"

Ms. Marvel smiled, understanding exactly what Spider-Man was thinking. She started typing into the hologram control panel on the wall—the same one that had created the holographic debate room. "You get the Goblin's attention."

Spider-Man shouted down the hall: "Hey, you green goon, your favorite wall-crawler is here!"

With a *whoosh*, the Green Goblin sped down the corridor on his glider. He stopped short at the cell doorway. Spider-Man and Ms. Marvel were waiting for him inside.

"A two-for-one deal—what a surprise!" he said with a sneer.

Spider-Man pointed his web-shooters at the Green Goblin.

Ms. Marvel held up her growing fist. "We're ready for you," she said.

The Green Goblin lobbed some pumpkin bombs toward the heroes. The bombs exploded at their feet, but to his surprise, Spidey and Ms. Marvel were unharmed. The Goblin's rage grew. He fired a dozen more pumpkin bombs at the duo. Still nothing.

But they did *flicker* ever so slightly. . . .

"Huh?" Goblin swung around to face the door, where the real Spider-Man and Ms. Marvel waited. They'd used holograms of themselves to trick him while they hid around the corner!

"How does it feel to be caught in your own trap, Goblin?" Spidey asked.

After everyone had been freed, Peter rejoined the other students, who were buzzing over the day's events.

"I'm glad you're okay," Kamala said.

Peter blushed. "Yeah, me too," he replied.

Kamala smiled. "So, seeing Spider-Man was pretty cool. . . ."

"Yeah, but not as cool as seeing Ms. Marvel," he replied.

"Okay, I won't argue with that," she said, laughing.

They shook hands and said good-bye, unaware of each other's secret identities . . . for now. . . .

SPIDER-MAN
The Amazing Spider-Kid

Zack lived with his brother, Jake, and his parents in a small town, and he loved Spider-Man. In fact, Spider-Man was his favorite Super Hero! Zack wore pajamas that made him look just like the famed wall-crawler. Every night as he drifted off to sleep, Zack imagined what it would be like to fight bad guys alongside his idol.

One Friday, as Zack was walking home from school, he felt a little prick on his arm. *What was that?* he thought.

He looked down in time to see a small spider scurrying away. He scratched at his arm and suddenly felt a surge of energy. *Is it the spider bite?* Zack thought.

The next morning, he went downstairs and told his family about it. "Think fast!" Jake yelled, and threw an orange right at Zack's head. Zack quickly caught it, surprising everyone. "Whoa!" Jake cried. "Rumor has it Spider-Man got his powers because he was bitten by a radioactive spider. What if it's happening to you, too?"

Am I turning into . . . Spider-Kid? Zack wondered. *I need to test this out.* Zack finished his breakfast, crammed some of his Spider-Man Halloween costume into his backpack, and set off to test his newfound powers.

Zack rode his bike a few blocks before he noticed his classmate Anna sitting on her porch. She looked upset.

"My spider-sense is tingling!" he said to himself as he rode up to Anna's steps. "What's wrong?" he asked her.

"I was playing with my dog, Chewie, and he saw a squirrel and ran away! Can you help me find him?" Anna said.

What would Spider-Man do? Zack thought. He scanned the yard and noticed paw prints leading to a bush. "Aha!" he yelled. The bush had thorns, so he carefully parted the branches. There was Chewie!

"Oh, Zack, thank you!" Anna cried. "You're my hero!"

"All in a day's work," Zack said, and he got back on his bike and rode off in search of another adventure.

Let's see what other powers I have, Zack thought. He continued riding and found his friend Gerald sitting on the curb beside a bike.

"Zack!" Gerald yelled. "I was just riding my brother's bike, and the chain fell off into this ditch. Can you help me reach it? He's going to be so upset if I bring it back broken."

"This looks like a job for Spider-Kid!" Zack said.

Zack noticed a dirt ledge that led down the wall of the ditch. He took out the boots of his Spider-Man costume. He didn't want his mom to get mad at him for dirtying his clothes again.

"There!" Zack said excitedly. He quickly retrieved the bike chain and took it back to Gerald.

"You saved the day!" Gerald shouted.

"Maybe I *am* Spider-Kid," Zack said to himself. "I can do anything Spider-Man can!" he yelled as he sped down the street on his bike, proud of his new powers. Suddenly, he ran straight into a set of long metal legs and fell off his bike.

It was Doctor Octopus, fleeing from a bank robbery! Zack was afraid, and he thought of running away. Doc Ock was a real villain. Could Zack stand up to him? *But Spider-Man would be brave,* Zack thought.

"Stop there! You shouldn't steal! . . . I'm not afraid of you!" he shouted at Doc Ock.

"Why, you are just a little boy!" Doctor Octopus mocked.

"I'm Spider-Kid, and you better watch out!" Zack responded.

Doc Ock grinned and said, "What could you possibly do to hurt me?"

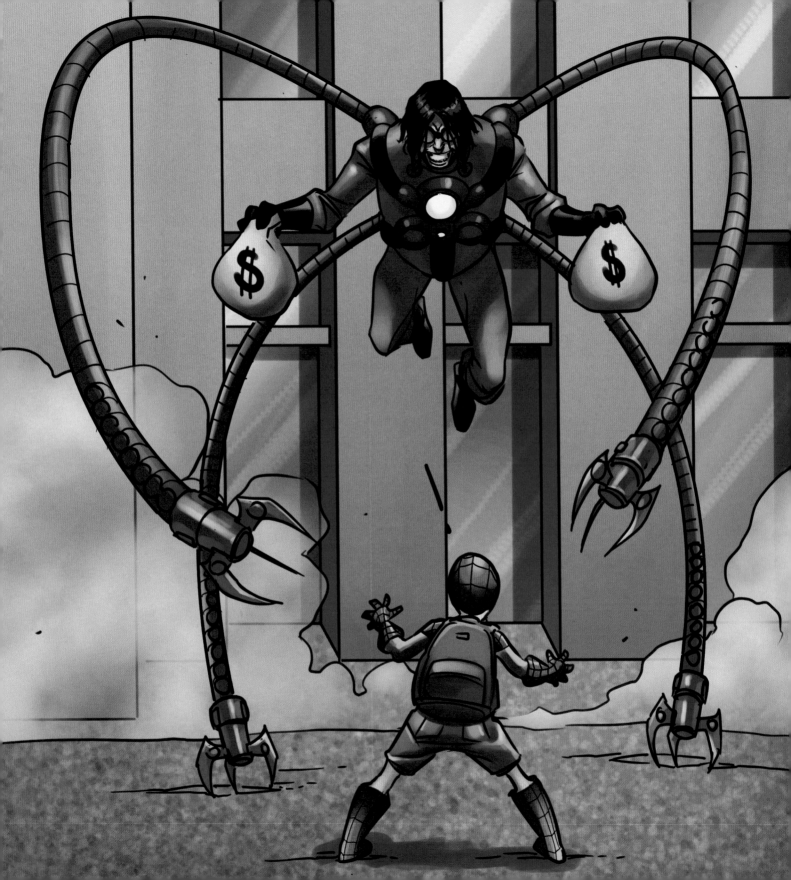

How would Spidey get out of this? Zack thought. "Yes!" he cried, getting an idea. "I've got something up my sleeve!" He stuck out his arms. "Here goes nothin'. One . . . two . . . three!" Zack closed his eyes and willed himself with all his might to shoot webs from his hands, just like Spider-Man! He opened one eye: nothing had happened. "One more try," Zack whispered in a panic, and then he shut his eyes and tried again.

"*Aaarrghhhh!*" Doc Ock cried.

Zack opened his eyes. Doc Ock was covered in webs! Zack stared down at his palms in wonder. He closed his eyes and thrust his hands out again. *Thwip-thwip! Thwip-thwip!* With each *thwip*, one of Doc Ock's tentacles was covered in webbing.

Then Zack heard a voice from behind him. "Looks like you need a hand . . . or eight." It was the *real* Spider-Man!

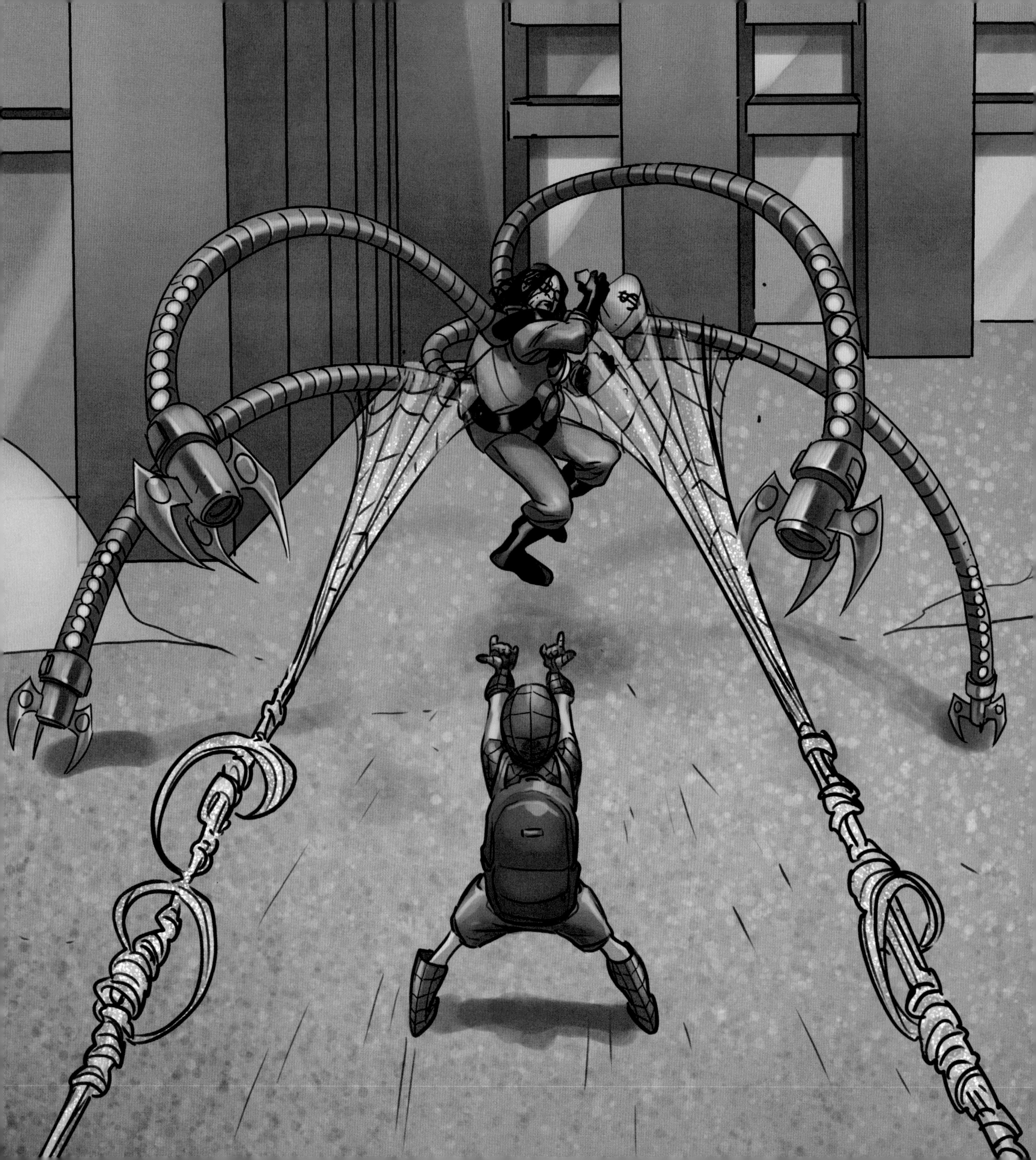

"Nothing can stop me!" Doc Ock yelled, breaking the webs.

"Come on, Spider-Kid, we can handle this one together," Spider-Man said. Zack beamed. He was finally fighting crime with his favorite Super Hero!

"I'll distract him!" Zack said excitedly.

"I like your style, Spidey-Kid. Let's go!" said Spider-Man.

Zack jumped in front of Doc Ock. "Hey, spaghetti arms! I bet you can't catch me!" He hopped on his bike and pedaled as fast as he could. The villain followed angrily.

Just as Doc Ock started gaining on Zack, Spider-Man swooped in.

"You did it!" Zack cried. "You saved the day!"

"*We* did it," Spider-Man replied.

He knelt down next to Zack. "You did a good job today. You learned that there's a Super Hero in all of us," Spider-Man said. "But sometimes even Super Heroes need help. And that's okay."

"Thanks, Spidey," Zack said.

Later that night, Zack thought about his day's adventures. The night before, he had only dreamt of fighting the bad guys with Spider-Man. That day, his dream had come true!

"It's tough being a Super Hero," he said, sighing. Zack climbed into bed and began to dream about his next adventures with his hero Spider-Man!

SPIDER-MAN
Power Trip

One morning, on the way to school, Peter Parker and his friend Mary Jane were surprised to find the subway closed.

"What happened?" Peter asked a nearby police officer.

"There was another off-duty train accident," the officer said. "First one happened under the City Art Museum yesterday, and today's was right below Brittany Jewelers."

Hmmm, Peter thought. *Two high-profile buildings in two days? Seems like more than a coincidence. I'd better check it out.*

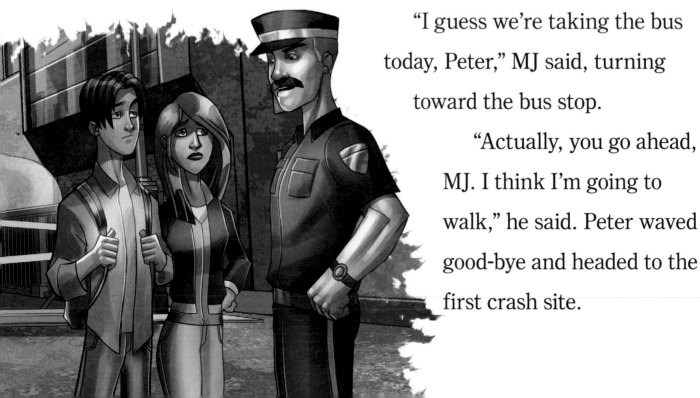

"I guess we're taking the bus today, Peter," MJ said, turning toward the bus stop.

"Actually, you go ahead, MJ. I think I'm going to walk," he said. Peter waved good-bye and headed to the first crash site.

Peter rushed uptown to the City Art Museum.

"I am getting photos for the Daily Bugle," Peter explained, then headed to the lower level. A massive train car was still stuck in the wall where it had crashed. Several museum workers were sifting through the mess.

"Our Michelangelo painting is missing!" said one employee.

"You know, people are saying the train was haunted. The security cameras prove it. Sure, it was empty because it was off duty—but there was no conductor, either!"

Peter wasn't sure about a haunted train, but he was certain those crashes weren't accidents.

Peter headed to the famous Brittany Jewelers next. The owner was very upset.

"The Empire Diamond is missing!" he shouted to the police. "It's one of a kind, worth millions! We've checked every bit of debris, but we can't find it."

"Do you think someone stole it?" an officer asked.

"Maybe. . . ." The owner whispered to the cops, "Can I show you something . . . odd?"

He pulled out his phone and showed a photo taken by the security camera on the night of the accident.

"At first it just looks like a blast, like an electrical short or something." He zoomed in on the picture. "But look closer, right there—doesn't it look like a man? Craziest thing I ever saw!"

Not that crazy, Peter thought, looking at the photo. It was his old nemesis—Electro!

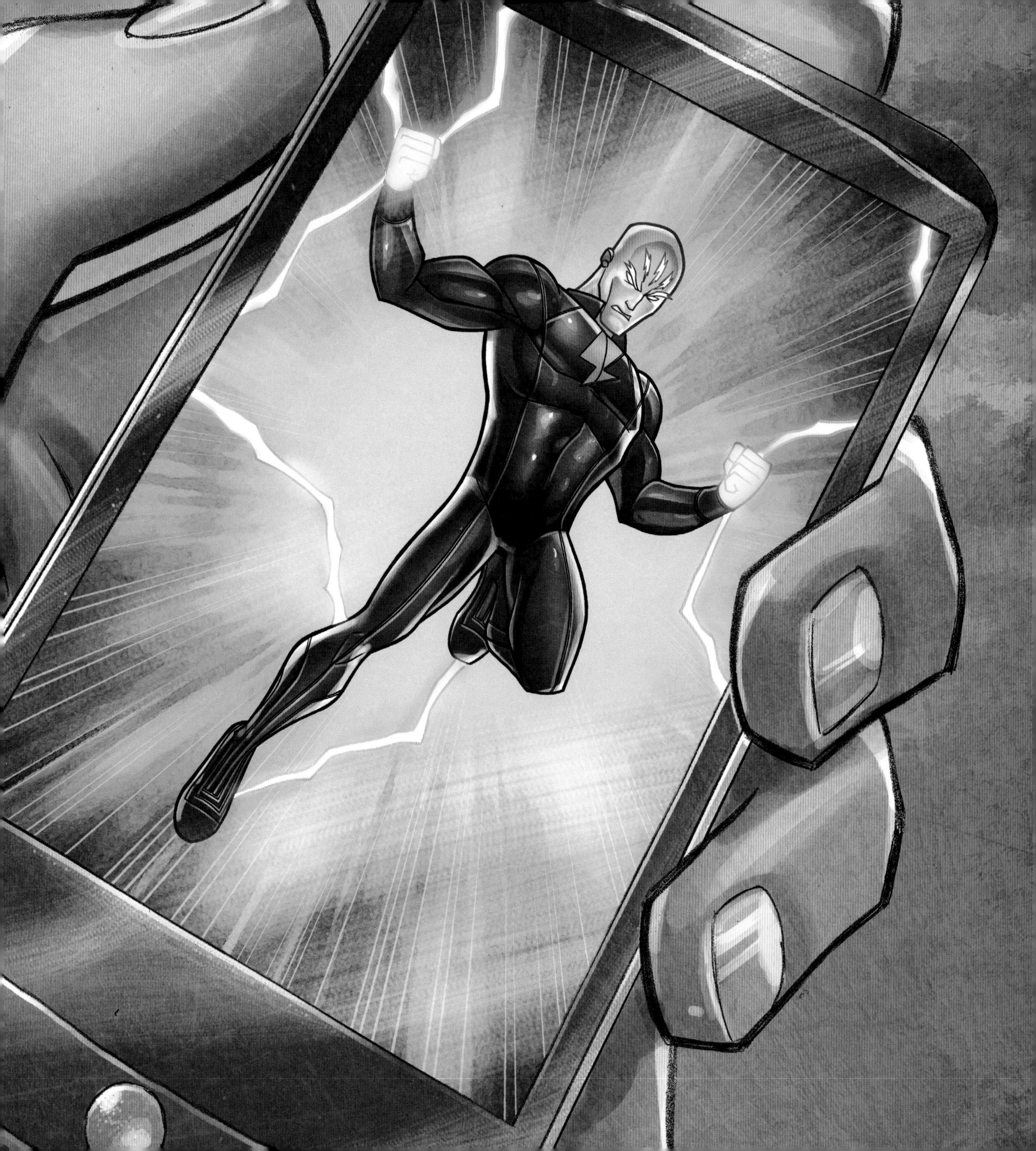

Just then, an emergency call came in on the cops' walkie-talkies.

"All units—we have another runaway train, uptown N," the dispatcher shouted.

Time for Spider-Man to get on board, Peter thought as he ducked down the stairs.

Moments later, Spidey was clinging to the subway ceiling, waiting for the runaway N train. He heard the train barreling toward him. As soon as it started to zoom past, Spider-Man dropped onto its roof.

The wall-crawler crept to the front of the train and peeked over the edge. Just as he expected, Electro was at the controls. Spidey wasn't going to let the electrifying villain get away!

"Don't you need a license to drive one of these things?" Spidey joked as he smashed through the train's window.

"Don't you just love the subway, Spider-Man?" Electro laughed. "It gets me to all the museums, stores, and banks I could ever want . . . *to rob*, that is." Electro pushed the throttle lever forward.

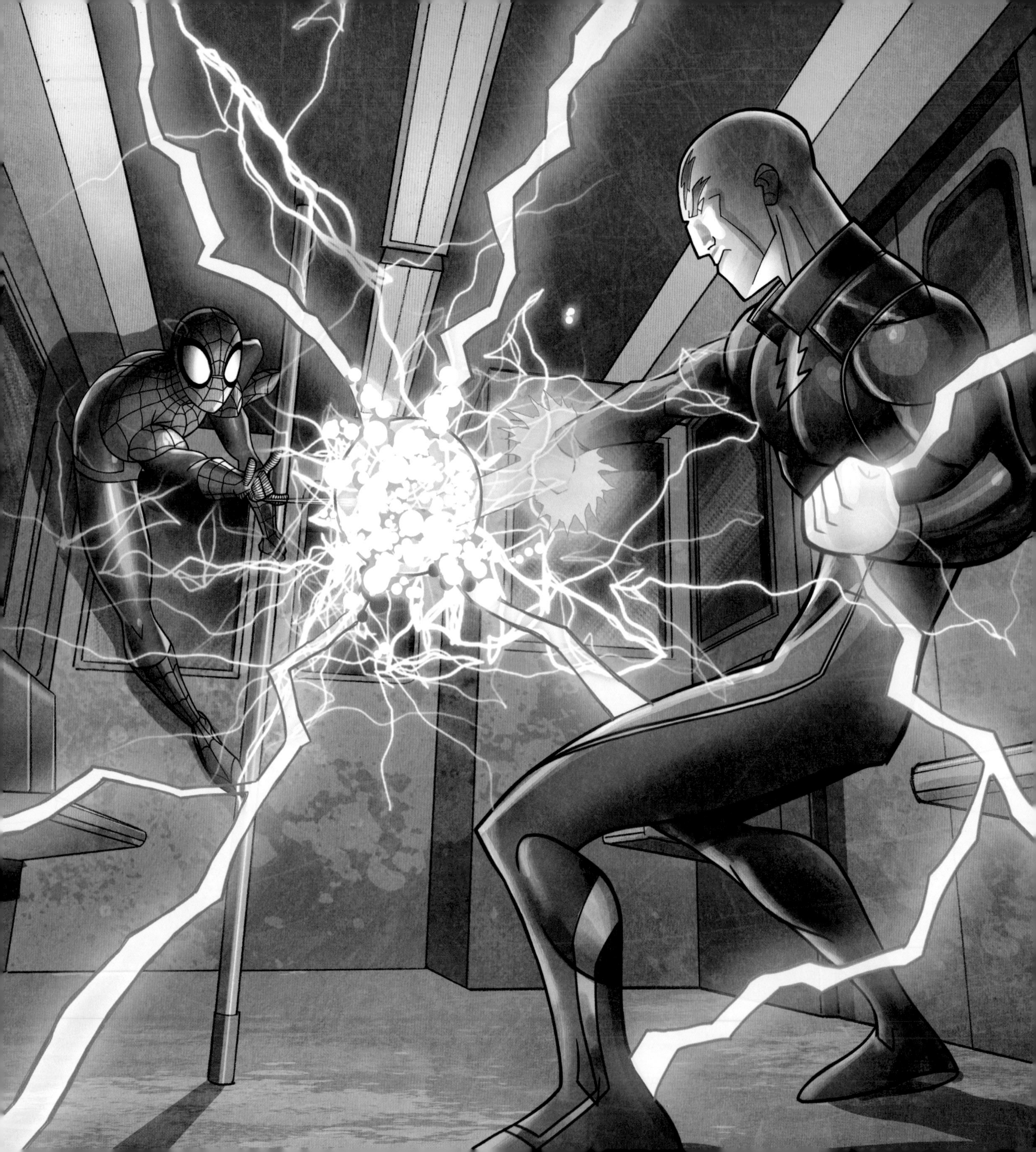

"Let's make this an express." Electro smirked as the train sped down the tracks.

"No way. I'd rather suspend service," Spidey said as he fired two web lines at Electro, but the villain fried the webbing in midair with a burst of lightning. The train went even faster.

"You shouldn't be wasting your time with me, Spider-Man," Electro said with a sneer.

"What do you mean?"

"This train isn't off duty like the other ones."

Spidey looked through the conductor's back window. The runaway train was full of terrified people! Electro cackled and pressed the intercom button. "Ladies and gentlemen, the next stop will also be your *last* stop."

Electro zapped the brake system, blowing it out. And just as easily as Spidey had gotten in, Electro leapt out the broken window and escaped through the electrified rail below the train.

Smoke was coming out of the brake system, and Spidey knew he'd have to stop the train before it crashed.

Good thing I can make my own brakes, he thought. Spidey climbed through the window and quickly shot bolt after bolt of webbing into the train's many wheels, creating temporary web brakes. Finally, the train began to slow and gradually pulled to a stop. The passengers cheered!

As he helped the passengers safely off the train, Spider-Man wondered what would be Electro's next target. There were hundreds of possibilities along the vast subway system.

Then Spidey glanced at a poster. The National Bank was advertising its new vault system. The ad read "So secure, even the *U.S. Mint* feels safe with us!" above a picture of a rare nickel locked away in the bank's new safe. The bank was conveniently located right above the 1 line. Spider-Man remembered Electro mentioning banks in his list of targets.

"Next stop, the National Bank," Spidey said to himself.

A little later, deep in the vaults of the National Bank, Spidey felt a rumble and suddenly a subway car burst through the vault wall.

"Right on schedule," Spidey said when Electro emerged from the dust and smoke.

"I'm not afraid of an itsy-bitsy spider," Electro growled.

He charged at Spidey—but after two lumbering steps, his feet would not budge. He'd walked right into Spider-Man's trap! Spidey tugged hard on the web net he'd set for Electro, pulling him into the air in a bundle of crackling rage.

But Electro wasn't going down without a fight. He ripped out a light fixture nearby, grabbing the sparking wires. He grew brighter as he fully charged. Then he sent a powerful sizzling current of electricity through the web toward Spider-Man! But with a quick *THWIP*, Spider-Man triggered the sprinkler system and the alarm. Within seconds, Electro's charge fizzled with a hiss.

Just in time, the police came running in with the bank manager.

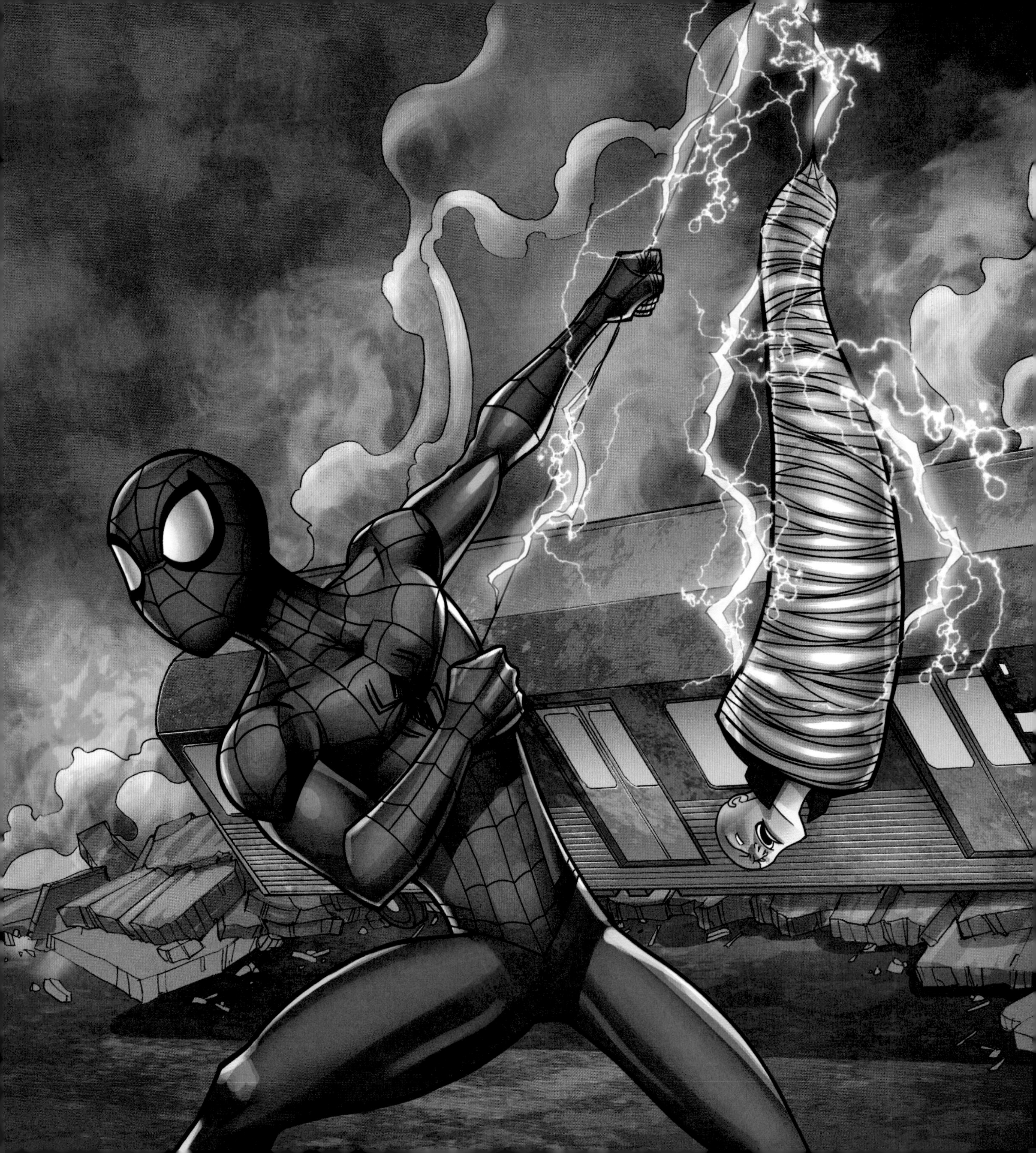

The next morning, Peter and MJ discovered the subway entrance was open and the trains were once again safe.

As MJ started to head to the station, Peter paused.

"Wanna walk with me, instead?" Peter asked. "I think I've had enough of trains this week."

MJ smiled, and the two walked to school together.

SPIDER-MAN
Black Ice

It was a bright winter morning when students of Midtown High arrived at Empire Mountain Ski Resort. Peter looked forward to having fun with his friends and maybe learning how to snowboard on the winter class trip.

But just as the kids were checking in, they heard a low, distant rumble.

"Avalanche!" shouted one of the ski instructors.

Everyone ran inside the lodge, but Peter ducked behind a rack of skis. Time for Spidey to hit the slopes.

From the lodge roof, Spider-Man saw the avalanche tumbling toward the resort. There had to be a way to keep the crushing wall of snow from hitting the lodge!

Spidey looked around and saw snow piled against some orange plastic safety nets that lined the beginner slopes.

My webs may not be orange, he thought, *but they'll do the trick.*

He worked quickly, attaching several large webs to the steel ski-lift poles that ran past the lodge. The avalanche roared down the mountain, faster than a speeding car. Spidey braced himself for the impact, but it never came. The nets had worked!

Just then, Spidey noticed a black shadow flicker in the corner of his eye. It was Venom! Venom was an alien made out of a gooey black suit that gave him powers just like Spider-Man's . . . and more. He was obsessed with crushing the wall-crawler.

Venom skulked along the ski-lift cables. The lift was empty due to the avalanche warning, but Spider-Man knew he still had to lure Venom away from the lodge. Spidey swung up to the ski lift and landed on the side that moved up the mountain.

"Look who it is," Spidey said, "my number one stalker. What are you doing here?"

"Spider-Man," Venom hissed, slinking over to join Spidey on the uphill lift. "I'm just here for the snow. What better place to dwell than a ski lodge? You know I don't care for the fireplace. . . ." He grinned, lashing his long tongue in the air. One of Venom's few weaknesses was extreme heat.

Before Spidey could make a plan, Venom charged at him.

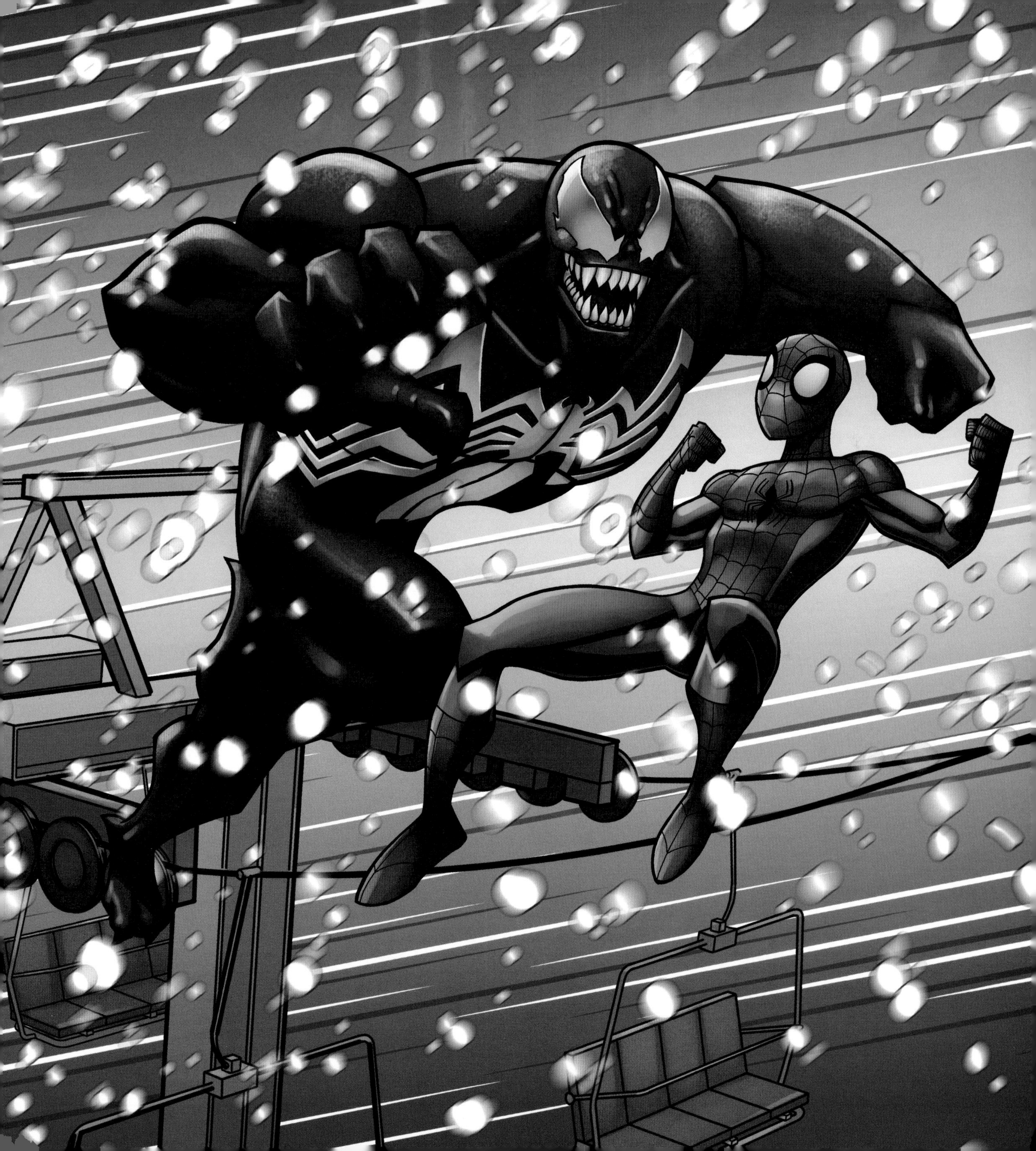

They were only a few yards away from the loop at the top of the ski lift. Soon they'd be heading back down the mountain, toward the lodge and the students. Spidey had to stop the lift—and fast! Instead of firing his webs at Venom, Spider-Man blasted two thick coils of web into the gears of the lift. The gears stuck. The engine creaked and groaned and shook—and then, finally, it jolted to a halt with a loud *BANG!* Spider-Man and Venom flew into the empty lift station, crashing through it just as the cables snapped!

Spider-Man pushed himself up a split second before Venom's fist pounded into the snow right where Spidey's head had been. Spidey grabbed a pipe from the wreckage to block Venom. *WHAM!* The pipe bent with the force of Venom's blow, but Spider-Man smacked it into Venom's chest. It stuck in the tarlike suit.

"Uh . . ." Spidey stumbled back. "That's okay, you keep it."

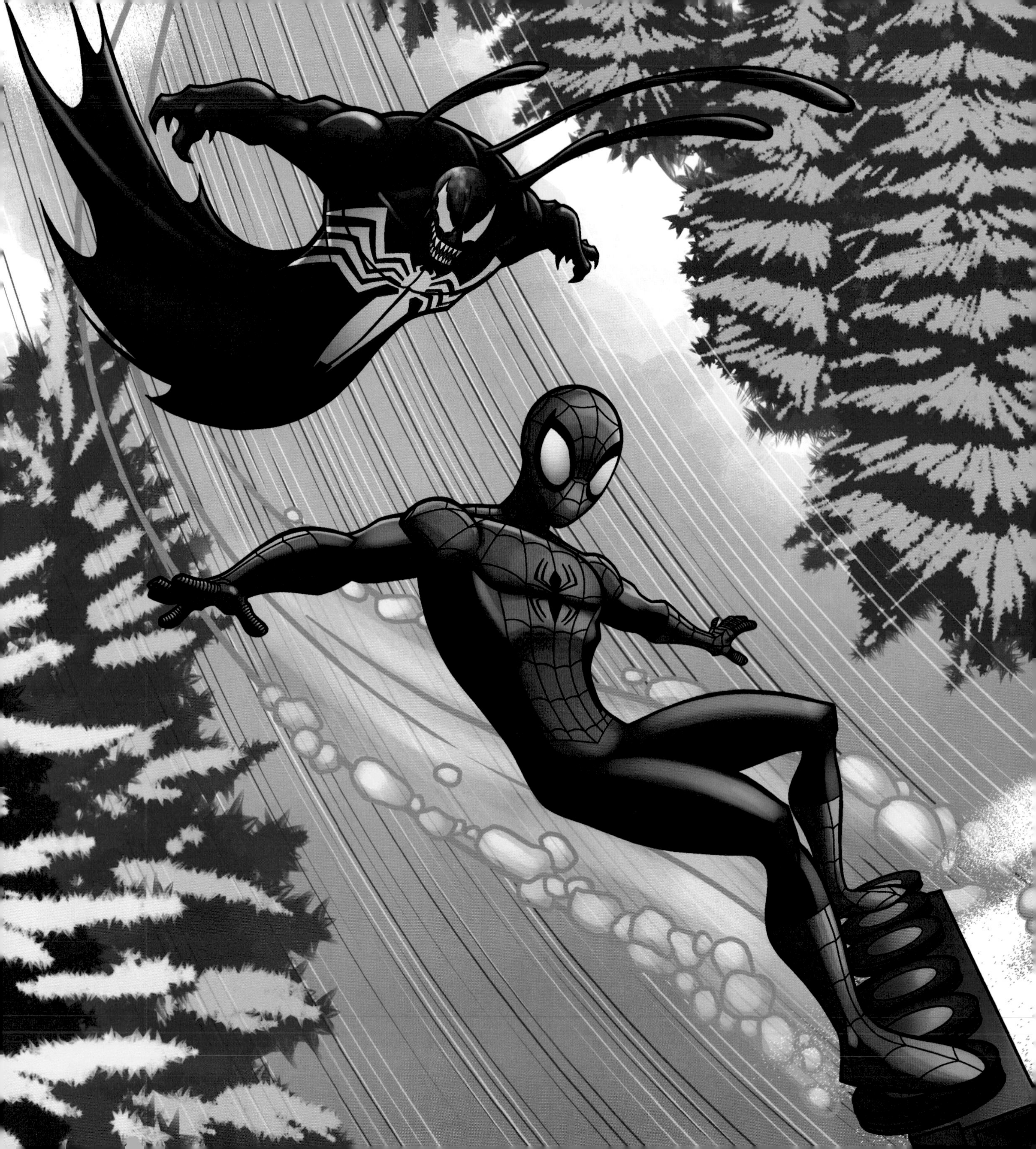

Spidey ducked, and the plank flew over his head. He had to stop Venom! "If only I'd packed a flamethrower," he grumbled as Venom grabbed a bright-red rescue vehicle and smashed it at Spidey's feet. *That's it!* Spidey thought. The rescue cabin at the bottom of the black diamond trail had a warming station—five thousand watts of blazing-hot lamps ready at the flip of a switch.

That should be enough to stop Venom, Spidey thought. *But first I've got to get there.*

Spider-Man snatched a long broken board and jumped on it. *Guess I'm learning how to snowboard now!* he thought, speeding down the steep black diamond trail.

Venom screeched and ran after Spidey. But with his makeshift snowboard, Spider-Man was faster. Suddenly, Venom stopped short. Spidey skidded to a halt and glanced behind him, worried that Venom was going to double back to the lodge. But Venom just stood there and grinned.

Venom tilted back his oily head, opened his vicious mouth wide, and gave a mighty roar. The sound echoed off the mountains around them. The ground began to shake and rumble. Venom had triggered another avalanche!

Venom cackled as he rode the churning crests of snow toward Spider-Man.

"Snow no!" Spidey said with a gulp, kicking his board back
into action. Venom shot sticky patches of thick black webbing at
Spidey, who swerved erratically to avoid being hit. The rescue
cabin was close. But Venom was gaining on Spidey—fast. It was
now or never. As Spidey leapt off the broken board, he shot two
bolts of webbing into the snow, creating a huge mound. Spider-Man
tumbled to a halt right by the cabin, landing hard on his elbow.
"*Oof!* That'll leave a mark," he muttered, scrambling to his feet.

Venom flew up Spidey's snow ramp and sailed over Spider-Man's head, hissing viciously as he went by. He landed in a deep drift beside the cabin. The avalanche tumbled past. Spidey yanked the warming-station switch just as Venom exploded from the snowdrift.

"Spider-Man, you've run out of mountain . . . and time." Venom hurtled toward Spidey.

He didn't notice the heat-lamp coils turning bright red over Spider-Man's head. *It's not heating fast enough!* Spidey thought as Venom closed in on him. Just then, Spidey heard a loud hiss. This time it wasn't Venom; it was the snow melting under the powerful lamps. Venom heard the hiss, too. He looked up, but it was too late. He gave one last roar as he began to melt away with the ice.

Spidey was happy to finally be rid of Venom! He hurried back to the lodge to change into his normal Peter Parker clothes before a crowd could form.

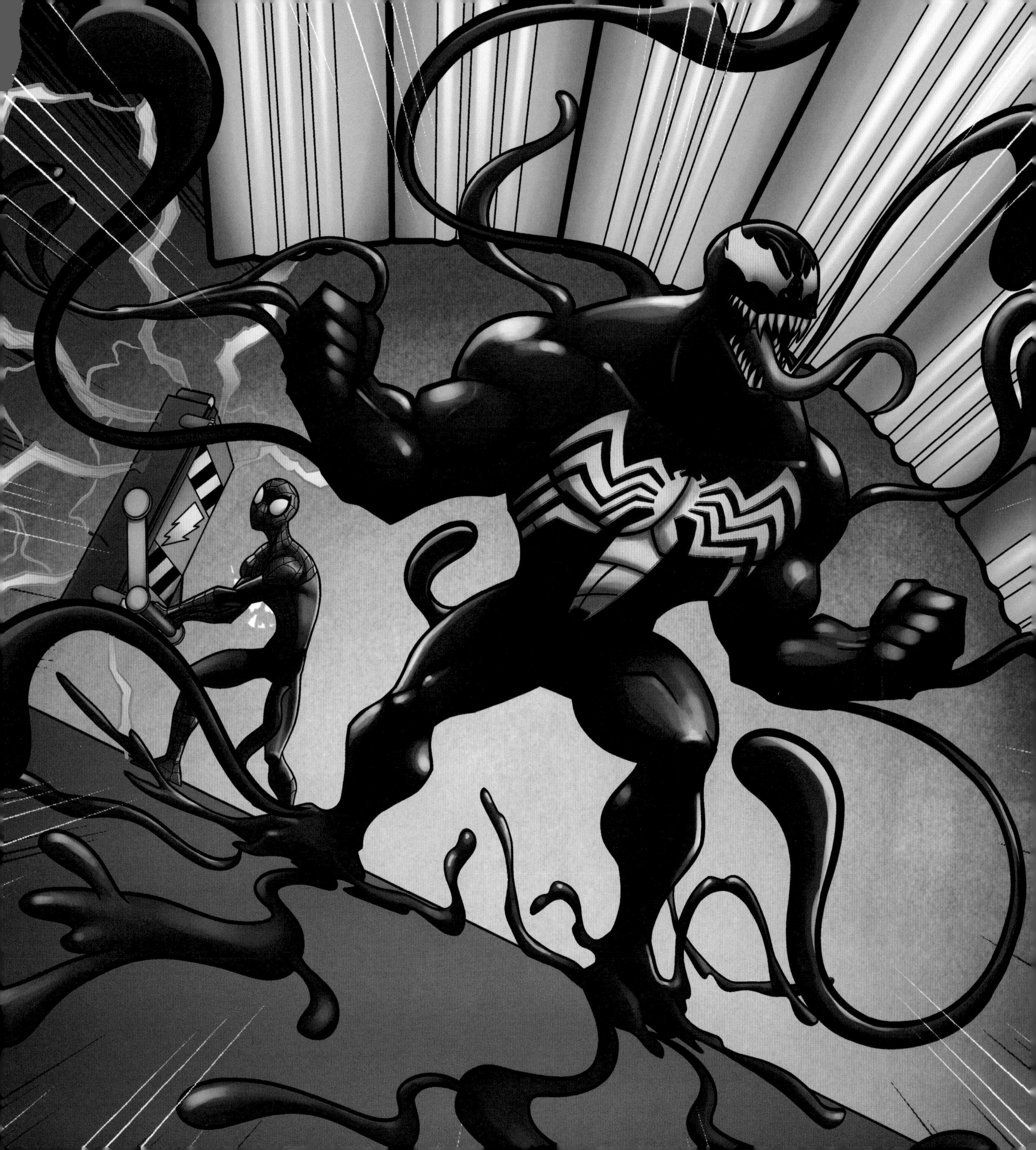

Later, MJ joined Peter by the fire pit in the lodge. "Too bad about the broken lift, huh?" she said.

"I'm just happy to be inside, where it's warm." Peter smiled. "And safe!"

SPIDER-MAN
A Hot Dog, a Real Dog, and an Octopus

It was a hot summer day. Peter Parker, the amazing Spider-Man, and Sam Alexander, aka Nova, were in the middle of a friendly but fierce competition to see who was the better Super Hero.

Nova thought he was better, because he had the ability to fly and release energy pulses. Spider-Man thought he was better, because of his agility and web-shooters.

Spidey's spider-sense alerted him to a girl's cry for help! They raced to the park.

"What's wrong?" Spidey asked the girl.

"My pet, Vicious, is stuck in that tree," she said.

Spider-Man made a web net and tried to coax Vicious down.

"You're wasting your time, bug breath," Nova shouted, flying up the tree.

Instead of a cat, Nova found a drooling little pug in the tree! Nova was shocked but plucked the dog from the branches.

The little girl was so happy to have Vicious back! She told Nova that he was the best hero she had ever met.

"Looks like I'm winning," Nova bragged to Spider-Man before rocketing into the sky.

"You've just peaked early, helmet head," Spider-Man shot back, webbing his way up a skyscraper.

Spider-Man noticed a long line of angry people by a hot dog cart. "This one's mine!" Spidey shouted as he swung over. "You need a hand?" he asked the owner of the cart.

"Yeah, I'm all outta hot dogs!" the vendor replied.

Spider-Man saw a shop nearby and noticed hot dogs on the first shelf. Before Nova could move, Spidey *thwipped* a web into the store and snagged some!

The shop owner looked confused as the hot dogs sped by. Seconds later, another web *thwipped* in with money.

Triumphant, Spider-Man handed the hot dogs to the vendor. But after he dropped them into his cart to cook, the vendor began drinking the hot dog water!

"Ah, nothing like hot dog–flavored water!" he said.

"Gross," Nova said.

Spidey shrugged. "But I still won that round."

The heroes needed a tiebreaker. Suddenly, Nova felt a tug on his arm. It was the little girl from the park.

"Excuse me," she squeaked. "Can I get your assistance again?"

She pointed up at a towering skyscraper in front of them.

At the very top was Vicious!

Nova was shocked. "How'd she get up there?"

"She was probably trying to get away from you. I know the feeling," Spider-Man teased. "I'm sure she'll stay put once she's felt the warm embrace of New York City's best Super Hero!"

"We'll see about that," Nova shouted as he started to fly.

Spider-Man shot a long web and pulled himself up. Nova thought it would be a cakewalk with his ability to fly, but Spider-Man had mastered the art of web-slinging. The two were neck and neck as they raced up the side of the skyscraper.

Nova had edged out in front of Spider-Man, but suddenly the helmeted hero collided with a flock of pigeons! "Ack!" Nova yelled, spitting out feathers. That distraction allowed Spidey to take the lead.

"Sorry, birdbrain!" Spidey joked. "Looks like this race belongs to me!"

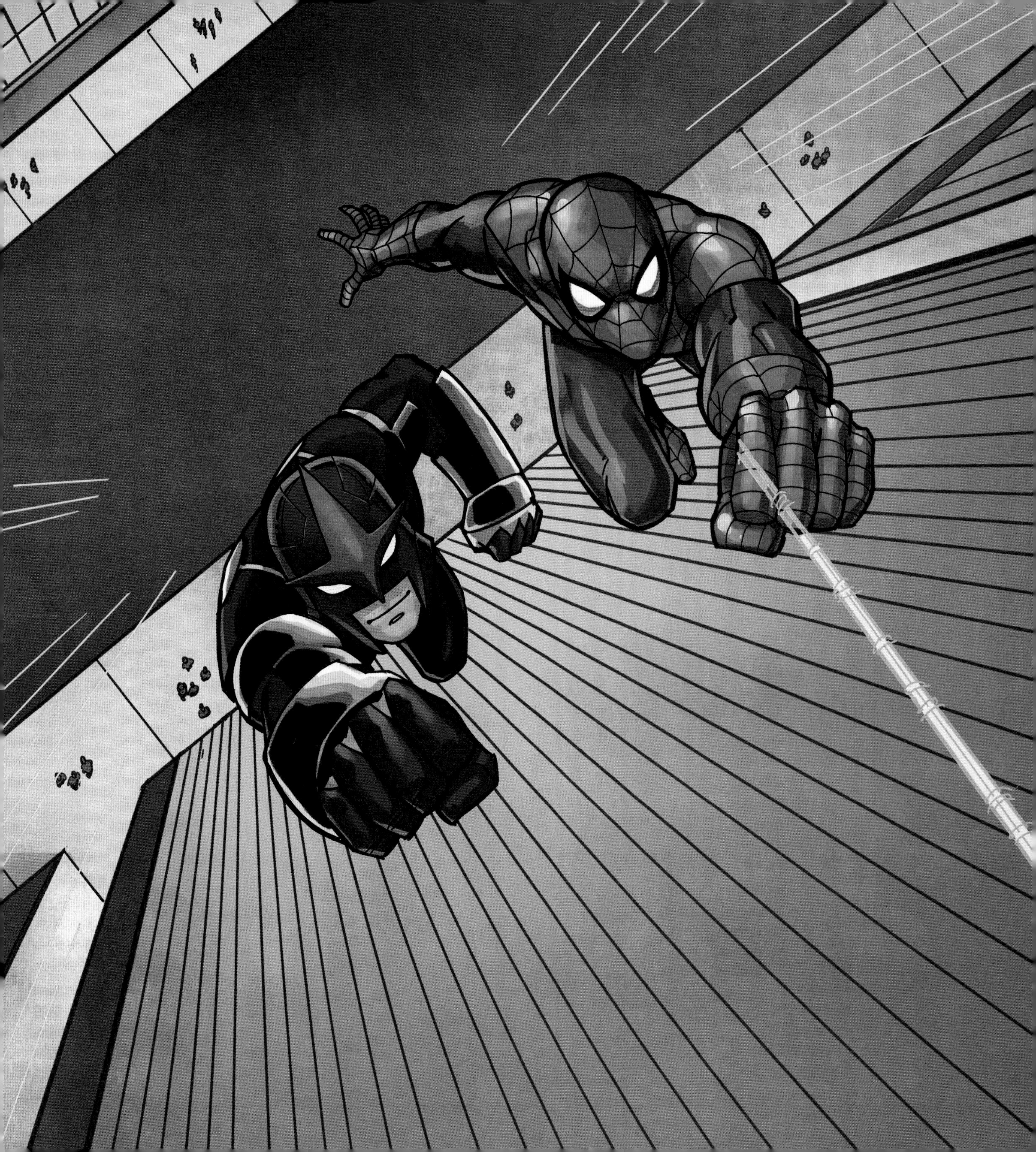

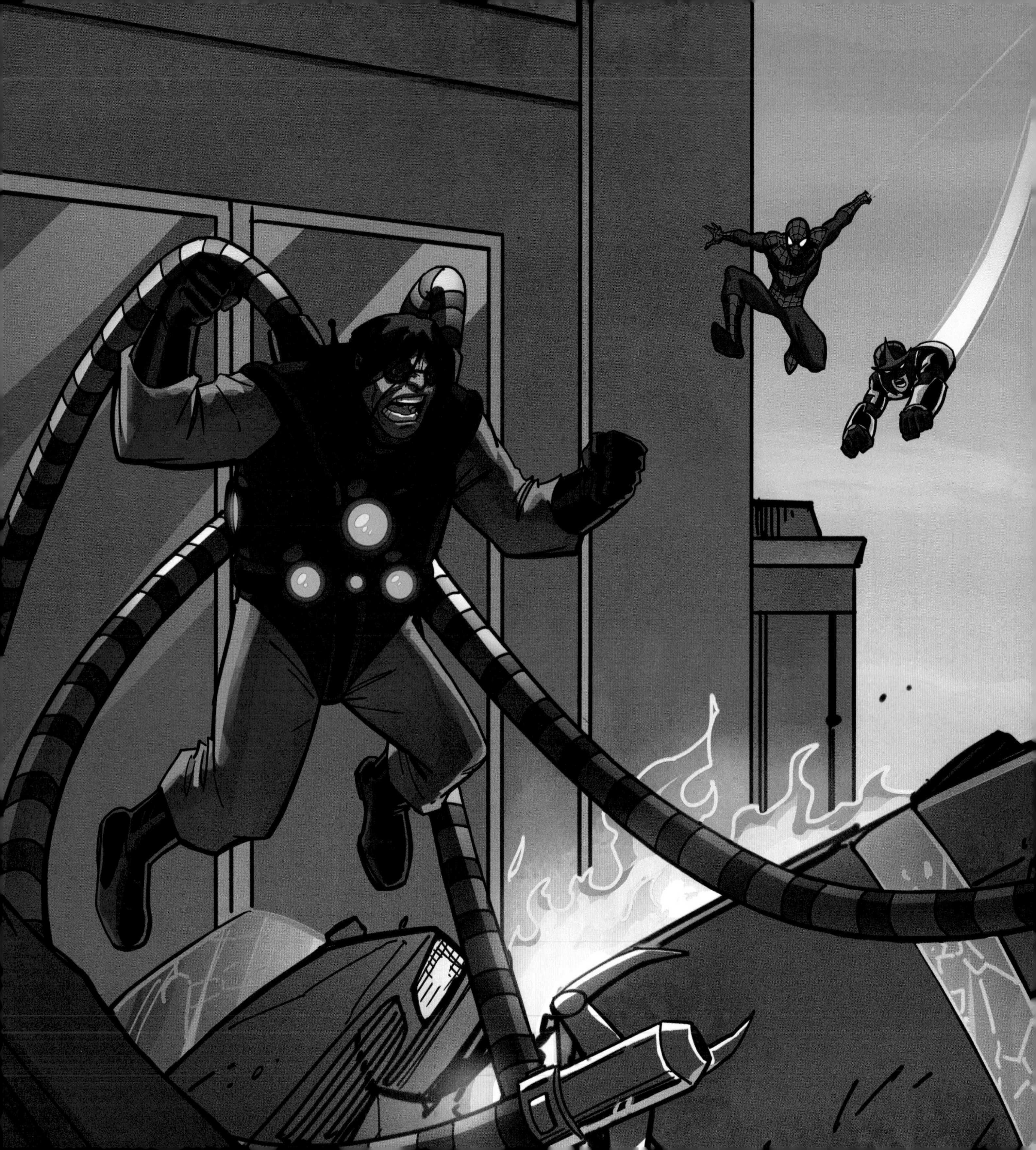

But his advantage was short-lived. Both heroes stopped when an explosion rocked the street below! It was Doctor Octopus and his Octobots. They were trying to destroy a coffee shop on the Upper West Side!

"Puggly-wuggly's going to have to wait," Spider-Man said.

"We have to get down there!" Nova agreed.

The duo dropped to the ground and confronted Doctor Octopus.

"No one likes decaf!" Doc Ock was yelling. "And your prices are outrageous!"

Spider-Man stepped up. "You leave that nationally renowned chain coffee shop alone!"

"Or what? You two against my Octobots and me?" Doc Ock laughed.

"Let's see how many of ol' mop top's bots we can stop," Spider-Man told Nova.

"Now you're on!" Nova yelled.

Spider-Man and Nova jumped into action and began to take out the Octobots. *THWIP! THWACK! KAPOW! KABOOM!*

Nova and Spidey had each destroyed an equal number of Octobots. Doctor Octopus was furious! Finally, he decided to join the fight.

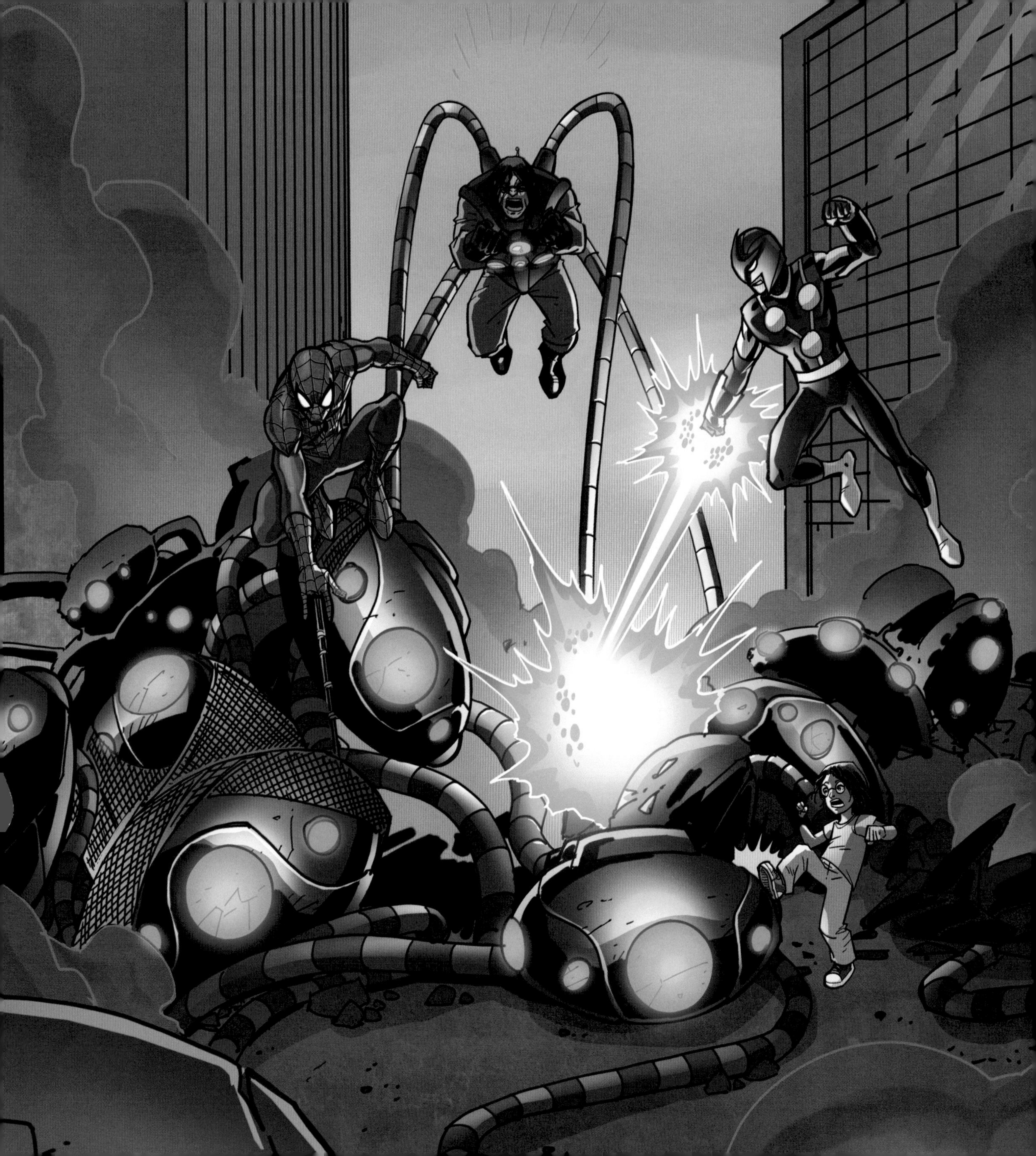

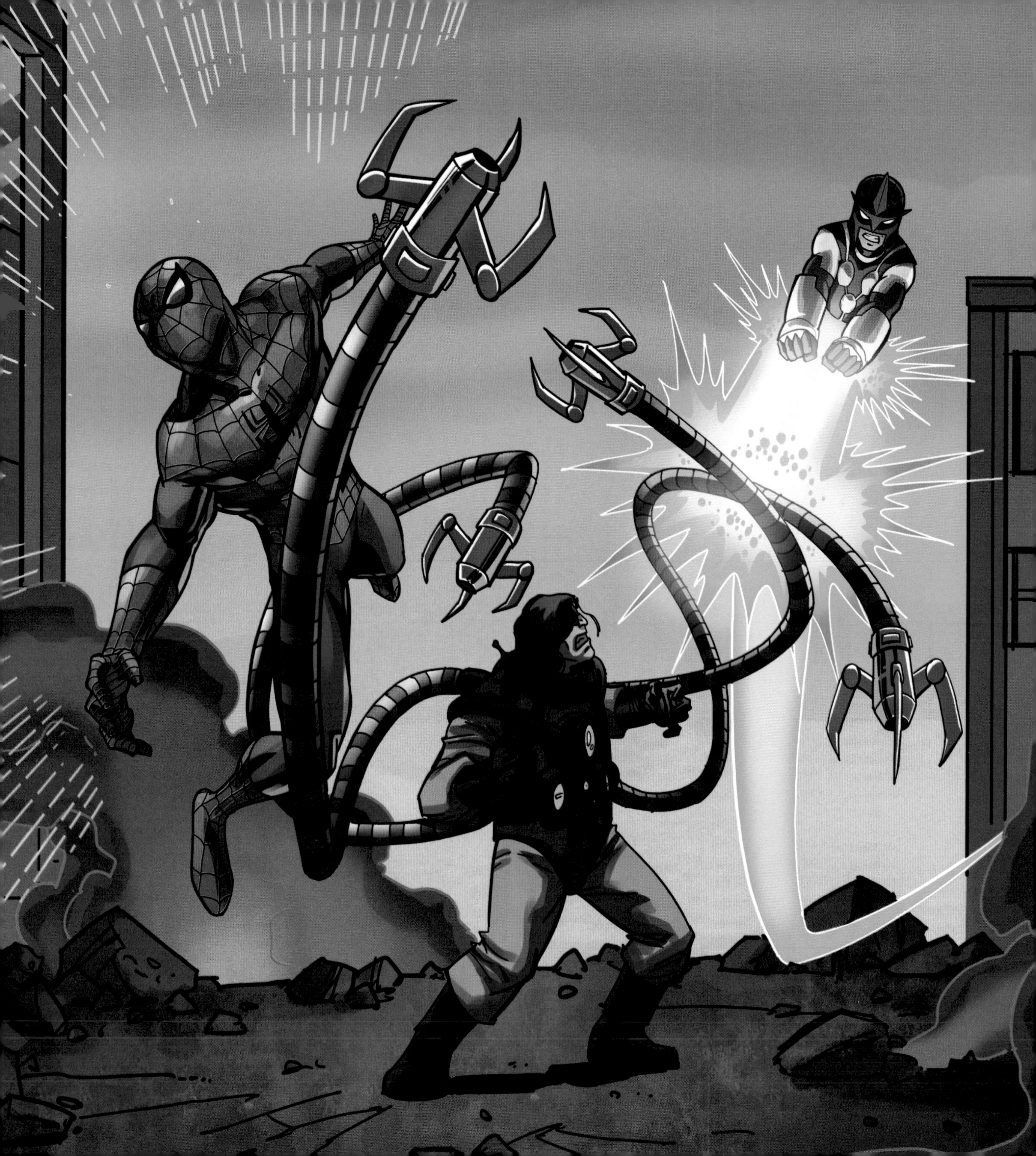

"I'm gonna grind you up and brew both of you!" he said with a cackle.

"Dude, that's totally gross!" said Nova.

"So uncalled for," agreed Spider-Man.

Doc Ock's metal tentacles swung and slashed at the heroes. Spidey leapt and rolled while Nova dove and dodged the attacks.

Working separately, neither hero could get a handle on Doctor Octopus's tentacles.

"I can't pin down his crazy arms!" Spider-Man yelled to Nova.

"They keep blocking my blasts!" Nova yelled back.

"We have to work together!"

"You thinking what I'm thinking?"

Spider-Man grinned. "Like a big sneaker."

Nova grabbed two of Doc Ock's tentacles, and Spider-Man grabbed the other two.

"First bunny ears, crisscross, loop-de-loop, and ta-da!" Spidey instructed.

Nova circled Doctor Octopus, wrapping the tentacles around him.

"Let's make it a double knot!" Nova said with a laugh.

Spider-Man swung around Doctor Octopus, mirroring Nova. Then he sealed the tangle of metallic arms with a sticky web.

"All tied up," he quipped.

"Man, we need to work on your puns," Nova said, shaking his head.

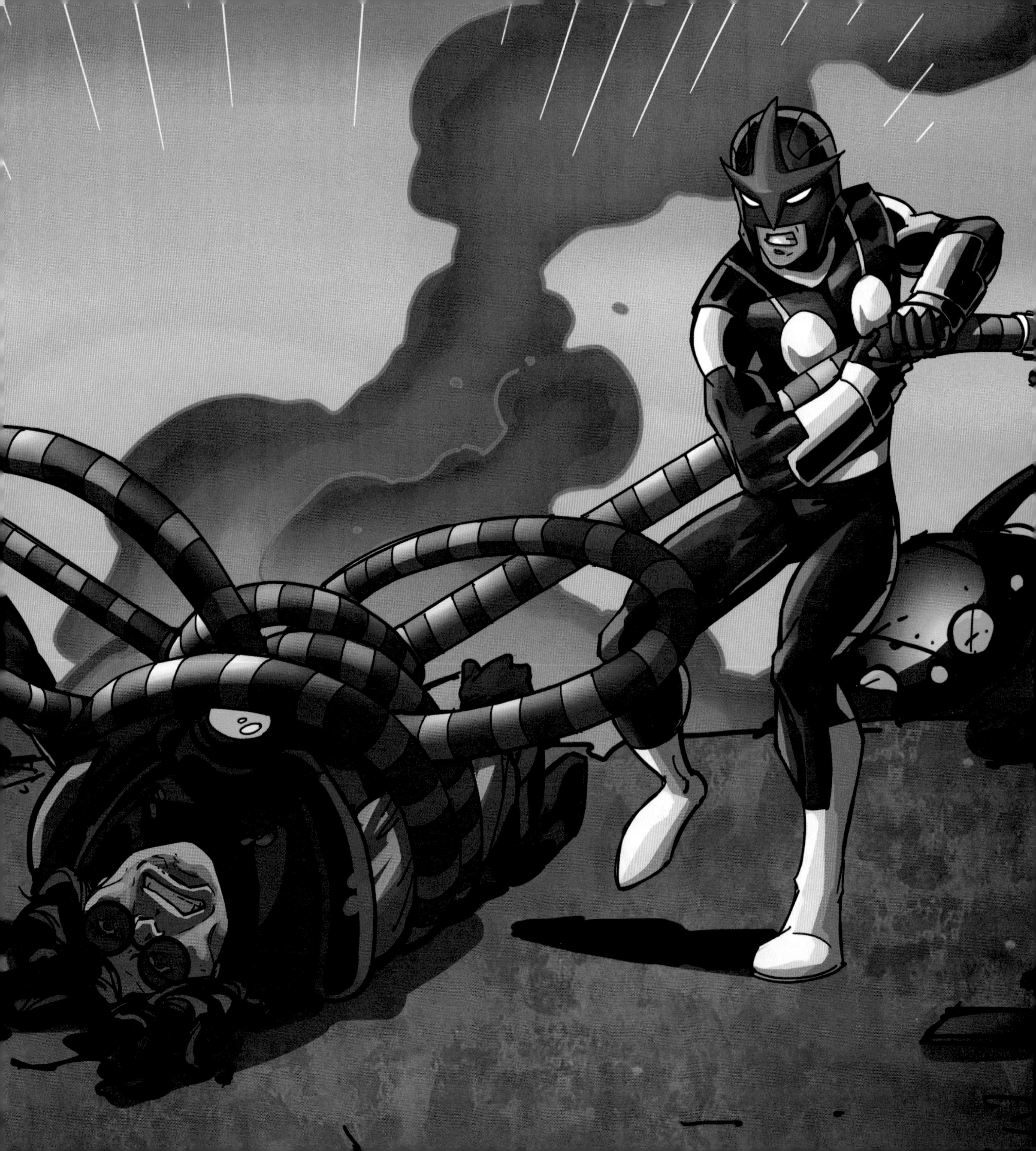

They had destroyed all the Octobots and left Doctor Octopus in a sticky situation. They had learned how important it was to work together, even though their abilities were different. But there was one thing left to do.

"We're still tied," Nova said.

"Who said the competition was over?" Spider-Man shot back.

"Race you to the pug!" they yelled simultaneously, heading to the top of the skyscraper as the little girl watched with a smile.

SPIDER-MAN
Super BUGZ!

"What a hack!"

Spider-Man groaned in frustration as the computer locked him out for the seventh time. He'd just caught Alexander Petrovski hacking into the secured network of the First National Bank. Now Spider-Man was trying to reverse it. But he wasn't having much luck.

"Maybe I could give you a hand with that?"

Spider-Man looked around, startled, but Petrovski's mouth was covered—and there was no one else in the room.

Spidey looked down but still saw nothing.

"Hold on," someone said.

A moment later, a man was standing in front of Spidey.

"Ant-Man!" Spidey exclaimed. "You sure know how to make an entrance. What are you doing here?"

"Same thing you are," Ant-Man replied, pointing over to Petrovski. "I've been tracking him for weeks now."

"Really?" Spidey said. "I just happened to be passing by a cybercafe when my spidey-sense started tingling. Petrovski ran off, and I followed him to this warehouse."

"Spidey-sense, huh? Must be nice."

"Oh, it's great, but it doesn't work for guessing passwords."

"Just leave that to me," Ant-Man said, shrinking and disappearing through the side of the computer.

"It should be a piece of cake," he called from inside. "Just push this wire here, press that switch there, and *presto*!" Spider-Man saw that the login had been bypassed. A few seconds later, Ant-Man was standing next to him again.

"Great work!" Spider-Man said. "You just saved a bunch of people a lot of money."

"Correction, Spidey—*we* just saved them a lot of money."

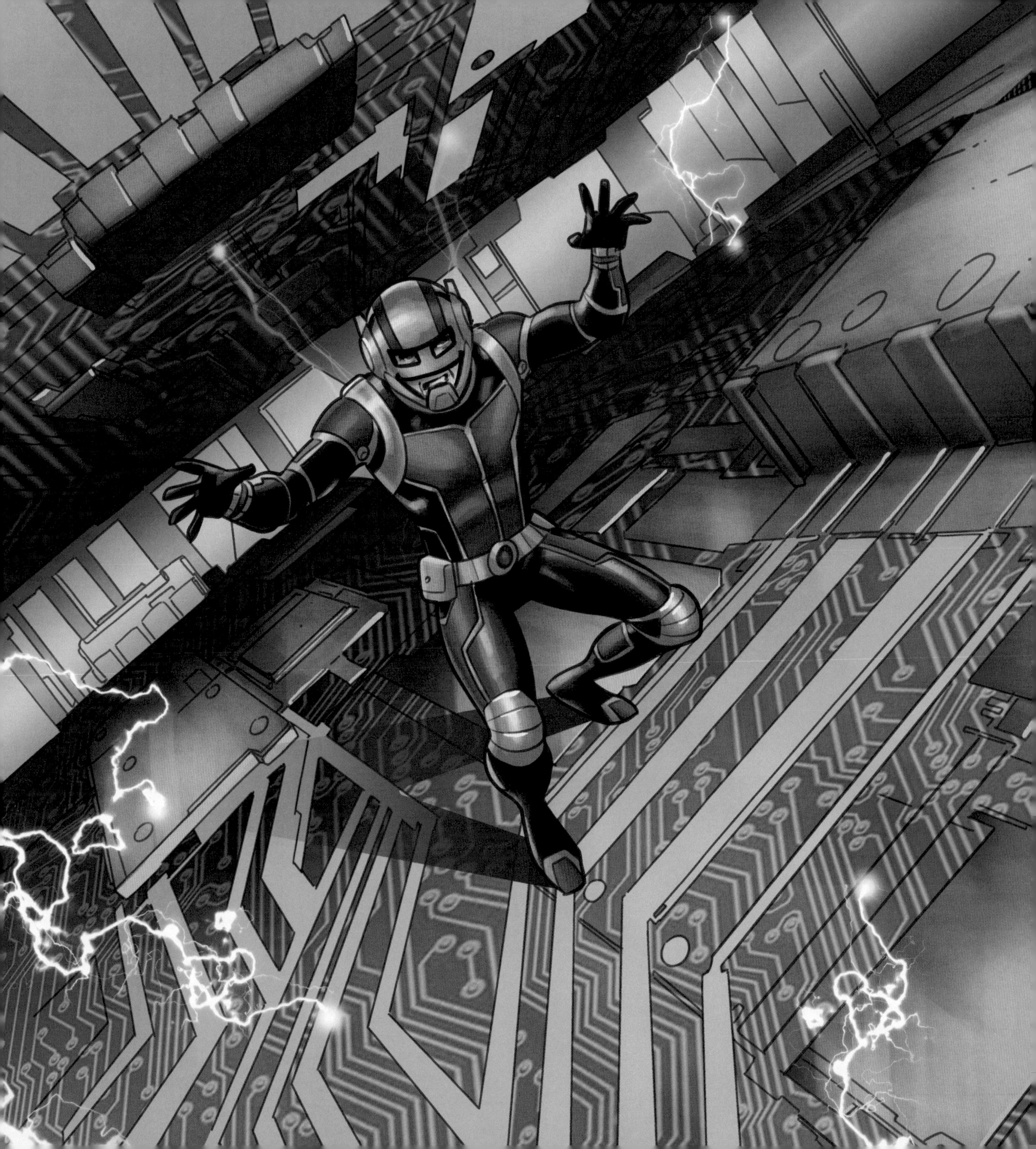

"Wait a minute," Spidey said. "Are you thinking what I'm thinking?"

Ant-Man stroked his chin and nodded. "Your spidey-sense, my shrinking ability . . ."

"We could be—"

"—the SUPER BUGZ!"

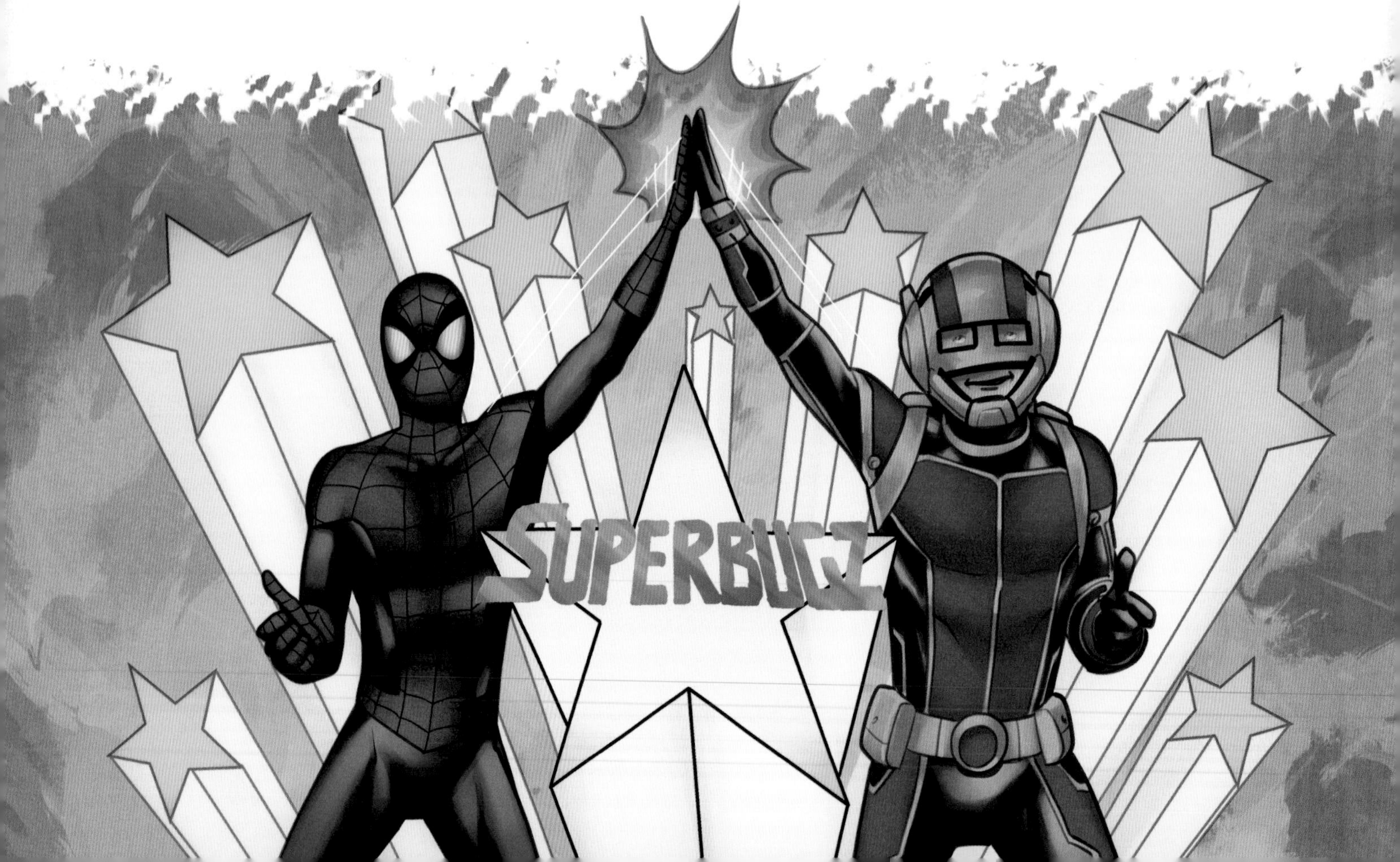
SUPERBUGZ

"Hold on, though," Spidey said. "I don't know if my spidey-sense still works if I'm ant-sized."

"Only one way to find out," Ant-Man replied. "Let's test it!"

They left Petrovski tied up for the cops and went outside.

Then Ant-Man sprayed Peter with Pym Particles.

Suddenly, they were both looking up at litter towering above them on the sidewalk.

"It worked!" Spidey cheered, looking around at the warehouse that now seemed like a skyscraper.

"Do you feel any different?" Ant-Man asked.

"A little hungry, but I skipped lunch. I think my spidey-sense still works—it's even tingling right now!"

"What? Right now?"

"Yes! Return us to regular size, quick!"

Ant-Man pressed the nozzle on his Pym Particles sprayer, but nothing happened. "Uh-oh."

"Let me guess," Spidey groaned. "It has a bug?"

Ant-Man nodded. "I can fix it, but I need a few minutes."

"I'm not sure we have that long," Spidey said, pointing to a sparrow that had landed a few feet away. It was only a regular bird, but it looked like a winged dinosaur from their perspective. A hungry bird of prey coming right for them!

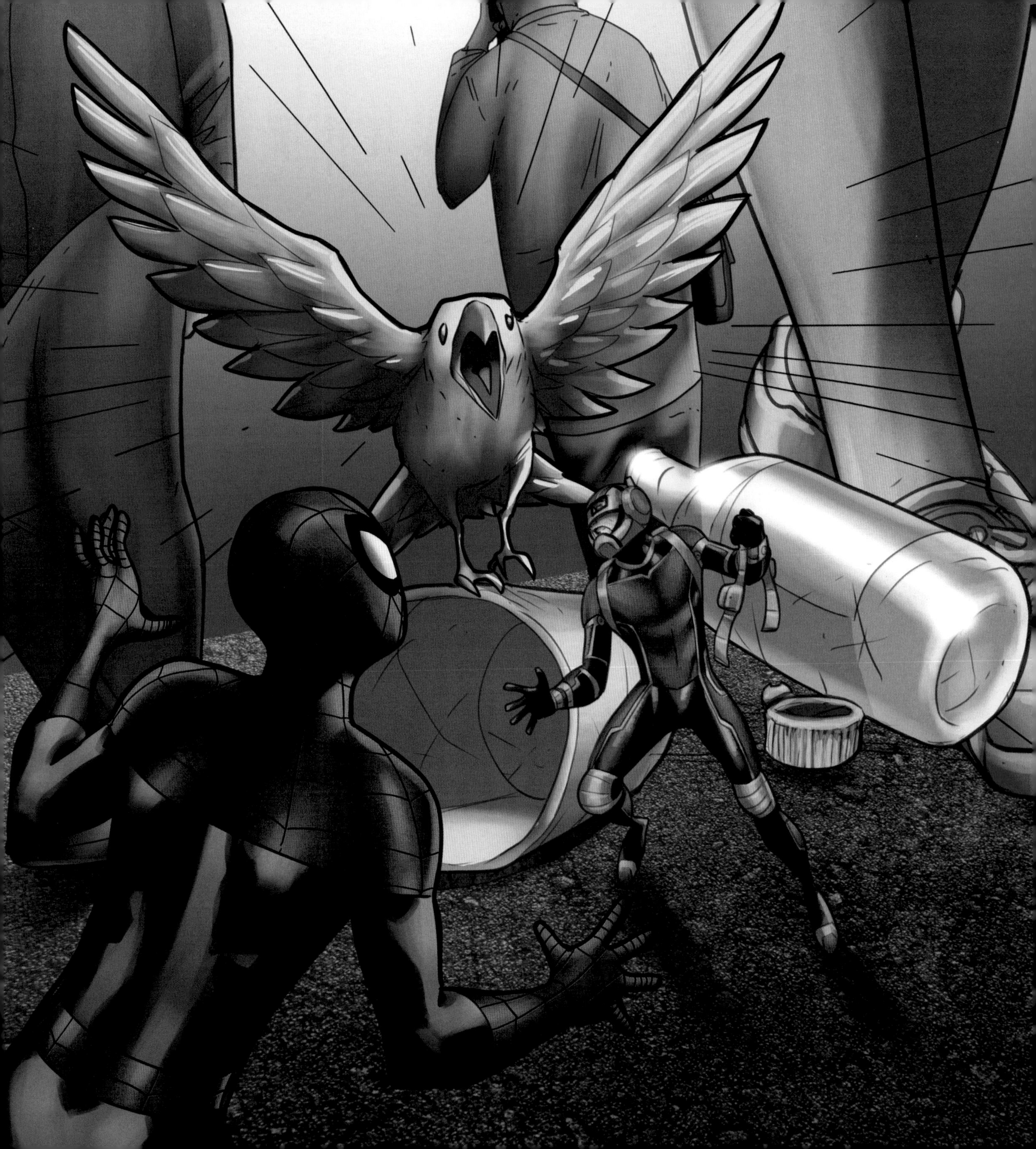

Spidey and Ant-Man jumped away just as the sparrow's beak snapped at them.

"I'll hold it off!" Spidey yelled. "You fix that!"

The bird flapped its wings and dove at them again. Quickly, Spidey shot a burst of webbing and hoisted himself onto its back.

"Hey, this isn't so bad," he said. "It's kind of like a ride at the carnival!"

Just then, the bird reared back and shot straight into the air. "Whoa!" Spidey shouted. "How do you get off this ride?"

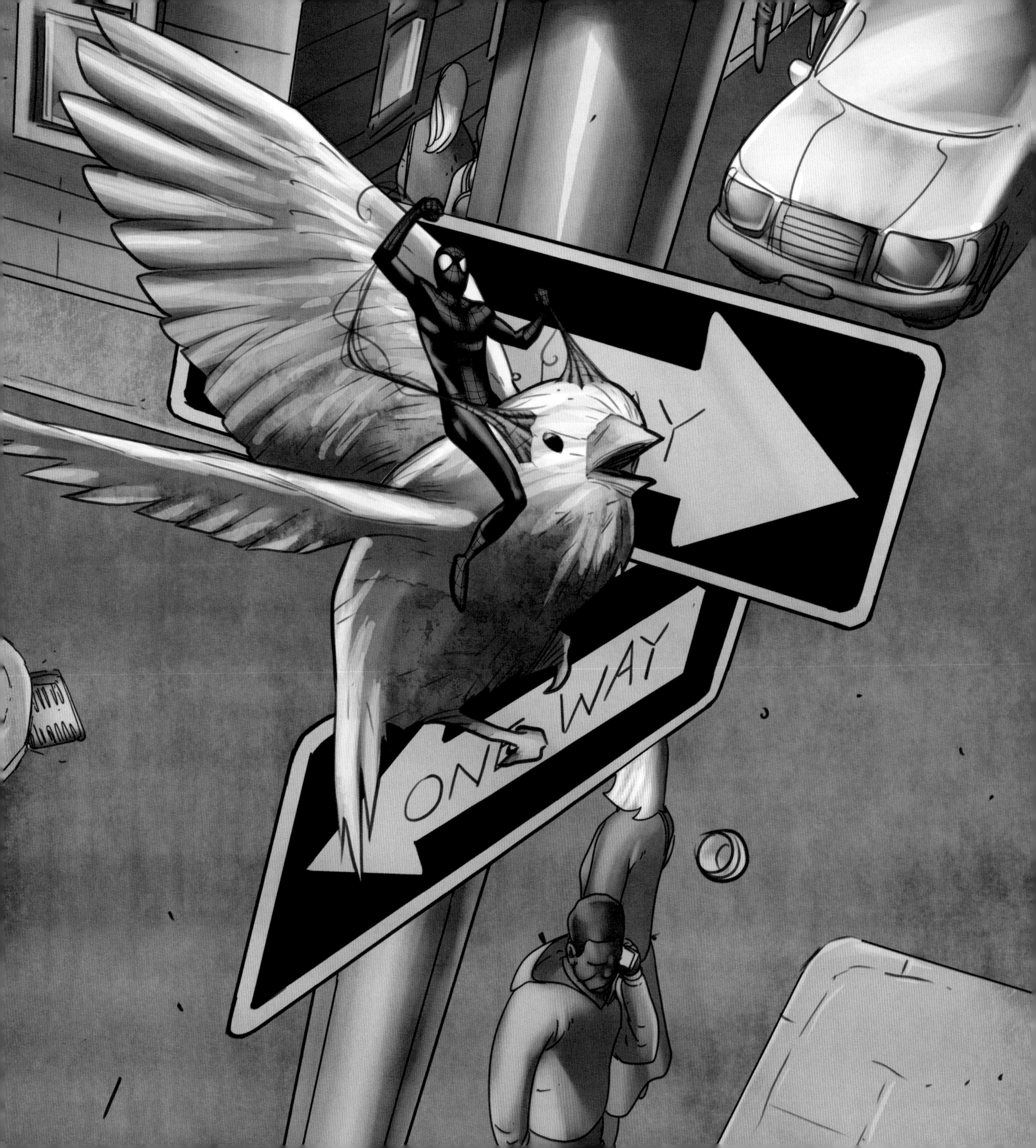
WAY

Spidey held tightly as the sparrow zipped under, over, and around. He wasn't afraid of heights, but then he'd never ridden on the back of a bird before. He hoped Ant-Man was close to fixing the device.

"Uh, one little problem . . . I can't spray you with the Pym Particles when you're so far away!" Ant-Man explained.

"Throw it to me! I'll catch it!" Spidey shouted.

"Are you sure? I don't want the bird to eat it. . . ."

"Just do it!" Spidey yelled.

Ant-Man shouted, "Hey, birdie! Down here!" The sparrow suddenly dove, speeding toward the sidewalk.

"Anytime you're ready, Ant-Man!" Spider-Man yelled.

"Get ready!" Ant-Man held up the belt. Without a moment to lose, Spidey aimed his web-shooter. It was his only chance!

"Here goes nothing," the wall-crawler whispered to himself. He snatched the belt seconds before the sparrow could!

Spidey sprayed himself with the Pym Particles and tumbled to the ground.

The world seemed to spin, and then he was on the sidewalk looking down at Ant-Man.

Ant-Man laughed. "You know what? Maybe that whole Super BUGZ idea needs a little more work."

Spidey chuckled with him. "We do make a good team, but I prefer to fly without a copilot—especially one with bird brains!"

SPIDER-MAN

Sand Trap

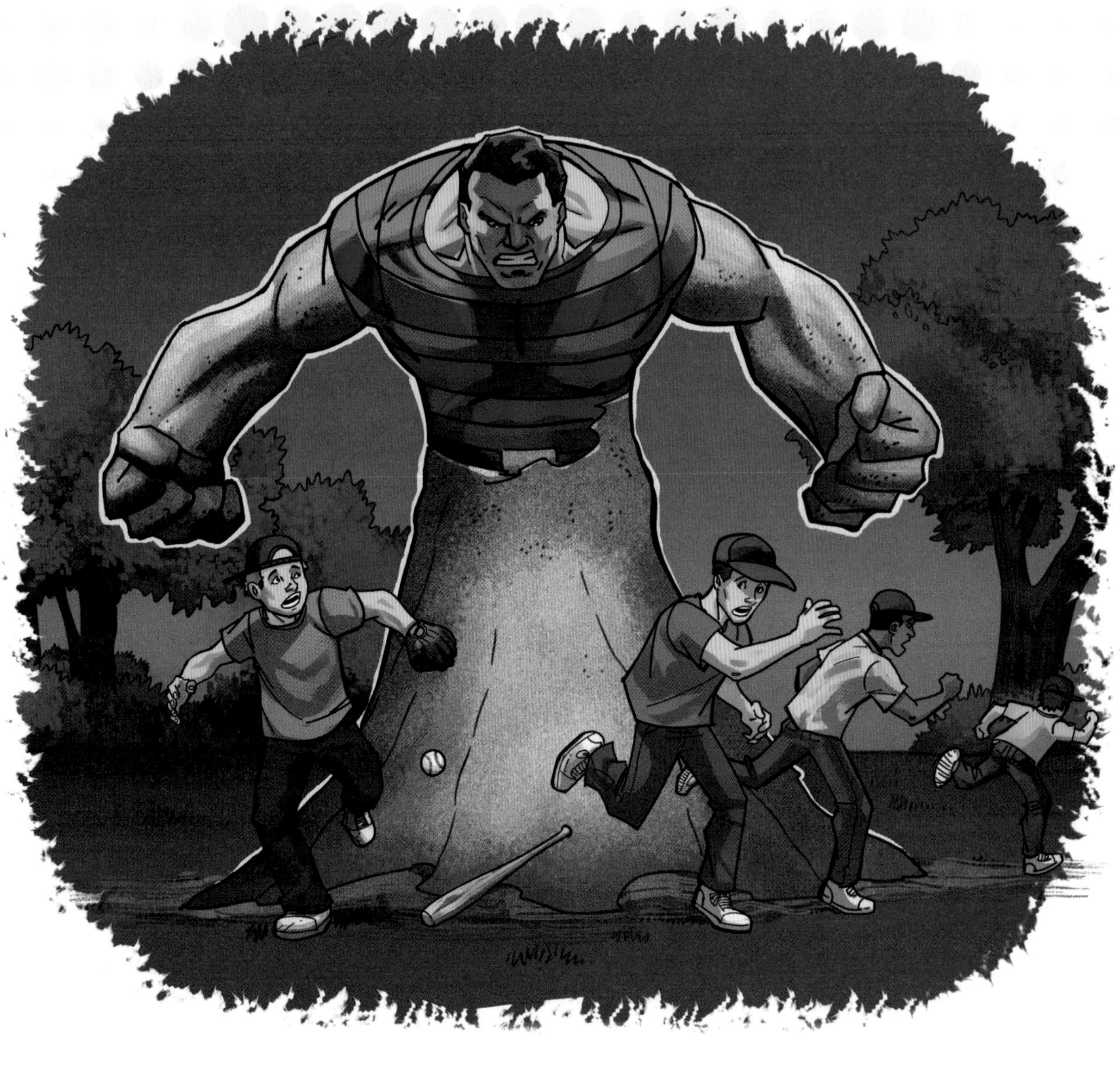

*T*he bank alarm wailed loudly as people screamed in fear.

Peter Parker was on his way to the nearby park to take some outdoor spring pictures for the *Daily Bugle* when he heard the alarm and ran toward the bank. *Sounds like someone decided to make an unauthorized withdrawal,* he thought.

Arriving in front of the bank, he saw a trail of sand disappearing into the entrance and knew exactly who was behind the robbery—Sandman!

Peter looked inside to see the bank vault open and empty.

Looking for a place to change into Spider-Man, Peter spotted the bank manager angrily shaking his head.

"Are you with the newspaper?" the bank manager said, pointing at Peter's camera. "You're too late—he's already gone! You could still take some pictures for the paper, I guess," he said, frustrated.

"Yeah," Peter sighed, disappointed. "I guess."

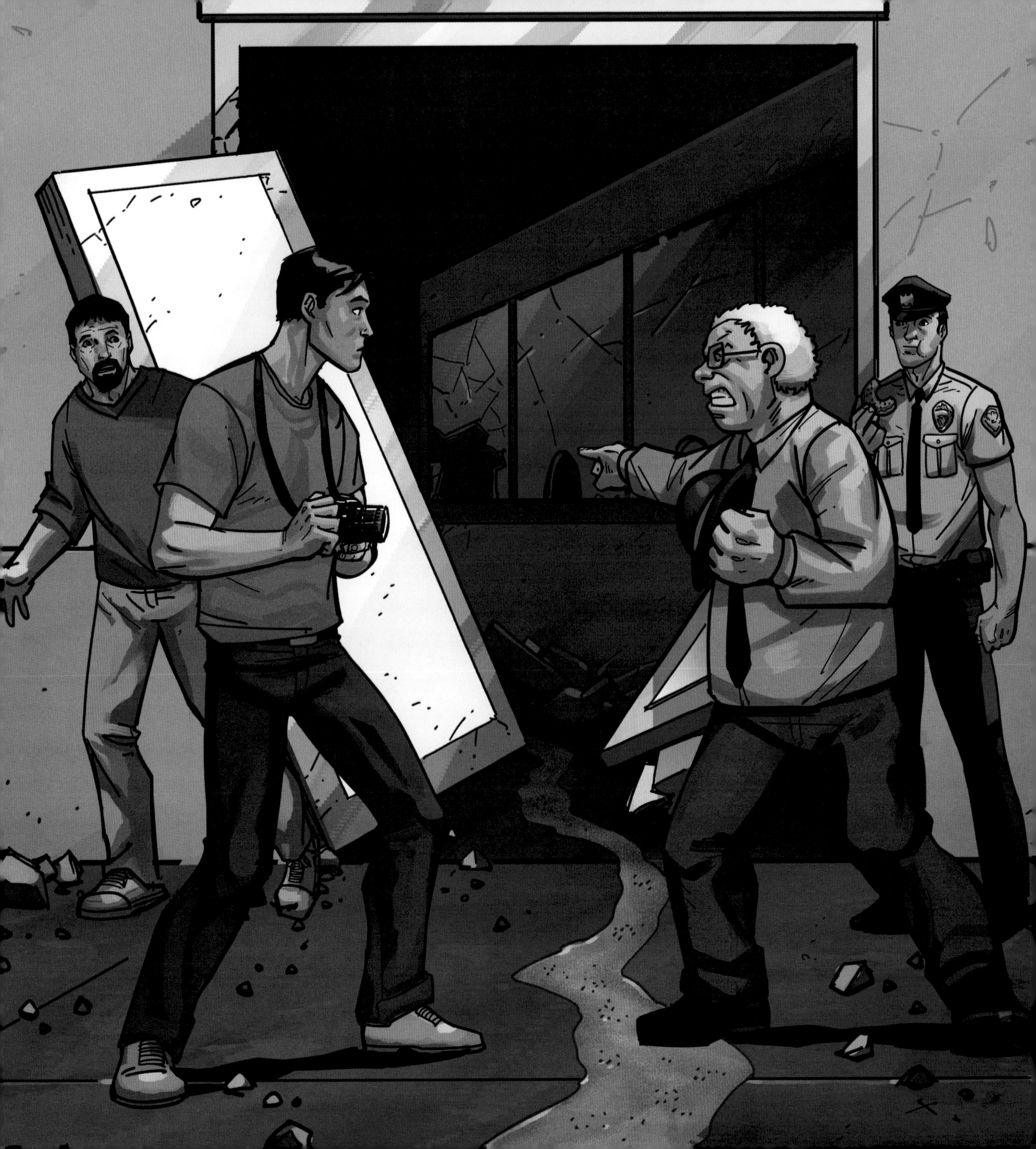

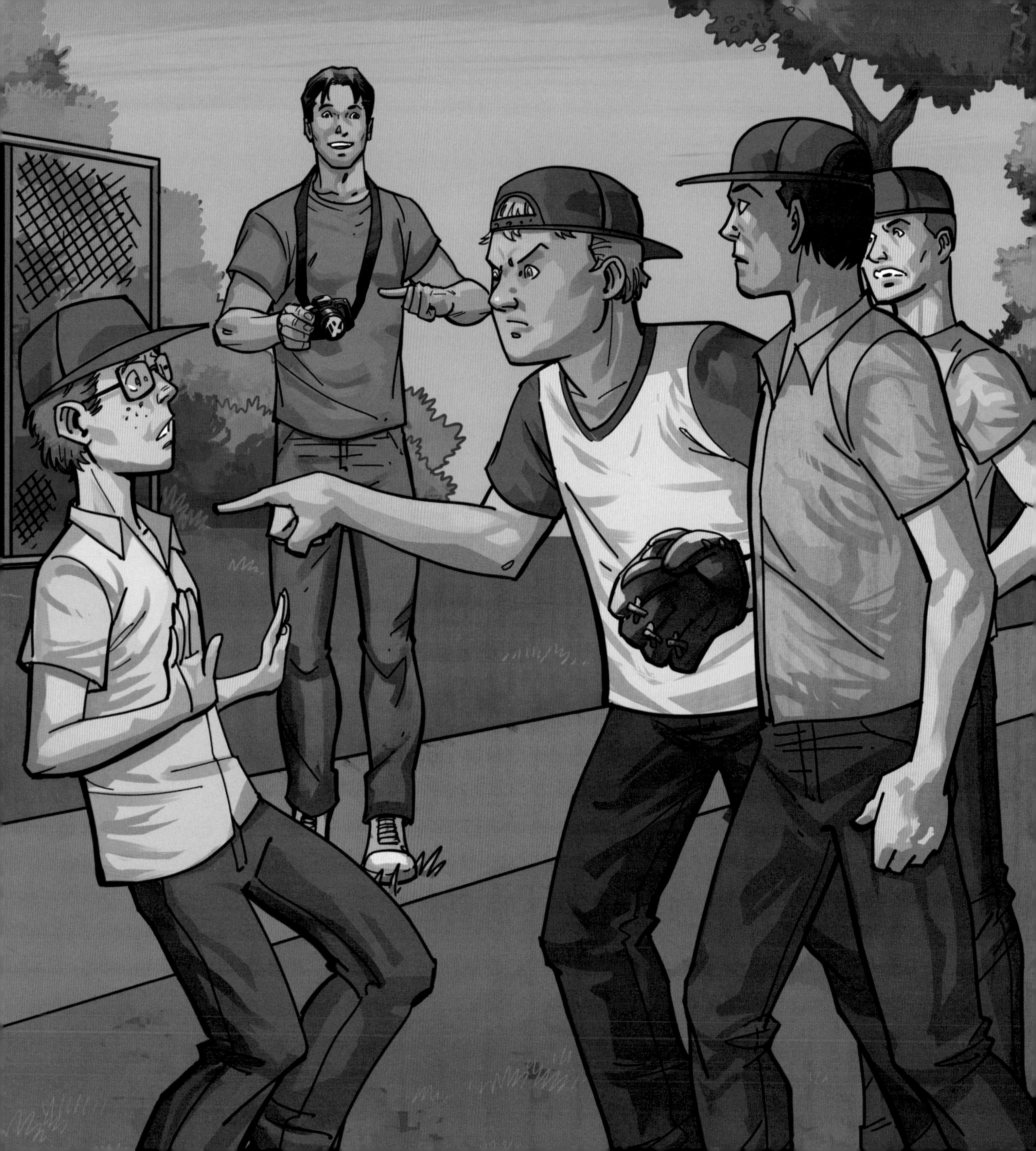

Peter was angry with himself for not preventing the robbery. "I could have stopped him if I didn't have to do that story for the *Bugle*," he muttered under his breath.

Frustrated, Peter continued on his way to the park. He snapped some pictures of ducks in the pond, then got one of a tree in full bloom. As he approached the baseball field, he heard yelling.

Peter saw a bunch of kids surrounding a smaller boy.

"See, dork-face? That's how you catch a baseball," said one kid.

"My own grandma can catch better than you!" said another.

Peter shook his head. *That's no way to talk to someone,* he thought. Maybe it was time to remind those kids about the importance of playing nice.

"Everything all right here?" he asked as he approached them.

"I wish," replied the tallest, who seemed to be the leader of the pack. "Nervous Neddy over here can't catch a ball to save his life!"

Peter knelt down and said, "Ned, is it? I know how you feel—I wasn't that great at catching when I was your age." He turned to the taller boy. "What's your name?"

"Barry," he said, turning his cap around. "I'm the best at baseball!"

"Well, Barry, my name's Peter, and I work for the *Daily Bugle*. I'd love to do a story on the young baseball players we have right here in the park. How about we help Ned become a *better* catcher, instead of making fun of him?"

Barry's eyes glazed over as he pictured himself in the newspaper. "You think I could make the front page? I'm game, but good luck with butterfingers over here!"

Peter got his camera ready as the boys took their positions on the field. Ned went to first base while Barry covered second.

"Okay," Peter yelled, "let's see what you got!"

The pitcher threw a fastball and the batter swung hard, hitting the ball between first and second base. Diving full stretch to his left, Barry scooped the ball off the ground and rolled to his feet to throw to first.

Ned was only a few feet away, at first base. All Barry had to do was lob the ball over to him and the batter would be out. Instead, he reared back his arm and rocketed the ball at Ned, who ducked out of the way just in time to avoid getting hit in the face! The ball went rolling away, and the batter safely rounded first and headed to second.

"Great job, wimpy!" Barry yelled at Ned, who was still on the ground. "You let him get to second base!"

"Wait a minute. That's not fair," Peter called out. "You threw that too hard for him to catch!"

Barry laughed. "He would've dropped it even if I'd handed it to him!"

Just then, out of the corner of his eye, Peter saw the sand on the pitcher's mound moving.

That's strange, he thought. A second later, it got even stranger: the pitcher's mound started rising, with a face taking shape. It was Sandman!

"Blasted kids! You're stomping all over my getaway hideout!" the villain yelled.

"Run!" Barry yelled at the top of his lungs, and disappeared behind a tree. Most of the other boys followed him—but Ned stood motionless, too scared to move.

Peter knew he had to do something, but there was no time to change into Spider-Man. He had to distract Sandman somehow.

"Hey, you, um, sandy guy—over here!" Peter cried as he clicked away with his camera.

"Oh, good, the media!" Sandman loved being the center of attention. "I always wanted to be the most famous Super Villain in the world."

It was working! Peter just had to figure out what to do next. He saw a fountain in the park and quickly came up with a plan.

"Barry!" Peter cried. "Throw the baseball at the bag of money!"

Barry gripped the ball. "I can't get the right angle!"

"Throw it to Ned!" Peter yelled.

Ned heard his name and opened his mitt but hunched behind it—afraid Barry might throw the ball at his face again.

Peter saw Barry adopt a pitching stance. "Remember—throw it so he can *catch* it!"

Barry nodded, then threw the ball directly at Ned's waiting mitt. Ned caught it!

"Okay, Ned," Peter called, "throw it at the bag of money—now!"

Ned took aim and threw the ball with all his might. He hit Sandman right in the wrist, and the thief dropped the bag!

That was Peter's cue. With everyone focused on Sandman, Peter quickly shot a strand of webbing at the fountain, then pulled back sharply. The fountain fell right off its base and shot a spray of water into the air, dousing Sandman!

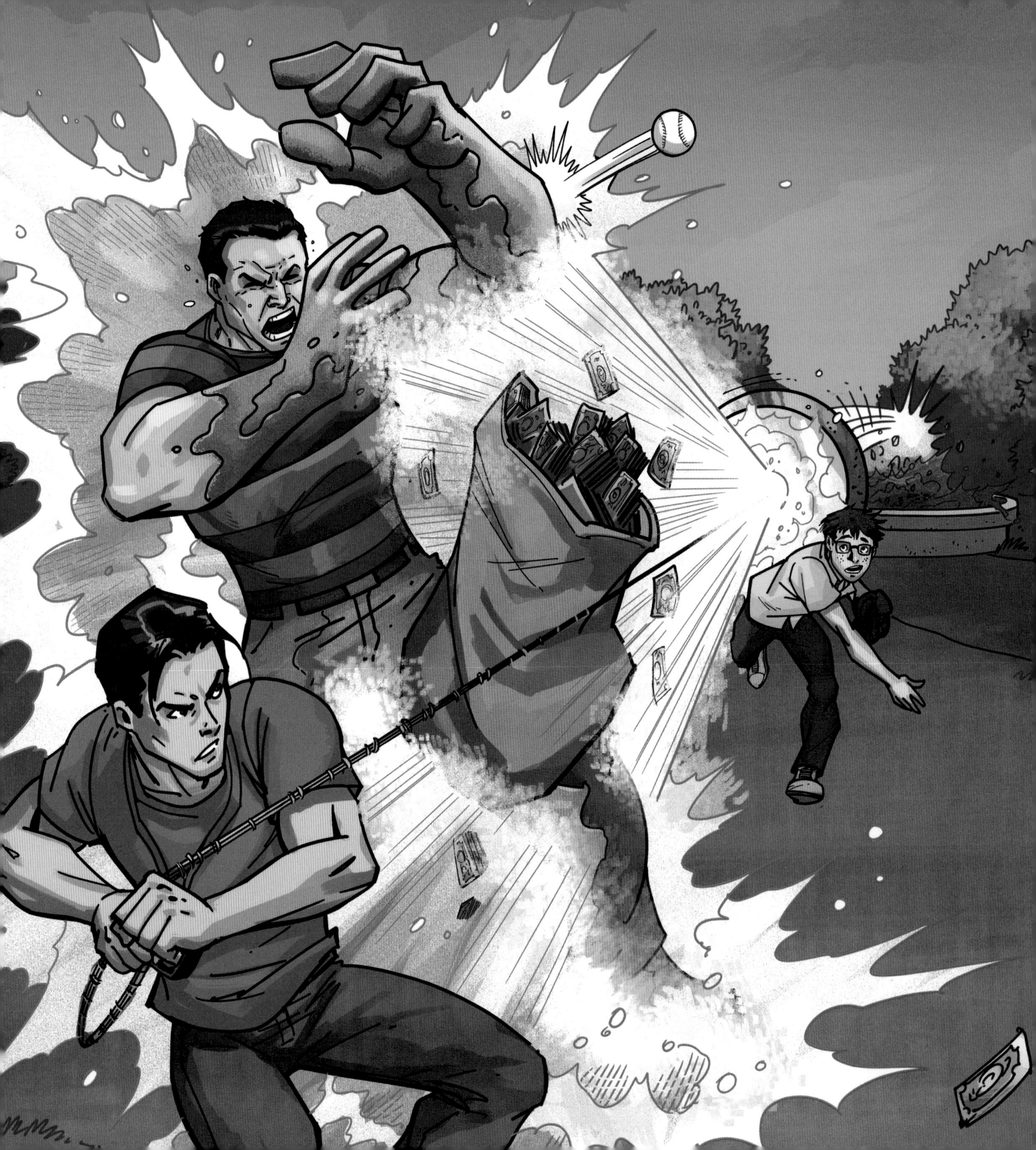

"Noooo!" Sandman cried, turning into a muddy puddle.

"Wow, dude, that was a cool 'double play'!" Barry went over and gave Ned a high five. "I didn't know you had it in you!"

"I didn't, either," said Ned, looking up and smiling at Peter. "Thanks!"

"We should all be thanking *you*, Ned," said Peter. "Now how about we get that front-page picture?"

"You bet!"

SPIDER-MAN
The Fastest Web in the West

Peter Parker was having an excellent day. He had just aced yet another history test. He even knew the answer to the extra-credit question: Billy the Kid, the Wild West outlaw, was left-handed. Peter had grown up watching classic western movies with his Uncle Ben, so he figured he was an expert on the Old West.

After school, Spider-Man zipped over to Avengers Tower. He had agreed to house-sit for the team, who were going on a mission. As Black Widow gave Spidey his list of chores, he found himself staring at an old pocket watch in Iron Man's lab. Widow explained that the watch was actually a mysterious object the Avengers had found. "Don't touch it," she said.

"Sure, my fellow spider-themed Super Hero," Spidey said.

When the Avengers left, Spidey fed Thor's Asgardian half-alien, half-goldfish pet. He dusted Iron Man's armor. He rearranged the Hulk's closet, which was full of purple pants. But after he was done, Peter was bored. He peered at the pocket watch.

It's just a watch. What could go wrong? Spidey thought. The wall-crawler lifted the watch's lid. *POP!* He disappeared.

Spider-Man reappeared in a ramshackle town. A tumbleweed rolled past. Nearby, a cowboy was shoeing a horse. Spidey heard a commotion. He turned to see two horsemen chasing after three bandits fleeing a bank . . . all heading directly at him! Spidey started running, too! But one of the crooks, a lanky teenager, bumped into Spidey. The impact sent the bandit's hat flying across the road. A crowd gathered. Pointing at the teen, the onlookers yelled, "It's Billy the Kid!" Spider-Man realized he was in the Old West! *Guess the tumbleweed should've been my first clue,* he thought. The pocket watch must have been a time machine. The pocket watch . . . Spidey had lost it!

Suddenly, Billy lassoed his hat . . . with his *right* hand. Peter thought, *Wow, guess I was wrong. Billy's not left-handed! But he is in all the movies. . . .*

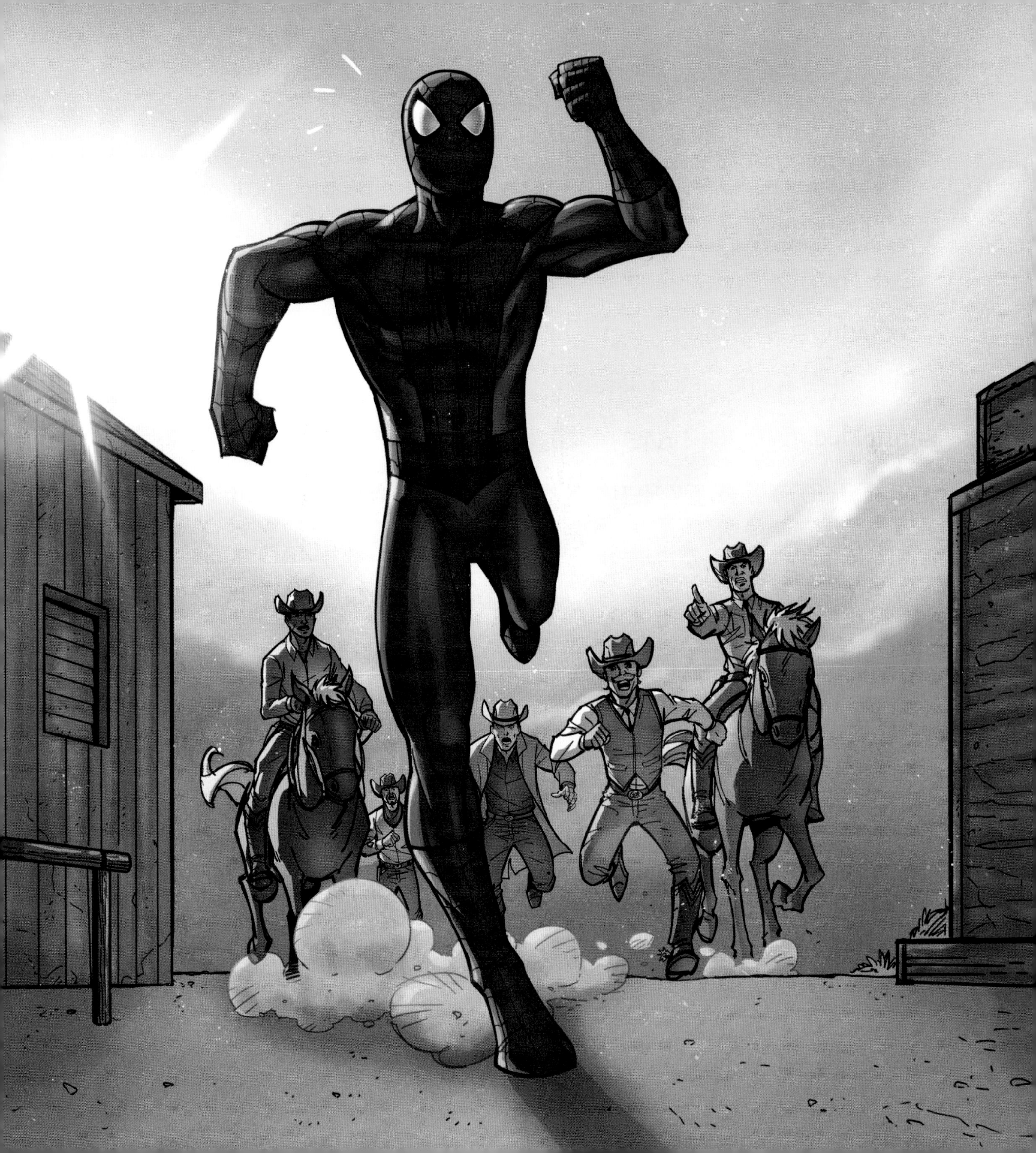

The crowd was so excited to see the famous criminal Billy the Kid, they hardly noticed Spider-Man, the young fellow wearing red-and-blue spandex. Nervous about the unwanted attention, Billy fled. As he ran, a scrap of paper fell out of his pocket. Spidey unfolded it. It was a map of stagecoach routes, with notes scribbled on it. Billy was going to rob the stagecoach at Romita Canyon!

Spider-Man decided to stop Billy. But right then he felt a hand on his shoulder. He spun around to see . . . *Nick Fury*?

"Howdy there. I'm Sheriff Fury," the man said. "And you are . . . ?" It had to be a coincidence. Spidey realized there was no way the man could be Nick Fury. Or could he?

Spider-Man talked like a movie cowboy to impress Sheriff Fury. "I'm the biggest, baddest galoot west of the Pecos," he declared.

"I'm not sure what *that* nonsense means, but I don't like masked bandits," Sheriff Fury said. "You must have been helping Billy!"

Before Spidey could respond, Fury's sidekick, Deputy Coulson, slammed into him. Spider-Man decided not to fight back. He didn't want to be misunderstood further. Spidey soon found himself in jail. But he had to go stop the stagecoach robbery!

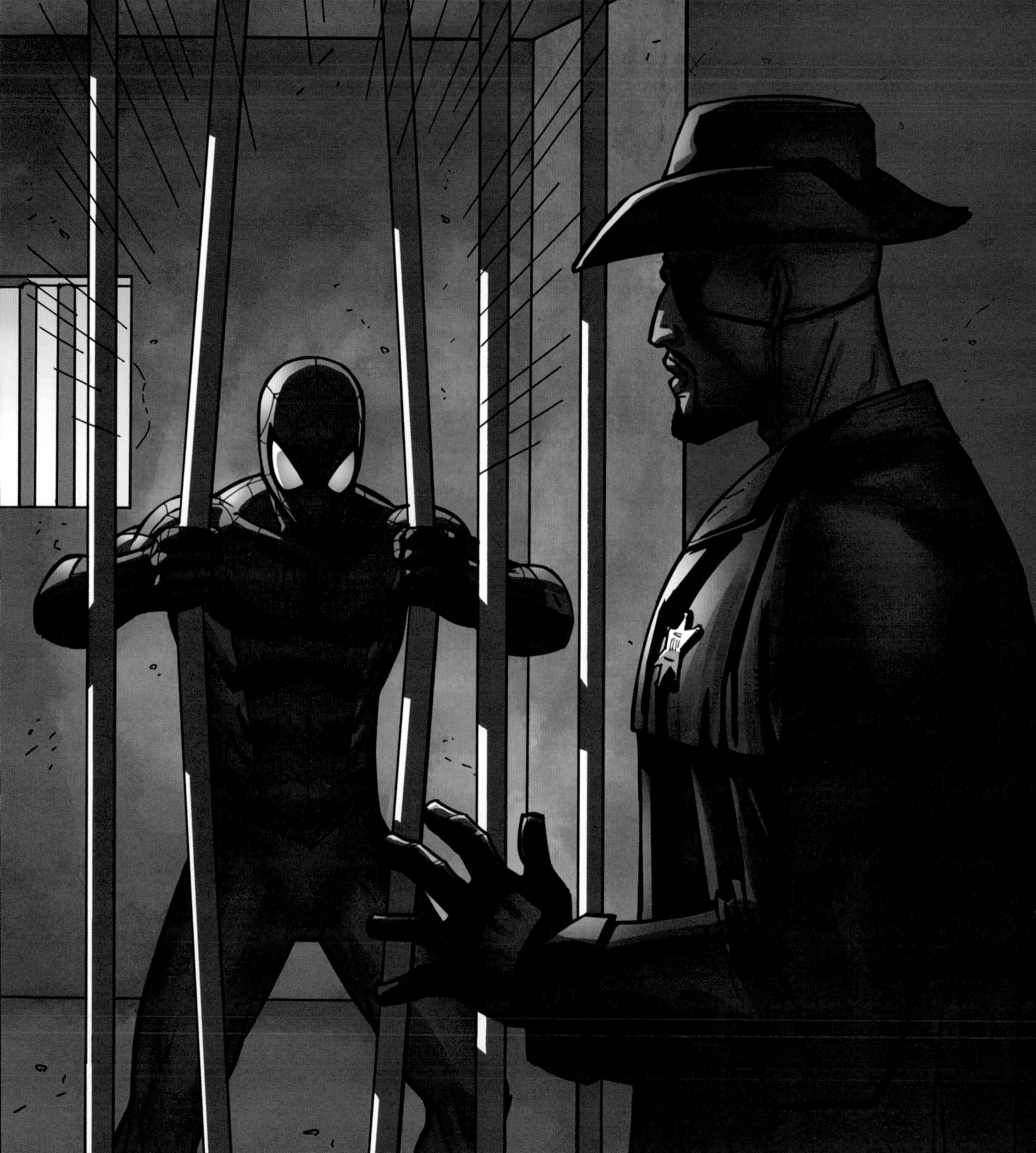

Using his super strength, Spider-Man bent the jail cell bars apart and walked out. Sheriff Fury was dumbfounded. To prove that he meant no harm, Peter walked back into his cell. This convinced the sheriff that Spidey was a good guy.

The wall-crawler explained that he was a hero from the future who had special powers and that he was called Spider-Man.

"They should call you Pajama-Man, because you run around in your pajamas," Sheriff Fury said. Fury plunked a cowboy hat on Spider-Man's head and stated, "*That's* better."

The sheriff explained that most masked men were *bandits*. Peter was confused. In cowboy movies, *heroes* such as the Lone Ranger and Zorro wore masks. Peter realized that all he knew about the Old West was a bunch of movie clichés. *Maybe I shouldn't always assume I know everything about a situation*, he thought.

Spider-Man showed Billy's map to Sheriff Fury. Fury told Spidey to go stop Billy while the lawman stayed to protect the town.

Soon Spider-Man reached Romita Canyon. Billy had the stagecoach's wealthy passengers tied up. His henchmen, Charlie and Tom, were looting a chest of valuables taken from the stagecoach. The crooks looked up to see Spidey glaring at them.

Spider-Man fired webbing at Billy's hands, sticking them

together. Charlie and Tom tossed their lassos at Spidey, but the wall-crawler dodged the ropes. "You guys couldn't catch a *cold*," Spider-Man said, taunting the thieves. But Peter couldn't keep this up forever. The crooks were lasso *experts*. What would he do?

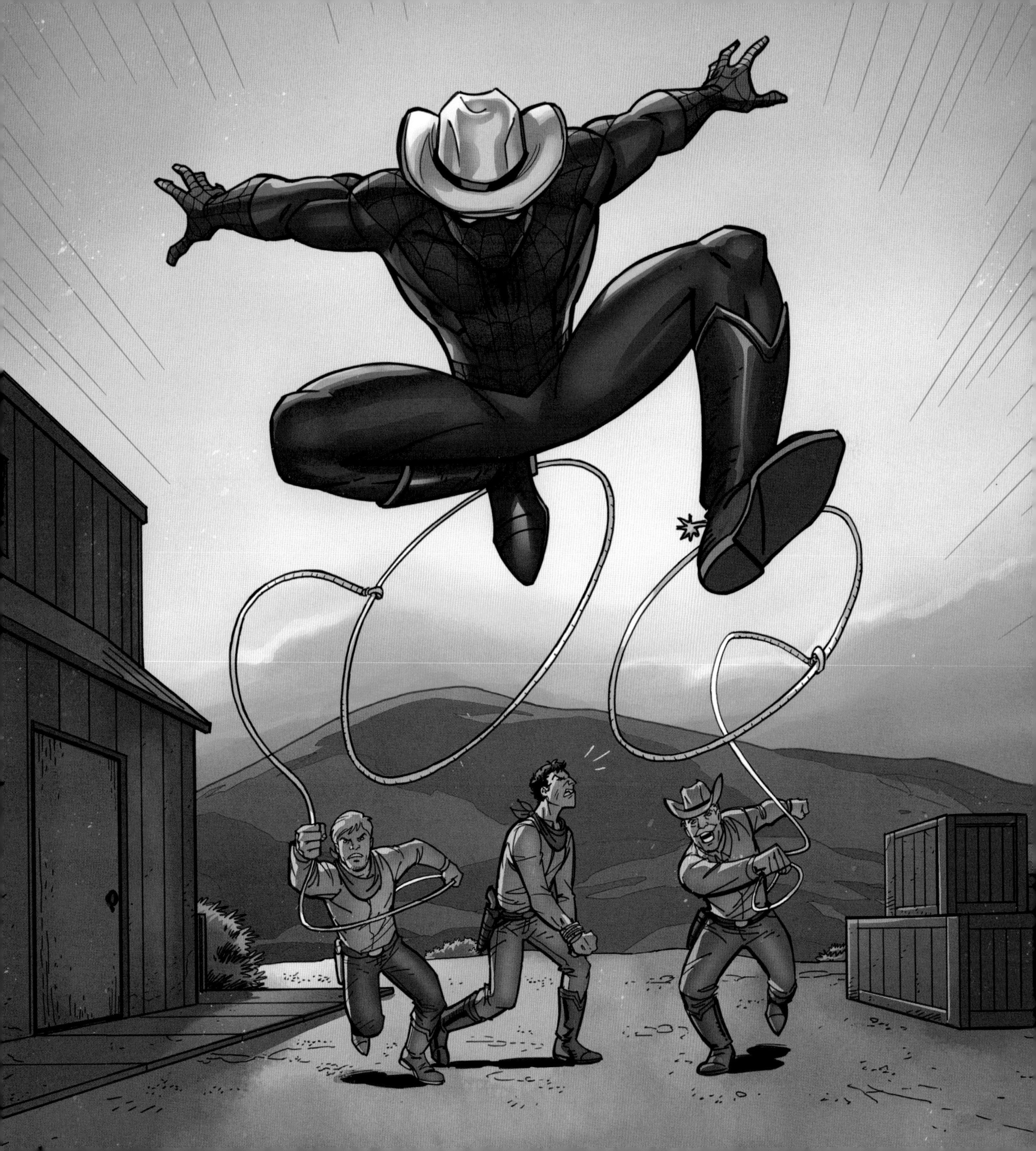

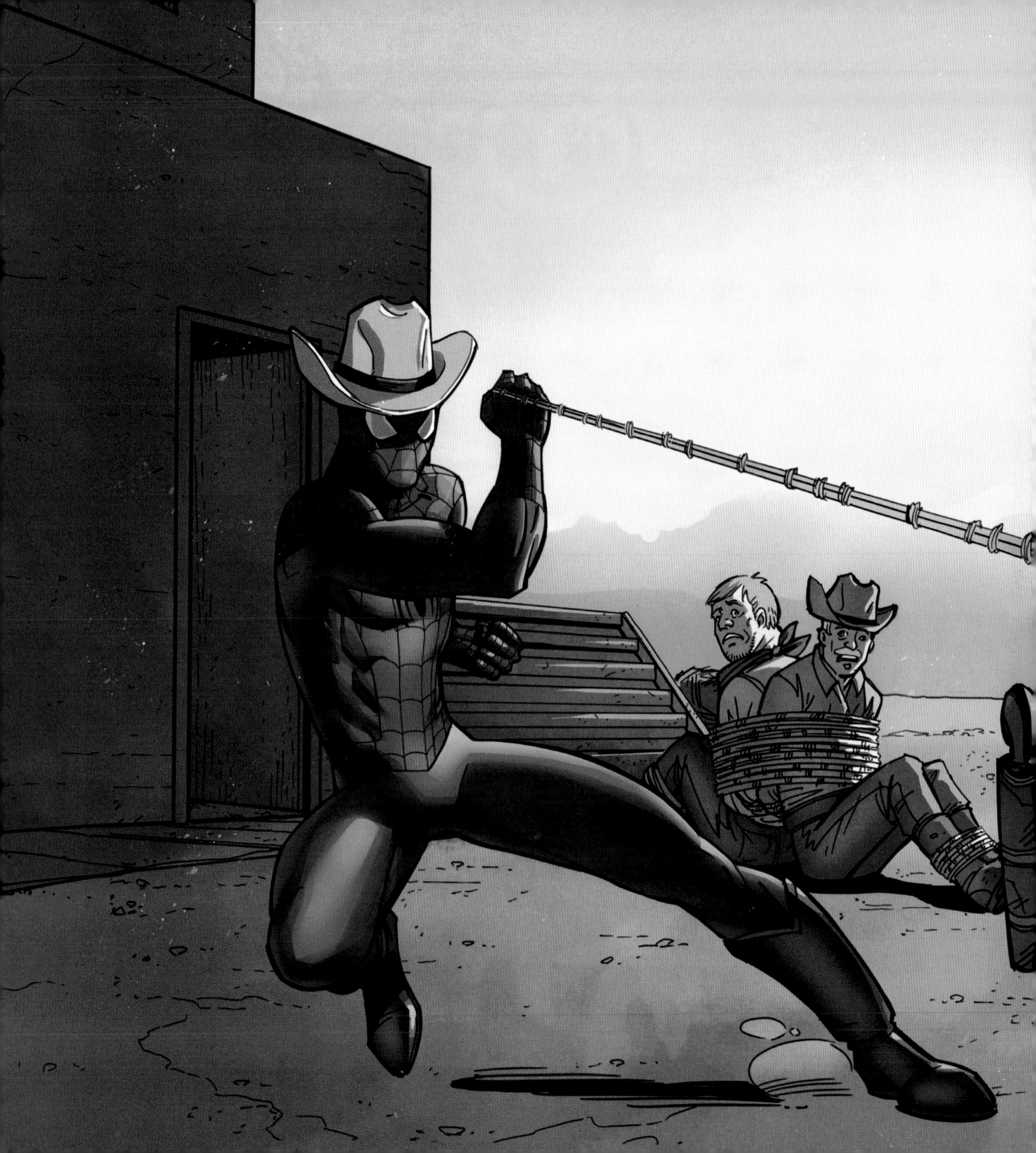

Then Spider-Man had an idea. This whole trip had taught him that he could learn new things from other people. So he decided to learn from the tricks that Billy's men were using. Maybe he could make a lasso, too! Fashioning his webbing into a makeshift lasso, Spidey bounced from bandit to bandit. He tied up Tom, then Charlie, and finally Billy the Kid!

Spider-Man delivered the criminals to Sheriff Fury. As the lawman took them, Billy yelped, "There's a snake in my boot!"

"Wow," Spidey laughed. "I guess some movie clichés *are* true."

Billy yanked off his boot. Both the snake *and* the pocket watch fell out! Billy had stolen the watch when he and Spider-Man bumped into each other outside the bank.

Spidey decided it was time to go back home.

"Good-bye, Pajama-Man! And thanks!" Sheriff Fury said.

Spider-Man arrived back in the twenty-first century with a loud *POP!* He was overjoyed to be home. But he felt bad that he had broken his promise to Black Widow. He wrote her a note.

MASKED MAN SAVES THE DAY!

The note read,
"Sorry I didn't listen.
Guess when you
said not to touch the
pocket watch, you
meant it." Then Spider-
Man placed something
beside the note. It
was a *Daily Bugle*
newspaper from the
Old West. And Spidey
was on the front page!
Spidey smiled. "That
guy must have been
amazing," he joked to
himself.

SPIDER-MAN
Museum Madness!

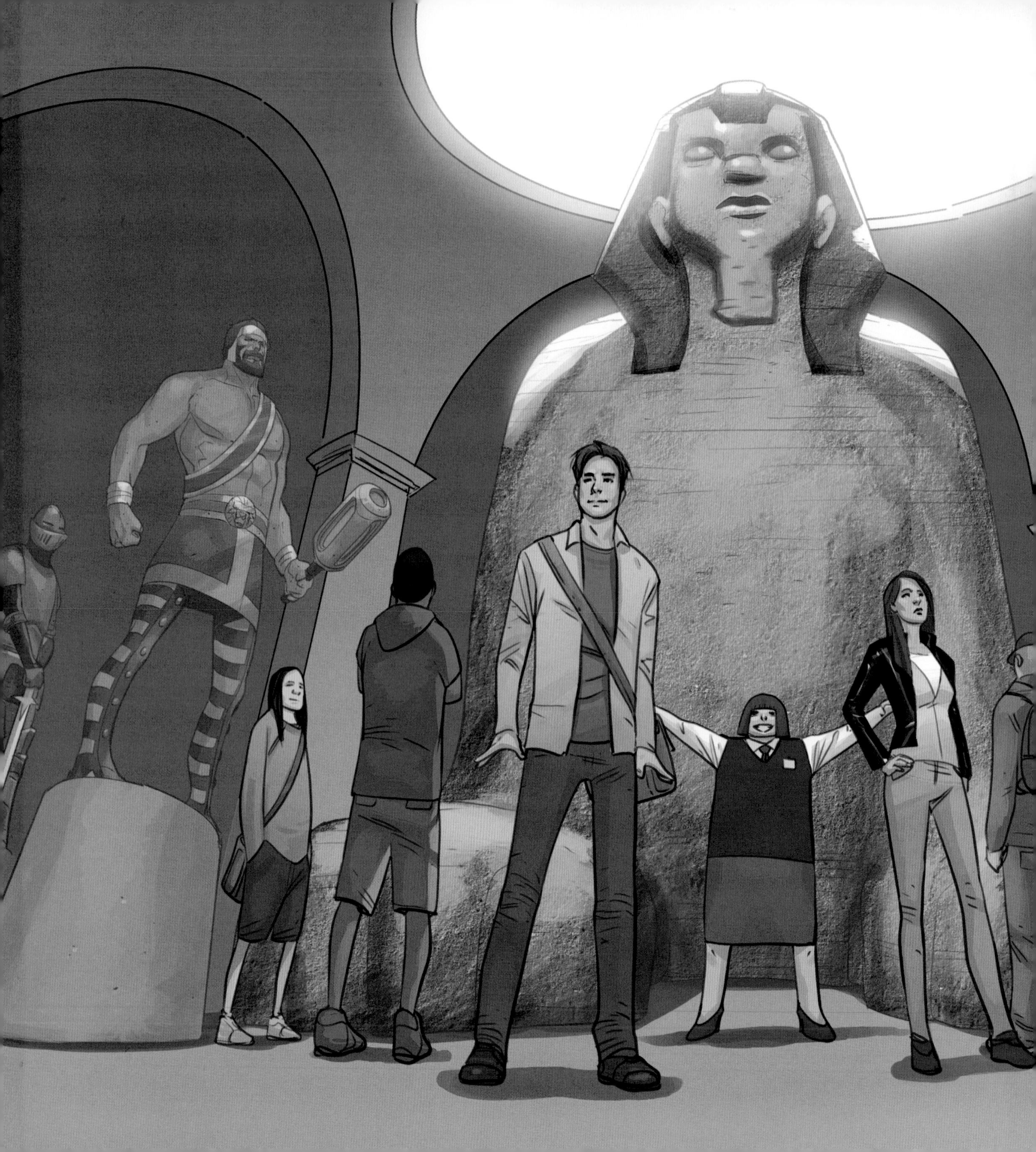

On a high school field trip to New York City's world-famous Metropolitan Museum of Art, Peter Parker and Mary Jane Watson were having two very different experiences.

Peter was thrilled to see ancient artifacts, such as the mummies, the knights in shining armor, the sword-wielding samurai, and the ancient Greek heroes of old, including Hercules! MJ was not as impressed.

"These things are *soooo* three thousand years ago," she said.

"That's exactly right, MJ!" Peter replied excitedly.

"Um . . . what's—" MJ started, but Peter just continued.

"That's what makes them so amazing! Most of these heroes didn't have super powers—any one of us could be a hero!" As Peter went on about the ancient Greeks, MJ watched the strange mist coming out of the museum floor and engulfing everything.

But neither of them noticed the statues were coming to life!

Just in time, Peter's spider-sense began to tingle.

The statues started grabbing Peter's classmates! A Japanese samurai and Egyptian mummy caught Dylan and Sofia. Across the room, a medieval knight snatched Owen.

When MJ turned to check on Peter, he was gone! She ran to find help.

While Mary Jane was distracted by the museum madness, Peter had run into one of the smoke clouds and changed clothes. He came out the other side as SPIDER-MAN!

"Hey! How exactly *did* you guys just come to life?" Spidey felt strange talking to inanimate objects that were now very animated. "Was it magic?" he asked. "I hate magic!"

"Spider-Man! Help us!" cried Dylan. The heroic wall-crawler knew the first thing he had to do was get his classmates to safety.

Careful not to harm any of the living artifacts, the web-slinger snatched his classmates and dropped them onto a giant web.

"Hey, Spidey!" Sofia called. "Did you see that samurai?" Spider-Man looked back and saw that the samurai had sprouted wiring!

"They're robots underneath the priceless armor!" Spider-Man exclaimed.

"You may be covered in history, but you're just so much metal and junk underneath," Spidey said as they closed in on him. "Catch me if you can!" He quickly created a shield of webbing that would help protect the artifacts . . . and himself!

Trying not to damage any of the automatons, Spidey raised his
cushiony shield and spun a web around all the statues' feet! "I'd
better move fast! My shield will only last so long," Spidey said.

Just before the knight's sword could rip through his shield,
Spider-Man webbed his last opponent's legs!

With all his spider might, the wall-crawler leapt into the air, holding tightly to the web.

The higher he rose the more his web tightened, pulling and dragging the automatons together by their ankles!

"Why don't you fellas hang out for a bit while I get to the bottom of this mystery?" Spidey said.

"Look no further, Spider-Man!" Spidey turned to see MYSTERIO—master of illusion—coming out of the smoke! "You've stopped my robots for the last time," Mysterio said. "Let us finish this game, web-slinger!"

Mysterio continued to rant: "Now you'll battle my masterpiece— the Sphinx!"

As the Sphinx churned to life, Spidey saw that MJ was back—and she'd called the police! "You know, Mysterio, with all your scheming, you always miss the small stuff," he said.

Spider-Man struggled with all his might against the Sphinx, barely able to hold it over his shoulders.

"For too long you have stood in my way, Spider-Man," Mysterio continued.

Mustering all his strength, Spider-Man gave the Sphinx one last push and hurled it away!

"No matter," Mysterio said as MJ snuck up behind him with Hercules's heavy mace.

"Do you *ever* stop talking?" MJ asked as she struck Mysterio over the head. *SMASH!* "You sound like Peter Parker!"

Spider-Man sheepishly approached MJ. "Thanks for your help," he said, trying not to sound too much like Peter.

"A friend told me you don't need super powers to be a hero," MJ replied, smiling.

SPIDER-MAN
Climate Calamity!

*T*here's always something for Spider-Man to do before he can get back to being regular old Peter Parker! On one wintry day, the Scorpion kidnapped J. Jonah Jameson—again—because the villain liked JJ even less than Spidey did!

"You're to blame for the Scorpion's attack, Spider-Man!" JJ yelled.

But Spider-Man saved the day, even though it meant helping someone he didn't like. That's what heroes do!

"Thanks, Spider-Man!" one of the police officers said.

JJ immediately shouted, "Yeah! Thanks for *nothing*, web-head!"

The snow was coming down harder than before! Spider-Man needed to get home to his Aunt May to make sure she was okay— and of course, to eat a big bowl of her famous chicken soup.

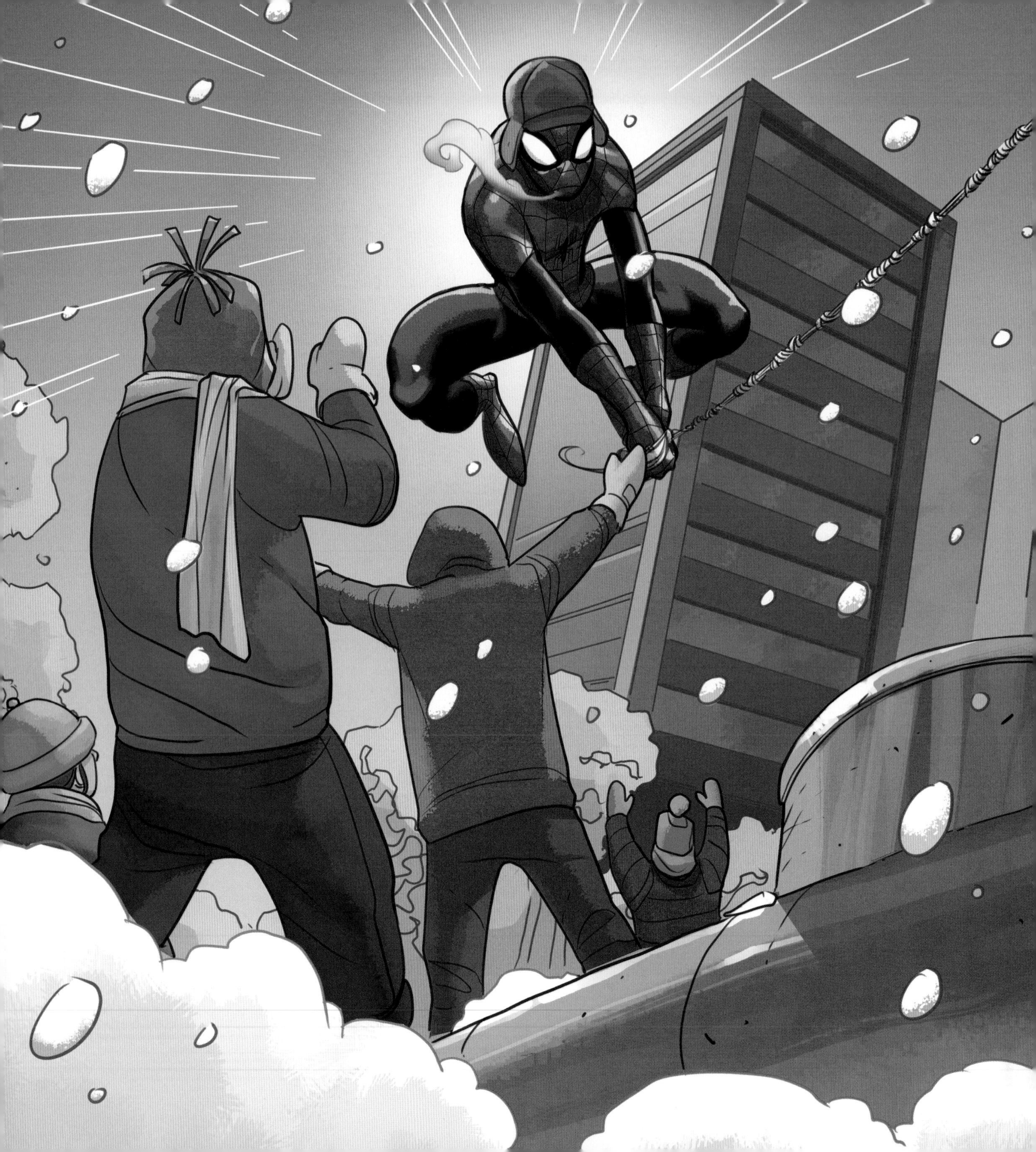

On his way home, Spidey heard someone calling for help from a playground. "My work is never done," Spider-Man said.

"Spider-Man! Skyler is stuck in the pipe," a young boy told Spidey. "She went in through the top, but she didn't know the ends were blocked by snow. She can't get out!"

Spidey dropped into the pipe and found Skyler, cold and scared. "Don't worry," Spidey said. "I'll get you out of here!"

Spider-Man pulled Skyler out of the pipe and returned her safely to the ground. "Thanks, Spidey," Skyler said as Cale, the eldest boy, gave her a big hug.

The kids told Spider-Man their names. Oliver was the one who had called out for help. Then there were Ellie, Gavin, Miles, and Skyler's younger sister, Riley.

Oliver said, "It sure is getting cold, huh, Spider-Man?"

The heroic web-slinger replied, "If it's getting cold, then we better get a move on, shouldn't we?"

Oliver looked around, a little confused. "You mean . . . you're going to help us get home?"

"I wouldn't be a friendly neighborhood Spider-Man if I didn't," Spidey said. "Now bundle up! You're not the only ones who need rescuing today!"

"I know we're small, but can we help, too?" Skyler asked.

"I'm sure we can find a way," Spidey replied.

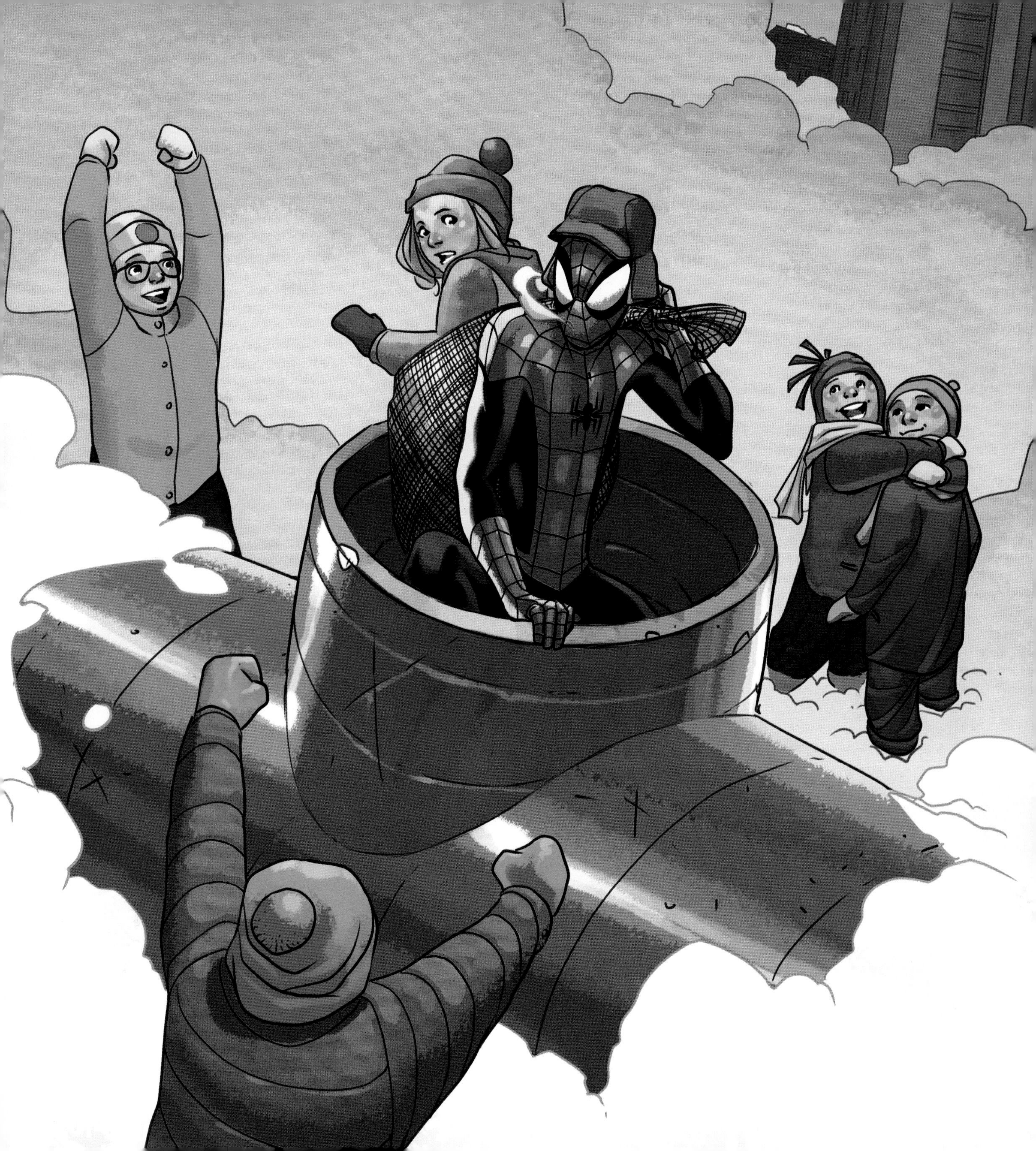

On their way to Gavin's house, the kids spotted Captain Stacy's police car caught in a snowdrift. "Well, we can't let the police get stuck in the snow when they're supposed to be helping everyone else," Spider-Man declared.

He spun his powerful webs and towed Captain Stacy's car free. The kids were sitting on top of the car, laughing with delight as it moved slowly through the snow! "But I don't want to go home," Gavin said. "This is too much fun!"

"I'm having fun, too," the web-slinger said. "But we've got to get everyone home tonight—and that includes me! I have family waiting, too!"

After dropping Gavin off, the wall-crawler and the remaining six children started to cross the Queensboro Bridge. But the road was slippery, and the fire department needed help melting the ice.

Spider-Man got an idea! Up and around the kids swung on his webs, sprinkling salt across the road. Riley yelled, "Now that's how Team Spidey melts ice!"

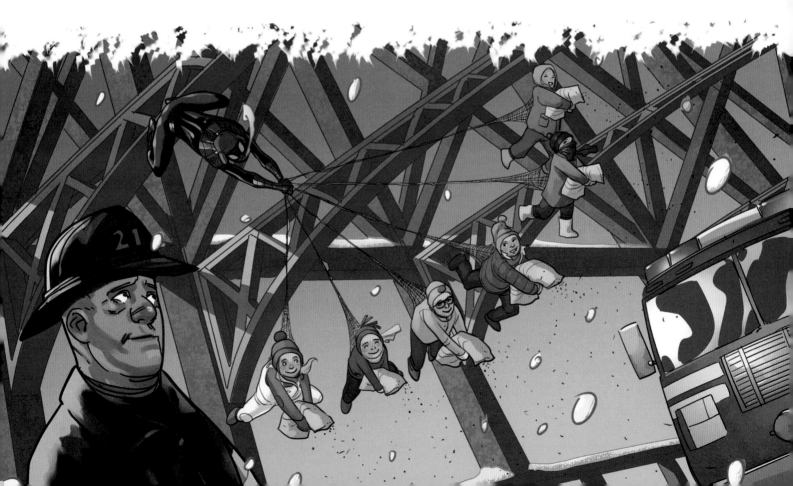

As the group left Skyler and Riley's house, Oliver noticed an elderly man shivering by himself. "Is there anything we can do to help that man, Spidey?" Oliver asked. Spidey thought for a moment and then took the kids to the man.

Spider-Man spun a coat and mittens and hat all out of webs! "I hope this helps keep you warm, sir," Spidey said. The man was happy to have the extra layers.

When Spider-Man saw a little dog shivering in an alley near Miles and Ellie's home, he stopped to help.

And the kids helped, too! It turned out that helping others was a great way to keep their minds off the cold. As Spidey made an igloo for the dog out of his webs, Miles kept the puppy warm and Cale got a blanket for it. Oliver found some food, and Ellie made a sign for the puppy's new house that read HAZEL'Z HOME SWEET HOME!

"Hazel?" Spider-Man asked.

Ellie giggled, and Miles smiled big and said, "She looks like a Hazel to me, too!" Spidey laughed.

Oliver and Cale were the last of the kids to get home, and boy were their parents glad to see them!

"Mom! Dad! Spider-Man got Skyler out of a pipe! And then we helped firefighters! And cop cars! *Can you believe it?*" Oliver said.

"Thanks for helping us get home," Cale said as he waved to their hero. Spider-Man was so proud of the kids. They were heroes, too!

As he swung home, Spidey realized he was late getting back to Aunt May.

After a quick change out of his costume, Peter Parker—goofy winter hat and all—finally arrived home to his Aunt May. But Peter knew he was late, late, late! Just as he started to say he was sorry, Aunt May said, "Now, don't you go apologizing to me, Peter!"

"You should know by now that I can take care of myself," Aunt May said. "But it looks like you're catching a cold! Sit down and let me take care of *you*."

Peter had spent the evening as Spider-Man, playing hero to people all over the city. But even Super Heroes need to be rescued sometimes—and Aunt May would always be Spidey's hero.

SPIDER-MAN
The Sensational Six!

"Parker!" bellowed JJ Jameson in an ear-piercing voice.

The publisher of the *Daily Bugle* newspaper yelled for his ace photographer, and Peter Parker came running. Inside Jameson's office, Peter saw editor Joe Robertson and reporter Betty Brant watching a giant television. They couldn't believe what they were seeing. The Sinister Six were attacking . . . *each other*?

"Why is Doctor Octopus fighting Electro?" Peter asked. It was true. Peter saw the Lizard battling the Beetle and the Rhino raging at Kraven the Hunter.

"That's what happens when Super Villain teams break up," said Robertson.

"Break up? But I thought—" Peter started.

Jameson cut him off. "I don't pay you to think. I pay you to take pictures. So why aren't you and your camera in Brooklyn taking pictures of that project I assigned you?"

Peter couldn't get over it. *Why* were the Sinister Six calling it quits?

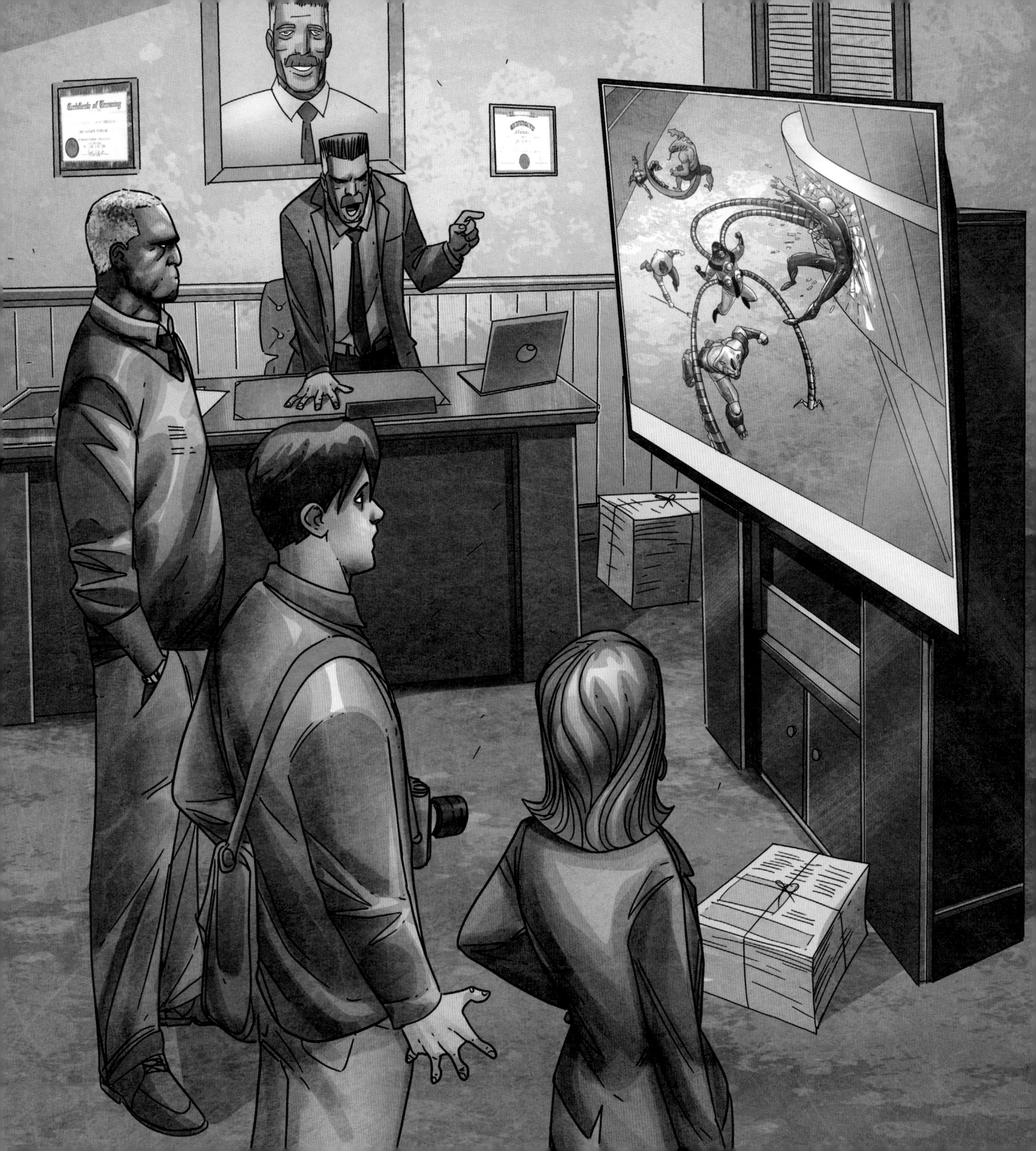

Peter swung high above Manhattan as Spider-Man.

"This is the life! No Sinister Six, no worries!" said Spidey.

Just then, his spider-sense started to tingle. Spidey saw Doctor Octopus on the prowl.

"I'd say, 'What's up, Doc?' but that's somebody else's line," Spider-Man said as he landed behind the tentacled fiend. "So what happened to your playmates?"

"I'm so glad you asked, Spider-Man," said Octopus.

Suddenly, the wall-crawler's spider-sense screamed. He sprung into the air as the Lizard appeared! The reptile swiped his tail at Spidey, barely missing him.

"No one asked you to bring the Lizard to our playdate!" said Spidey.

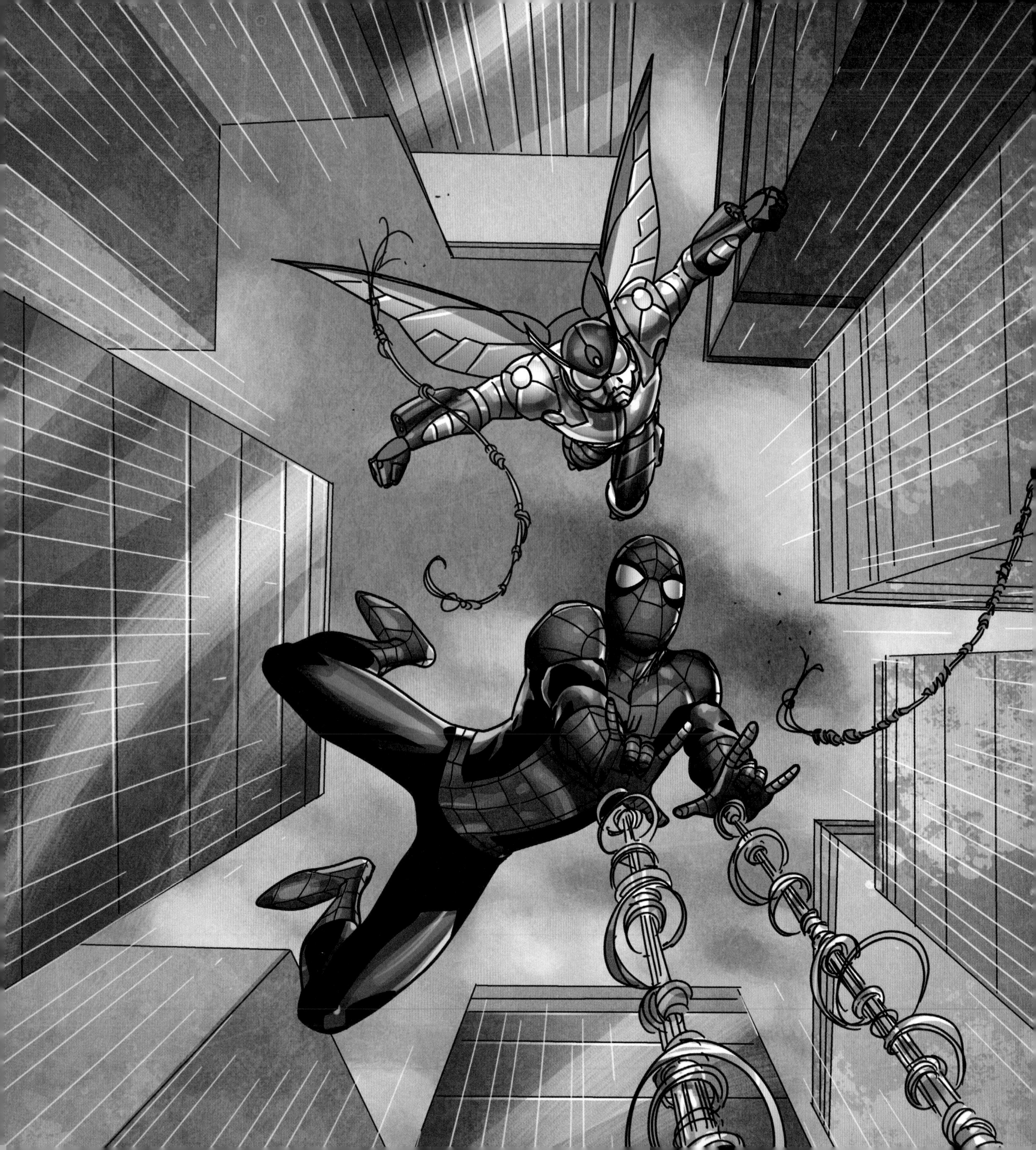

Spidey plunged over the side of the building and shot a web line to break his fall.

"So the Sinister Six broke up, huh?" said Spider-Man. "Rrrrright. Who else is gonna rain on my parade?"

Right on cue, the Beetle soared past Spider-Man, slashing the web with one of his wings!

"Tell the street I said hello, spider-splat!" said the Beetle.

Thinking fast, Spider-Man spun a web net to break his fall.

"My arm!" Spidey shouted as pain shot from his left shoulder to his hand. "I can't even move it!"

"Too bad," came a voice from behind Spider-Man. "I expected a more challenging hunt!"

"Kraven!" Spider-Man exclaimed as the Hunter threw spears at the injured hero. Thinking fast, Spidey used his webbing to make a sling for his left arm and evaded the attack!

"How can I beat the Sinister Six like this?" Spidey asked himself.

"Oh, wow—it's Spider-Man!"

"Who is that?" Spidey asked. He turned and came face to face with Ms. Marvel!

"Are you okay? Let me give you a hand!" said Ms. Marvel. Using her powers, she enlarged her right hand and carried Spidey away.

"That's some handy power," Spider-Man said, making Ms. Marvel laugh. "Sorry about the jokes. That's kind of my thing."

"No, it's totally cool!" said Ms. Marvel. "I'm, like, a big fan. So what's going on with the Sinister Six? Didn't they break up?"

"Not so much," said Spidey. "I'm definitely gonna need some help to stop those guys. You up for it?"

Before Ms. Marvel could answer, a bolt of electricity struck the roof near Spidey!

"Time to settle our score, web-head!" said Electro.

"I was wondering when battery boy was going to show up," Spider-Man said. "Any bright ideas, kid?"

Ms. Marvel looked behind Electro and saw an old water tower. Smiling, she enlarged her right hand and raced toward the tower.

"You look a little thirsty, Electro. Have a drink!" said Ms. Marvel. Using her huge hand, she smashed open the tower. Water rushed out, drenching Electro. Sparks flew everywhere as the villain's power shorted out.

"And I thought jokes were *my* thing," said Spidey. "Way to go, Ms. Marvel!"

Just then, Spidey and Ms. Marvel heard an enormous *BOOM* from below and felt the building rumble.

"What was that?" said Ms. Marvel.

"That would be the Rhino," said someone from above. "I think he doesn't want you two hanging out here anymore!"

It was the Falcon! Swooping through the sky, the Falcon carried Ms. Marvel and Spider-Man to the street below. The Rhino stopped bashing into the building and started running right for Spidey.

"These feet were made for stomping spiders!" said the Rhino.

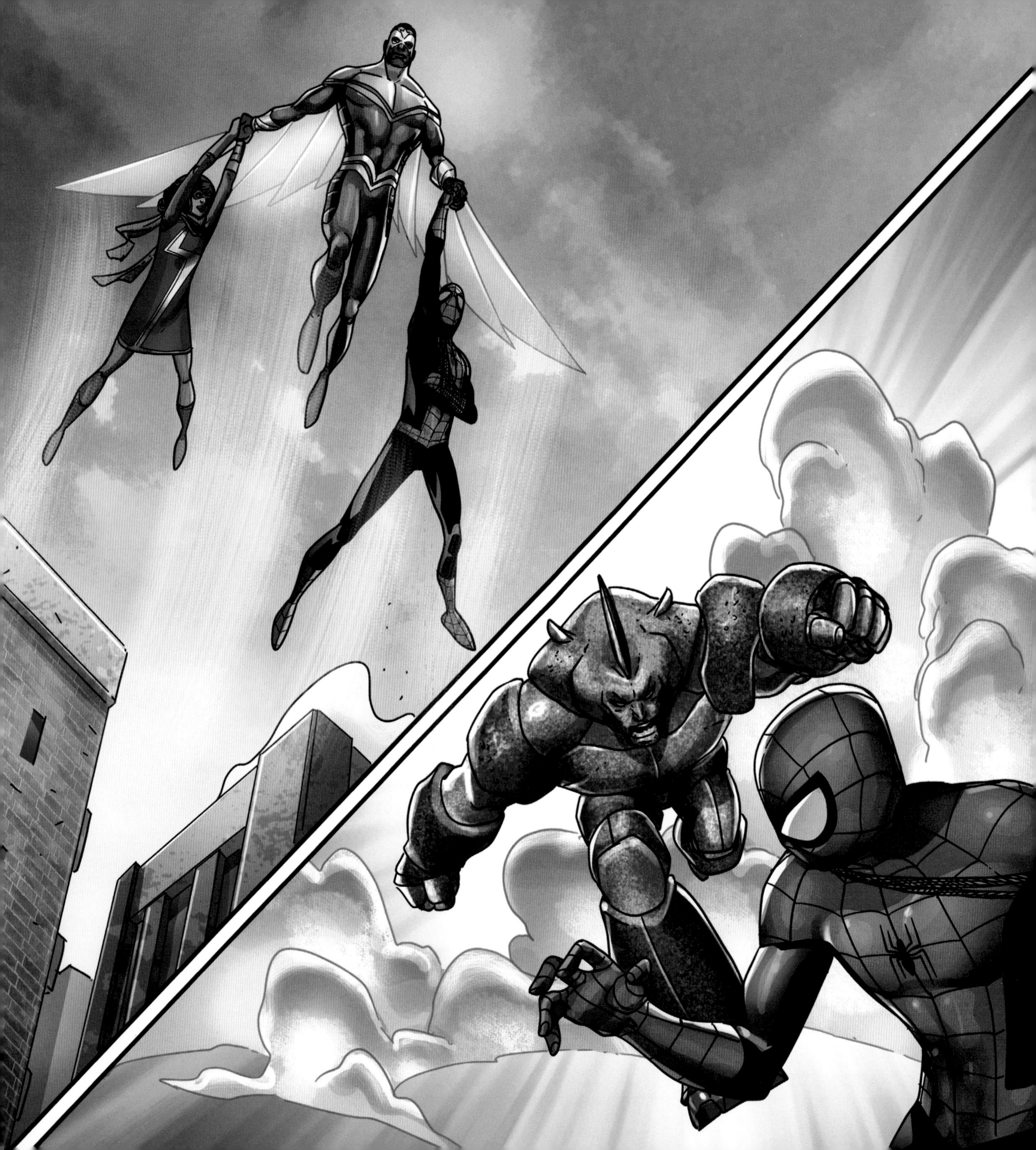

"What about ants?"
someone asked in a tiny voice.

As the Rhino raced toward
Spider-Man, he suddenly
found himself running
slower . . . and slower . . .
and slower, until he came to
a full stop!

"What's going on here?"
said the Rhino. When he looked down, he had his answer. He was
up to his ankles in ants! But they weren't just any ants—they were
following the commands of the astonishing Ant-Man!

"Ant-Man!" said Spidey. "Boy, am I glad to almost see you!
Thanks for the save!"

As Ant-Man ordered his ants to knock over the Rhino, he gave
Spidey a quick salute. "Anytime, Spidey! Happy to help!"

The rest of the Sinister Six caught up to the heroes as Spider-Man took his place next to Ant-Man, Falcon, and Ms. Marvel.

"Do you really think four little heroes are a match for the Sinister Six?" said Doctor Octopus, his tentacles poised to attack.

"Actually, it's *five* 'little heroes,'" said Black Widow. The Quinjet had appeared above Spidey and the others! Widow jumped down to join them. "And one *BIG* hero."

"Hulk smash!" said the Hulk as he crashed into the street, knocking out the Lizard and Rhino.

"The Hulk's here? Now this is what I call a party!" said Spider-Man. The wall-crawler summoned all his strength and gave Doc Ock a mighty kick. "We got this, guys!"

One by one, the heroes took down the villains. The Sinister Six were no match for Spider-Man and his amazing friends!

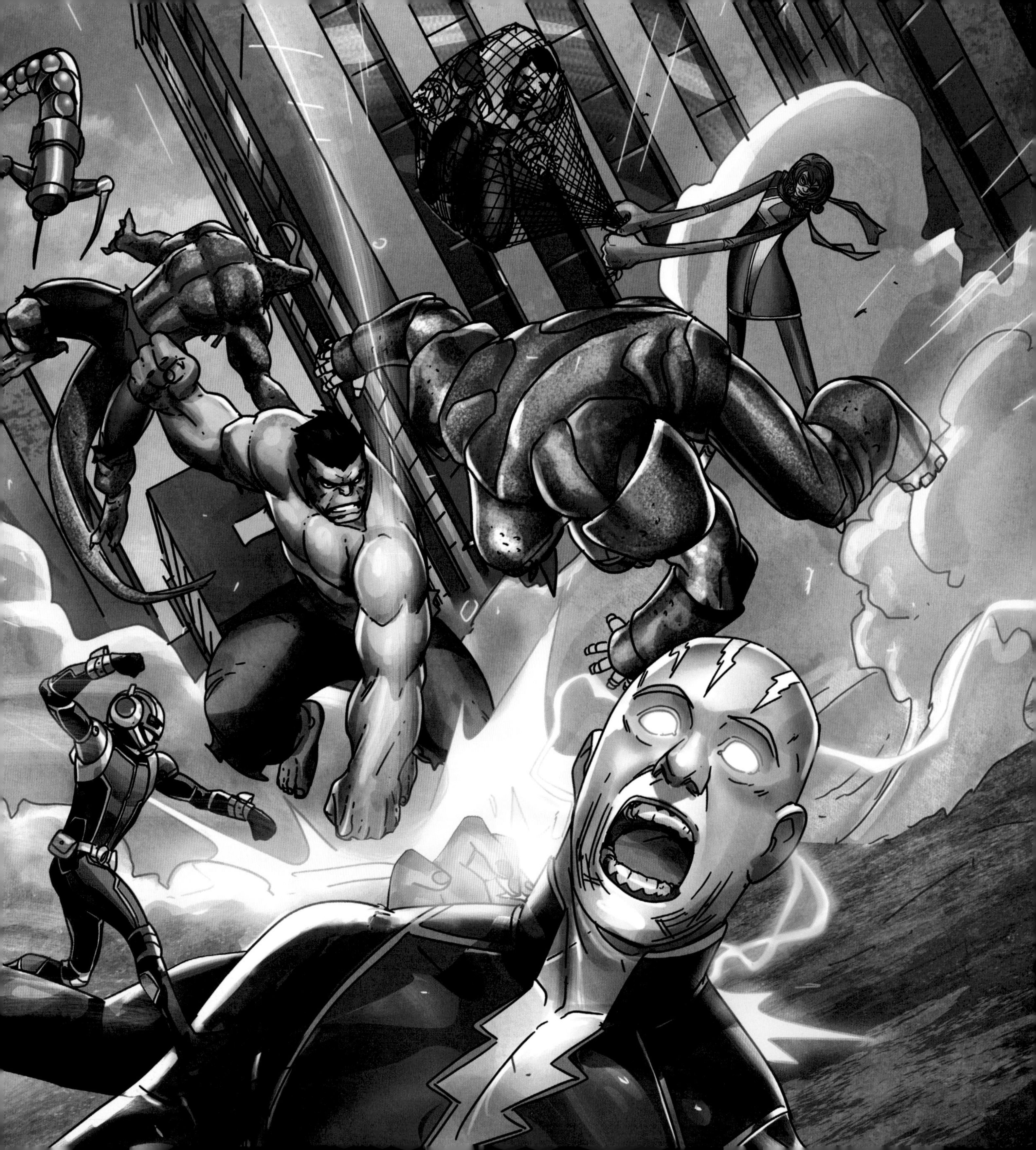

With the villains subdued, the police took the Sinister Six to jail, and Spider-Man thanked the Super Heroes. "I couldn't have done it without you," said Spidey. "You guys rock!"

"What did you expect from the Sensational Six?" said Ms. Marvel.

The End

page 13

page 77

page 38

page 55

page 85

page 109

page 52

page 121

page 177

page 136

page 161

page 144

page 255

page 197

page 207

page 217

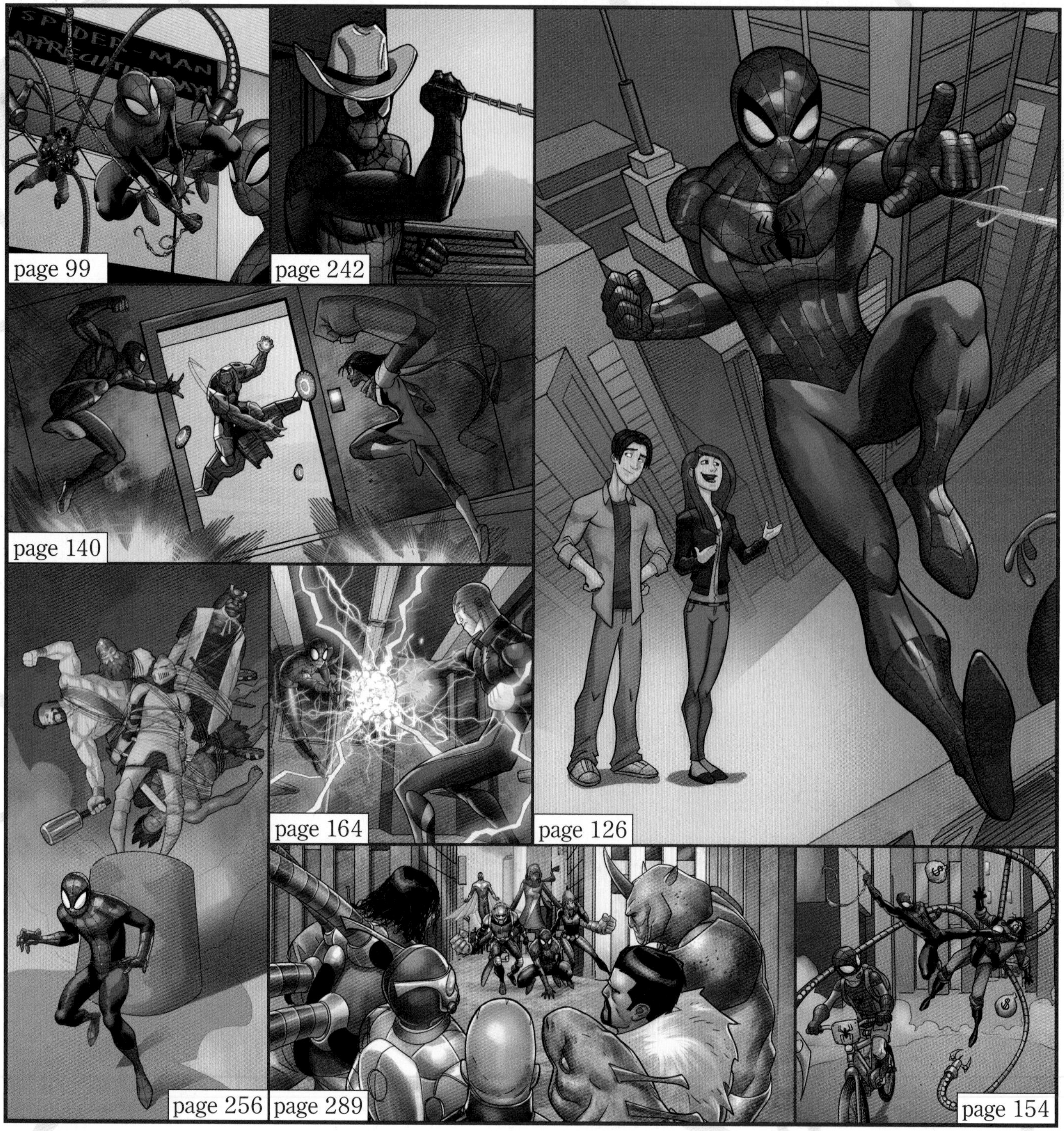
SPIDER-MAN
page 99
page 242
page 140
page 126
page 164
page 256
page 289
page 154

page 261

page 278

page 5

page 82

page 25

page 87

page 60

page 36

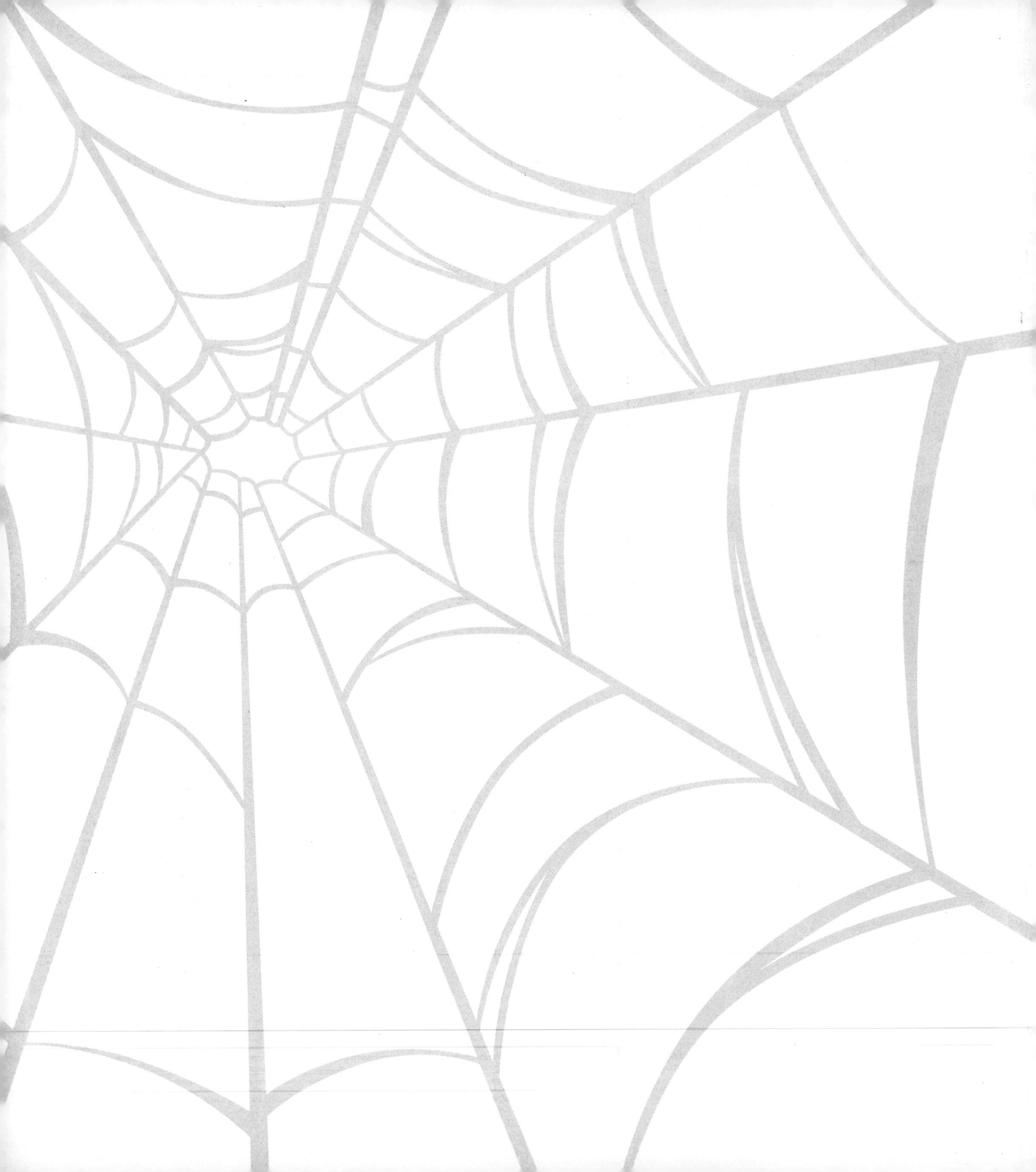